A Dinner Party Turned Sour

I was beginning to get the picture. Sarah wasn't home. If I weren't so thorough (some people might say *anal*), I never would have looked into the bathroom. It was at the end of the hallway, and I was right there. Besides, the door was closed, and I could see the glow of light from under it.

Call me crazy, but that struck me as a bit strange, considering no one was around but the dog. I knocked. Just in case. I didn't expect an answer, so I wasn't disappointed when I didn't get one. I turned the knob and walked inside.

I'm not the dramatic type, so I don't think I screamed when I saw the body in the bathtub. But I guess I must have made some kind of noise. Eve and Foster came running.

Sarah's head was thrown back against the rim of the tub. Her eyes were open and staring. Her skin looked waxy and pale. As if in some macabre, slow-motion dance, her body bobbed in the maroon-tinted water that filled the tub nearly to its brim.

The color struck me as odd. Until I saw the bloody knife on the floor next to the tub.

My own blood whooshed like a torrent inside my ears, but I could still hear Foster say something about calling 911. And Eve's scream.

Cooking Class Mysteries by Miranda Bliss

COOKING UP MURDER
MURDER ON THE MENU

Murder
on the
Menu

MIRANDA BLISS

BERKLEY PRIME CRIME, NEW YORK

THE BERKLEY PUBLISHING GROUP
Published by the Penguin Group
Penguin Group (USA) Inc.
375 Hudson Street, New York, New York 10014, USA
Penguin Group (Canada), 90 Eglinton Avenue East, Suite 700, Toronto, Ontario M4P 2Y3, Canada
(a division of Pearson Penguin Canada Inc.)
Penguin Books Ltd., 80 Strand, London WC2R 0RL, England
Penguin Group Ireland, 25 St. Stephen's Green, Dublin 2, Ireland (a division of Penguin Books Ltd.)
Penguin Group (Australia), 250 Camberwell Road, Camberwell, Victoria 3124, Australia
(a division of Pearson Australia Group Pty. Ltd.)
Penguin Books India Pvt. Ltd., 11 Community Centre, Panchsheel Park, New Delhi—110 017, India
Penguin Group (NZ), 67 Apollo Drive, Rosedale, North Shore 0745, Auckland, New Zealand
(a division of Pearson New Zealand Ltd.)
Penguin Books (South Africa) (Pty.) Ltd., 24 Sturdee Avenue, Rosebank, Johannesburg 2196,
South Africa

Penguin Books Ltd., Registered Offices: 80 Strand, London WC2R 0RL, England

This is a work of fiction. Names, characters, places, and incidents either are the product of the author's imagination or are used fictitiously, and any resemblance to actual persons, living or dead, business establishments, events, or locales is entirely coincidental. The publisher does not have any control over and does not assume any responsibility for author or third-party websites or their content.

PUBLISHER'S NOTE: The recipes contained in this book are to be followed exactly as written. The publisher is not responsible for your specific health or allergy needs that may require medical supervision. The publisher is not responsible for any adverse reactions to the recipes contained in this book.

MURDER ON THE MENU

A Berkley Prime Crime Book / published by arrangement with the author

PRINTING HISTORY
Berkley Prime Crime mass-market edition / June 2007

Copyright © 2007 by The Berkley Publishing Group.
Cover art by Stephanie Power.
Cover design by Rita Frangie.
Interior text design by Kristin del Rosario.

ISBN: 978-0-425-21607-1

BERKLEY® PRIME CRIME
Berkley Prime Crime Books are published by The Berkley Publishing Group,
a division of Penguin Group (USA) Inc.,
375 Hudson Street, New York, New York 10014.
The name BERKLEY PRIME CRIME and the BERKLEY PRIME CRIME design are trademarks belonging to Penguin Group (USA) Inc.

PRINTED IN THE UNITED STATES OF AMERICA

10 9 8 7 6 5 4 3 2 1

One

✖

"HE HAS SHIFTY EYES. AND THEY'RE SET WAY TOO close together. I read somewhere that's a sure sign of a criminal. What do you think, Annie? What do you suppose he's up to?"

If I was a better/less-harried/not-so-incredibly stressed friend, I would have paid more attention to what Eve was saying. More than none, that is. As it was, I was staring at invoices from food suppliers, beverage distributors, and the janitorial service that took care of the floors and bathrooms in Bellywasher's, soon to be Alexandria's best, trendiest, and (if only the culinary gods would smile on us) most successful new restaurant.

The part of my brain that wasn't taken up with being nervous about what would happen in a few minutes when we finally opened the doors for our first day of business was filled with numbers. Lots and lots of numbers. As quickly as they flashed through my head, I tallied them up and balanced them against how much I knew was in the restaurant's checking account.

My stomach clenched. My breath caught.

We weren't in red-ink territory. Not yet. But we were

skirting the edges, pretty much like Bellywasher's did, poised as it was on that invisible line that divided the upscale, gentrified part of Alexandria, Virginia, and the slightly seedier neighborhood farther from the Potomac River.

I tossed out an answer to Eve's question, eager to appease her, because I knew that until I did, she wouldn't leave me alone. "Criminal? Sure. Whatever you say."

"I mean it, Annie." It didn't work. The beauty pageant Southern drawl Eve usually reserved for good-looking men and social occasions had a way of rearing its ugly head when she was miffed. Or, come to think of it, when she was under pressure, under the weather, or over the moon about anything. "I'm telling you, girl, he's up to something. And don't tell me I'm imagining it."

I checked the clock hanging on the wall above my desk. Thirty minutes and counting, and I still needed to double-check the change in the cash register. "You're imagining it."

Eve snorted her opinion. "You don't even know who I'm talking about."

I didn't, and I guess realizing that fact was what made me aware of how inconsiderate I was being. Harried or not, there was no excuse for that.

"I'm sorry." Eve was my best friend and Bellywasher's one and only hostess. We'd been through a lot together, Eve and me. Good times and bad times. Middle school, high school, and now almost middle age. Any number of engagements (Eve's), one disastrous marriage (mine), a divorce that wasn't as acrimonious as it was just plain awful (again, mine), and if we counted what happened the summer before at Très Bonne Cuisine, where we went to cooking school together, a couple of murders, too.

I owed her better.

I pushed back from my desk and spun my chair around. "All right, I give up. Who's the shifty-looking one?"

"Shh! Not so loud. He'll hear you." Eve had been standing in the doorway of my office, and she shot inside, looking to hide. Easier said than done. As the restaurant's business manager, I had the luxury of the biggest office in the place, but of course, *biggest* is a relative word.

The room was only ten by twelve, but thanks to the dark wood paneling that had been de rigueur back when Angus MacDonald first bought the place, it looked and felt even smaller. There was a desk jammed into one corner, and it was piled with so many papers, I could barely get to the keyboard of the computer I'd brought from home. No big loss there. The computer, it seemed, did not like the move from Arlington to Alexandria. It was fidgety and these days it liked to give me error messages and mysteriously reboot in the middle of important projects more than it did anything else.

The rest of my office was taken up with file cabinets. I had one guest chair, too, but at the moment, it was a little hard to locate. It was awash with catalogues from restaurant supply houses, boxes of matchbooks printed with the Bellywasher's name, and sample place mats in every material imaginable including plastic, paper, and a product the sales rep who was trying to sell it to me swore was made completely from recycled truck tires.

The mess was unlike me, and it was a constant source of irritation. So was the fact that someone had yet to invent a way to cram more than twenty-four hours into a day.

I sighed. Eve might have noticed and come to the conclusion that I had better things to do than play into her warped fantasies if she wasn't so busy peeking around the door and into the restaurant.

"Him," she said in a stage whisper, pointing toward where an ordinary-looking guy in an ordinary blue work shirt and pants was going about what was probably an ordinary day for him, hauling in armloads of shrink-wrapped napkins. "The guy from the linen service," she added, in spite of the fact that he was the only one in the restaurant at the moment. "You know, Gregor."

I did know, though I hadn't picked up on the fact that his name was Gregor. Leave it to Eve. In addition to being tall, blonde, willowy, and gorgeous, her ability to make friends with everyone who crossed her path was exactly the reason I suggested she work as Bellywasher's hostess and precisely why Jim MacDonald, the restaurant's new owner, had agreed.

"Gregor is not a criminal," I told Eve, and I peeked into the restaurant, too. Gregor saw me and waved. I waved back.

"There's not a thing wrong with him or with the linen service he works for," I reminded her, careful to keep my voice down. "I checked them out before I contracted with them. I got plenty of references."

"References don't mention how shifty people look. His eyes—"

"Look brown." I took another gander at Gregor, just to be sure. "At least from here. But of course, I can't be certain from this distance."

"And the fact that they're so close together?"

"Is a sad twist of genetic fate."

"Which has also been cited as a cause of criminal behavior."

"Except Gregor isn't doing anything criminal. He's bringing us napkins."

"And you think he should what, wear a sign around his neck? One that says, Look at me! I'm a bad guy!" Logic had never been Eve's strong suit. She should have learned that by now. Alas, she apparently thought of her Gregor theory as flawless reasoning. "Believe me, Annie, I know what I'm talking about. I've got experience with these sorts of things."

I didn't have to ask. I knew the experience Eve was talking about had to do with the aforementioned cooking class. More specifically, with the murder we'd investigated while we were students in that class. Before that, the closest Eve had ever been to a bad guy was watching Anthony Hopkins in *Silence of the Lambs*. And as I recall, through most of the movie, she kept her eyes shut.

I let out a long, slow breath that teetered on the edge of impatience. "Just because we were unlucky enough to run into one mystery last summer—"

"Unlucky?" Eve's golden brows dropped low over eyes the color of Virginia bluebells. She was wearing a skirt in the same shade and a white blouse that hugged her surgically enhanced chest in all the right places. Call me shallow, but I couldn't help but compare my body to hers.

She's tall and gorgeous. Me? I belong in the short and cute category. I've got way-too-curly-to-be-contained hair, a turned-up nose, and a body that's too curvy to look good in anything even half-fashionable.

Of course, Eve wasn't thinking about any of that. "Do you think we were unlucky?" she asked. "I don't. We solved a murder. And caught a real bad guy. I think it was exciting."

"Almost getting killed is definitely not exciting," I reminded her, though it was clear I was wasting my time. There was nothing like a couple months of peace and quiet to make somebody forget that only a short while earlier, we'd spent our time dodging arms smugglers, bullets, and one particularly nasty poisoner. Especially when the somebody in question was Eve.

I, however, had not forgotten. Nor was I likely to. Call me crazy, but I don't need my adrenaline kicked into high gear by life-and-death situations. Everyday life is excitement enough for me.

I pulled in a breath, but as much as I tried, I couldn't bite back the same lecture I'd been repeating these last few months. Ever since Eve started seeing mysteries around every corner.

"There's nothing weird or evil about Gregor, Eve. He's not a bad guy. He isn't planning anything, except maybe how to get a free cup of coffee out of us before he leaves. There's nothing suspicious or criminal happening with anyone around here. We're regular people, just like all the other regular people in the world. Regular people working through a regular day. Just because we solved one mystery doesn't mean we're likely to ever run into another one. There aren't bad guys lurking everywhere."

"Sure, that's what you said before."

It was. I admit it. But facts were facts: I was a bank teller by day and Bellywasher's business manager on nights, week-ends, and holidays when the bank was closed. I did not have the pedigree to be a crime fighter.

"When someone ends up dead—" Eve began.

I didn't give her the chance to get any further. Before she could say anything else, I popped out of my chair and headed into the restaurant. "Nobody's going to end up dead," I told her, just like I'd been telling her for months. "Nobody's going to jail. Nobody's being sneaky or crooked or felonious. Our crime-fighting days are over, Robin, park the Batmobile in the cave."

She was still thinking about the metaphor when I swept past her.

"See you, Gregor," I called to the linen man as he walked through the restaurant and back toward the kitchen.

"If you want, grab a cup of coffee on your way out," Eve added. I doubt she made the offer because she felt guilty about labeling him an offender before he ever had a chance to do anything even mildly offensive. This was part of her South-ern hospitality upbringing, and though I was concerned about our bottom line and thus not happy about giving away free coffee, I knew Eve's warm and welcoming personality would serve us well in the long run.

It was working already.

Gregor smiled his thanks, promised he'd be back for lunch one day soon, and disappeared into the kitchen. I knew Heidi, our one and only waitress, was back there with Damien and Marc, the two young men who helped Jim with the cooking. They'd take care of him.

That handled, I checked the clock one more time and gave the restaurant a final once-over.

When I first arrived to see the place Jim had inherited from his Uncle Angus, Bellywasher's was . . . well, how can I say this delicately?

Bellywasher's was, in a word, a disaster.

The bar and restaurant was one part dive, one part neighborhood hangout. It had a menu that featured things like wieners, grilled cheese sandwiches, and the occasional blue plate special. Legend has it that thanks to Uncle Angus's nearsightedness and his tendency to not rotate kitchen stock as effectively as he should, on one particularly unfortunate occasion (and much to the dismay of the health department) blue food really did make an appearance on the plates. Lucky for Angus, no one got sick, and the regulars took it all in stride.

Bellywasher's attracted what Jim generously called a local crowd—mostly older than middle-aged guys, the kind who wore beat-up army jackets and talked about the good old days over shots and beers. While they might not have appreciated the blue food, they did apparently enjoy what passed for ambiance.

Uncle Angus had been the proprietor and barkeep almost since the day he set foot in this country from Scotland. Over the years, he'd filled the caramel-colored paneled walls with a collection of memorabilia that included photos of the Scottish countryside, even one he swore showed an authentic Nessie sighting. The pictures hung side by side with broadswords, kilts, and (I swear this is true) an autographed picture of Mel Gibson in blue face paint. The tablecloths were plaid, there was a mural of a thistle over the bar, and more often than not, there was a bagpiper on one of the barstools who was happy to play in exchange for a wee drop of something to wet his whistle.

It was eclectic to say the least, and while I'm not a snob, it took only one visit for me to recognize that as it stood, Bellywasher's wasn't going to bring in the kind of upscale crowd Jim wanted to attract.

Fortunately, in the months since he'd taken over, reason (not to mention good taste) had prevailed. The paneling was gone, replaced with clean white walls, and all of Angus's Scottish ephemera was stored in the basement. There wasn't a scrap of plaid in sight. The tables—there were only ten of them and twice that number of seats at the bar—were covered with crisp cloths. The chairs were ebony and sleek. The ceramic tile floor was white, too, with just a touch of gray in it, and thanks to the spare, clean colors and windows that looked out onto King Street, the lighting was good even at the bar at the back of the room.

We'd done well. At least, as well as we could with a limited budget and one odd legal constraint. Under the terms of Uncle Angus's will, Bellywasher's it was, and Bellywasher's it had to stay. According to Jim, a bellywasher was a drink, and though these days we were more interested in providing our clientele with fine food and fresh ingredients than we were in shots and beers, we were learning to live with the name even though we (well, actually, *I*) hadn't quite yet made peace with it.

"Are we ready, do you think?"

Some time while I'd been lost in thought, Jim had come out of the kitchen. I heard his voice right behind me. I turned and tried for a smile that told him everything was under control and I wasn't the least bit apprehensive about what the day would bring.

Fat chance.

I could no more pretend I wasn't nervous than I could make believe that being anywhere close to Jim didn't make my hormones flare like a kitchen grease fire.

Jim MacDonald is himself a born-and-bred Scotsman, and he has the knee-melting accent to prove it. Jim is tall and rangy. Mahogany hair. Hazel eyes. Athletic body. We met at that cooking class; he was the instructor. And if it sounds like I'm head over heels about him?

I tamped back the thought and those out-of-control hormones.

Sure, Jim is good-looking. Sure, he's decent and kind, and he has a great sense of humor. Yes, he's made it clear that if I'm interested, he's plenty interested, too.

But . . .

I twitched aside the thought and told myself to get my mind off my disastrous romantic track record and back on the restaurant where it belonged.

"We're ready," I told Jim. I guess I didn't look all that convinced, because he laughed.

"You're not being made to march in front of a firing squad. Loosen up, woman! If you forget to breathe, we're going to have more trouble on our hands than just some missing radicchio." He drew me closer and kneaded my shoulders.

Jim has strong hands.

Expert hands.

Warm and gentle hands.

I nearly fell under the spell, until reality hit like a ton of made-out-of-recycled-tires place mats.

"What do you mean no radicchio?" Before I even realized I'd shot out from under his grip, I was on my way back to my office to find the appropriate paperwork. "I know you ordered it. I know I paid for it. I can find the invoice to prove it. The rest of the produce came, didn't it? We aren't out of lettuce? Or tomatoes? Oh my gosh, how are you going to make the mozzarella salad without tomatoes?"

"Annie."

Jim's voice barely penetrated the panic-induced fog that filled my brain. I didn't pay him any mind. Already in my office, I shuffled through the papers on my desk.

"It's here," I mumbled. "I know the invoice is here. I know I marked it as paid. I saw it yesterday."

"Annie."

"It was with all the other bills I've paid." I was babbling now. Stress and fear and first-day jitters were bound to produce some sort of phobia in a person like me who treasures nothing as much as predictability. "If you give me a minute, I'll find it and call them and—"

"Annie!" This time, Jim wasn't taking any chances. Putting his hands back on my shoulders, he spun me around to face him. The heat of his skin penetrated the black blazer

I'd chosen to wear that day along with black tailored pants and a creamy blouse. OK, so I was no more daring when it came to fashion than I was about anything else in life. That didn't change the fact that Jim's touch warmed me through to the bone. He was far taller than me, and he bent down to look me in the eye.

"I don't care about the radicchio," he said, speaking low and slow, the way a mother does to a small child. Or a trainer does to a dog.

I swallowed a gulp of dismay.

"I've already worked around the missing radicchio," he continued. "I'll use endive in the salads instead. We've got it. It's fresh. It isn't as colorful, but we'll make do." He gave this news time to sink in. It wasn't until he was sure it had and that I wasn't going to start rooting through the papers on my desk again that he loosened his hold.

Loosened, not let go.

He linked his fingers at the back of my neck and tugged me a little closer. His thigh brushed mine. His breath was soft against my cheek. "Feeling better now?" he asked. His gaze dipped to my lips.

I nodded.

"You're sure?"

I wasn't, but I nodded again, anyway. How could I do anything else? It was hard to think rationally when Jim was this close and when—according to the clock I could just catch a glimpse of if I twisted ever so slightly—we had exactly ten minutes to go until opening.

"You don't want to forget this whole restaurant thing and just go back to working only at the bank?"

The bank? I didn't. But—

"I just want to make sure everything is perfect!" I wailed.

Jim chuckled. "Aye, as do I. But we've done all we can, Annie. And let me remind you, we've done it all well. We're as ready as we're ever likely to be, and now is not the time to worry about little things like radicchio. If you're going to succeed in this business, you're going to have to learn to roll with the punches. Radicchio that hasn't been delivered, that's not a crisis. Just a bit of an inconvenience."

"You're right." I willed the tension out of my shoulders and felt the knot in my stomach ease. "I just want things to go well."

"And they will; you'll make sure of that. Heaven help us all if they don't. Anything goes wrong today, and you'll have my head on one of Angus's old crockery platters."

"Will not." He'd gotten his way and coaxed a smile out of me. I forced myself to keep it firmly in place even though, when I looked, I saw that the clock had ticked away another minute. "It's just that—"

"You're nervous and excited." Jim nodded. Like a diver preparing for a leap off the high board, he drew in a deep breath and let it out slowly. "So am I," he admitted. "This restaurant . . . it's what I've always wanted."

"Which is why I need to make sure—"

"No." The glimmer in his eyes settled into a smoldering spark. "*You* don't need to make sure everything goes right. *We* need to do that. There's another thing you'll have to learn if you're planning to last in the restaurant business. It's a team effort, you see. Kitchen, front of the house, business end. We all need to work together. It isn't any one person's fault if things don't go right. Even when that one person is a certain woman who takes far too much responsibility on herself." One corner of his mouth pulled into a smile that revealed a dimple in his left cheek. I knew what was coming, and I braced myself for it.

"You might feel less stressed," he suggested, "if you quit your job at the bank."

The subject had been a bone of contention between us all summer, and truth be told, I understood Jim's point of view. Though his position could be construed as being cold and calculating, I knew he wasn't thinking of the restaurant and how much of my undivided attention it got. He was worried about me, about how I put in eight hours a day at the bank, then another five or six at Bellywasher's. Stress? I had it in spades. But that didn't mean I was willing to budge an inch. Taking on the obligations of a new business was risk enough. I didn't need to compound it by quitting a job that offered stability, a steady paycheck, and decent benefits.

Another look at the clock and I sidestepped around Jim and toward the door. "Maybe someday," I told him. Just like I'd been telling him all summer. "When things here are more stable. That's when I'll quit my job at the bank. You know, when this job is more dependable."

"Aye, you mean when you don't have to take any chances."

I didn't know why he had to make that sound like a bad thing. "There's nothing wrong with being careful."

"There is, if you spend so much time being careful, you forget to live life while you're at it."

Something told me we weren't talking about Belly-washer's anymore.

The familiar thread of uncertainty coiled in my stomach. "Look, Jim, it's not that—"

"Not that you don't care. Not that you don't like me. Not that I don't like you as well. And not that we didn't try."

He was talking about the last few months, about how we'd actually given the whole dating thing a go. And honestly, dating Jim . . . well, that was pretty much right up there with salt-and-vinegar potato chips. Or a bag of those dark chocolates from Dove.

Irresistible.

Delicious.

And loaded with pitfalls.

Hand in hand, we used to walk around my neighborhood. Jim would tell me about his plans for Bellywasher's. And me? I talked about my dream of owning a home. Nothing wrong with that, right? Until I realized that every time I revealed some personal piece of myself, I flashed back to my relationship with Peter and how he'd always shared my dreams.

Of course, that was before he ran off with the girl from the dry cleaner's and took half of my house down payment with him.

Other nights, Jim and I stayed in, and he cooked dinner using the recipes he planned for the Bellywasher's menu. I know, lucky me. Jim is a fabulous cook, and staying snug and cozy at home had always appealed to me more than a night on the town. But no matter how hard I tried not to, those nights made me think about how I'd taken all the snug and cozy nights I'd spent with Peter for granted.

We went to ball games and to a couple concerts and to the movies. I'll admit it, I loved sitting there with Jim's arm around my shoulders.

And all I could think about was how lonely I was going to be once he moved on.

As much as I missed our friendship and the sizzle that streaked through me every time I thought about taking our relationship to the next level, I'd slowly begun backing out of the relationship even before the demands of the restaurant swamped us both.

As if he was thinking about the same things, Jim sighed. "Back when we met at Très Bonne Cuisine, you wouldn't have gone scampering away when I put my arms around you."

It was true. But that was before I came to my senses and remembered that romance and I . . . well, the word *heartbreak* comes to mind. So do the phrases, *don't go there, who are you kidding*, and *don't take any chances*.

Because I knew if I did go there, if I risked everything as I had with Peter, and if things didn't work out the way they hadn't with Peter, then my heart would be broken in so many pieces a truck full of super-duper glue wouldn't be enough to even begin to stick it back together.

And I had the nerve to criticize Eve for her lack of logic? How about trying this argument on for size: I couldn't date Jim; I liked him too much.

I didn't try to explain. Jim wouldn't have understood, and besides, we didn't have time. Instead, I stood there like a lump. I guess Jim felt as if he had to jump in and fill the silence.

"It's my fault," he said, and honestly, it wasn't what I was expecting. I guess he interpreted the blank look on my face for disbelief. He was wrong. What that look really was, you see, was total surprise. He couldn't possibly think the fact that I liked him so darn much I couldn't stand the thought of things going wrong between us so I'd decided that I'd never let our relationship progress far enough for me to be devastated when it finally fell apart had something to do with him. Could he?

Once bitten, twice shy, as they say, and the big ol' bite of divorce still hurt like hell.

When I didn't protest the way he apparently expected me to, Jim went right on. "I've been so consumed by this place, I haven't paid nearly the attention to you that I should have these last months. We hardly talk except about the restaurant. We hardly see each other except passing to and from the kitchen. You stay late, and I have to be at the food terminal early, or I'll be left with what the other chefs won't touch. I know, it's hard, and I'm sorry, Annie. I really am. Things will get easier one of these days, and when they do, I swear I'll make it up to you."

"That's really nice." It was, and I wasn't about to ruin the moment by explaining that even when that rosy one of these days came along, I wasn't going to be any more willing to chance myself and my heart than I was now. I glanced at the clock instead.

"We'd better get out there," I told Jim. My voice jumped to the rhythm of the drumbeat of nervousness that started up inside me again. "It's showtime."

"That it is."

So why was Jim smiling?

"A kiss for luck?"

He asked the question, but he never really expected me to say no. And I couldn't, could I? After all, he was about to embark on the dream of a lifetime. Who was I to throw a damper on the day?

Our lips brushed and met. I didn't need to be reminded of how good a kisser Jim was or how much I enjoyed his kisses. I knew it couldn't last, but I melted into the moment and the odd feelings that enveloped me head to toe. It happened every time I let my guard down and let Jim get close (literally and figuratively)—that tiny spark of fire, the tingling that erupted in every cell in my body, the tranquillity that somehow managed to make itself felt, even through the herd of rampaging hormones. It felt good to be in Jim's arms.

I might still be there if not for the sound of Eve's voice calling from out in the restaurant. "I unlocked the door," she said. "Here they come!"

"Here they come." Jim's eyes glittered. For the first time since he'd inherited Bellywasher's and made the commitment to turn it into the restaurant of his dreams, I heard the same tension in his voice that rushed my blood through my body like a torrent. "Smile, Annie." He kissed me again, quick and hard, and headed for the kitchen. "It's a wee small restaurant with a wee small menu and a staff that's as good as they come. What can possibly go wrong?"

Two

✠

WHAT CAN POSSIBLY GO WRONG?
The words spun around in my head and started my stomach gyrating, too. Was I paranoid? There was a little part of me that wanted to believe that's all it was. But remember that cooking class. And those murders. Somebody starts talking about things going wrong, and I can't help but flash back to it all. Poison. Exploding stoves. Mayhem and mix-ups.

And that wasn't the worst of it.

Have I mentioned that I can't cook?

No, really. Just thinking about going within an arm's length of a stove sends me into fits of panic, and with good reason. Where others sauté, I scorch. While others boil, I burn. And when others bake? Well, let's just say that the one and only loaf of bread I made in Jim's cooking class has since been donated to an architectural firm for use as a building cornerstone.

And Jim had the nerve to ask what could possibly go wrong?

Annie Capshaw in a restaurant, for one thing.

Annie Capshaw working in a restaurant, for another.

Me having anything to do with Bellywasher's in any meaningful way was akin to thumbing my nose at the culinary powers that be. I'd never been much for tempting fate.

Honest to a fault, I tried to explain all this to Jim when he first asked me to be his business manager. Needless to say, he didn't listen, citing instead my facility with numbers, my (usual) inclination for organization, and my all-around common sense.

Maybe, but I wasn't taking any chances.

When I looked out of my office to see who the *they* were of Eve's "Here they come," I was careful not to even glance in the direction of the kitchen. This was neither the time nor the place for my bad cooking luck to rub off on Jim.

As it turned out, *they* were three guys in beat-up army jackets who milled around outside the front door for a minute or two, looking unsure about stepping inside. A tall guy with glasses was obviously the leader of the pack. He pointed toward the Open sign as if to prove to his friends that what he'd heard about the restaurant's resurrection was actually true. The others didn't look convinced. A shorter, rounder African American double-checked the Bellywasher's sign above the front door (newly painted in a tasteful shade of green) and glanced at the window boxes we'd added and the copper-colored spider mums Jim had planted only the night before. A heavyset man with a beer belly shuffled behind his friends, waiting for them to make the first move.

Apparently, their thirst conquered their fear. Glasses Man pushed open the front door, and he and his friends gingerly stepped into the corridor we'd created by partitioning off the main portion of the restaurant with delicate sandalwood and mother-of-pearl screens.

"Why, good morning, y'all! It's so nice to see you." Eve chirped an eager greeting. Though it was clear when they looked at her that the men appreciated the view, it was also clear she wasn't what they were expecting. Then again, from the looks on their faces, I don't think they were expecting the white walls, the clean floors, or the linen tablecloths, either.

"What the hell happened to this place?" Glasses Man spoke, and his friends nodded in unison. "Where are the pictures? And the swords?"

Eve's laugh echoed against the high tin ceiling, and rather than explain about ambiance and chic, she took over as only Eve can. She wound one arm through Glasses Man's and led the men to a table. "You just have a seat right here," she told them, her accent dripping with Southern belle charm. "And don't you worry about those nasty old pictures and such. I'll go on back and get Heidi for you. She's going to be your waitress today, and I just know she's going to take real good care of you. Now, what can I get you nice fellows to drink?"

I couldn't hear what they ordered, but I know one thing for sure: when Eve walked back to the kitchen, she left them smiling.

I let go the breath I hadn't even realized I'd been holding.

Maybe Jim was right, and there really was nothing to worry about. Maybe our first day would go smoothly and herald a dozen years' worth of profitable weeks and a restaurant filled with polite and appreciative customers, cooperative and hardworking employees, good food, fine wine, and nothing in the way of trouble.

Maybe?

Maybe not.

BY TWELVE THIRTY, THE ICE MACHINE HAD SUDDENLY and mysteriously stopped functioning, we'd had one fiery flare-up at the grill that didn't do any real damage but did set off the smoke alarms, and Larry, Hank, and Charlie—the guys in the army jackets—were on their sixth cup of coffee.

Each.

"Do they have any idea how much a cup of coffee costs?" I had been minding my own business, bringing some extra pens up to the bar, when I saw what was going on, and I stood frozen—not to mention incensed—in my tracks. Jim was mixing a martini for a woman in a black hoodie, hot pants, and flip-flops who sat alone at the end of the bar. He poured the drink, delivered it with a smile, and returned to my side.

"It's coffee, Annie," he said, in that oh-so-reasonable tone of voice that told me I was being anything but. "Just coffee. Don't worry about it. They'll order lunch sooner or later. That will make up the difference."

"They haven't even ordered lunch?" I did some quick mental calculations and cringed. If these guys were regulars, and if regulars came in on average four times a week . . . if there are fifty-two weeks in a year . . . and if on each of their visits they drank this much coffee and never ordered another thing . . .

Before I could stop myself, I was reaching for a stack of menus with one hand and a Sharpie with the other. "We need to make a note. That's what we need to do. 'First two coffee refills free.' How does that sound? Or maybe we should be more subtle. How about, 'We'll be happy to refill your coffee cup two times'? That's a little more politically correct, don't you think?"

"I think you forgot what I said about taking deep breaths." Jim plucked the menus out of my hand. He grabbed and pocketed the Sharpie, too, just to be sure I didn't decide to go do anything like scrawl my new coffee edict on the wall. "It's coffee, Annie. Just coffee. Let them drink all they want. They'll be back. They'll tell their friends. You'll see. It's good PR."

"Maybe," I agreed. Reluctantly, but I agreed. I glanced around at the other full tables. There were only two, so it didn't take long.

I sent a laser look to where a man in a navy suit sat across from a woman in a mink coat, and another at the table where three teenagers were sharing a pitcher of Coke. "They ordered, didn't they?" I asked. "They're not just sitting there drinking and getting free refills, are they?"

"They're not just drinking." Jim wound an arm through

mine and turned me around so that I was facing the kitchen and not our customers. "The man and woman are waiting for their orders, two bowls of sweet potato bisque, crab cakes, quiche. The kids are here to apply for jobs. I know, I know . . ." He stopped me before I could comment. "We don't need anyone right now. I told them that. But let's face it, this is the restaurant business, and it's not known for stability or for people who like to stick around long. I told them that we might someday need to do more hiring. And I let them know that when it comes to employees, you make the final decisions. I figured it wouldn't hurt to have them fill out applications."

"And the Coke?"

"They ordered it. They paid for it. Happy?"

I was. Sort of. I'd be happier if more of our tables were filled. As if a second look might change things, I flipped around and took another quick inventory. I was just in time to see the front door open and a young woman rush inside.

She was about thirty, an attractive strawberry blonde in a Burberry raincoat. When she caught sight of Eve, she smiled and waved.

"Well, aren't you the sweetest thing, ever?" Eve folded the woman in a hug. "You said you'd be here today—"

"And here I am!" The woman laughed. "I can't stay, though," she added. "I've got a meeting at two and a ton to do to prepare for it. You have a takeaway menu, don't you?"

Eve assured her we did and led her to a table. She didn't bother calling Heidi over. Eve took the woman's order herself, scampered to the kitchen with it, and waved me over on her way back.

"Annie, you remember Sarah, don't you?"

I didn't, and maybe my expression said it all. Eve propped her hands on her hips. "Oh, come on! It wasn't that long ago. Sarah Whittaker? Charlene's sister? They look so much alike, they could practically be twins. I know you remember Charlene. She was—"

"In our home room in high school. Of course!" The light-bulb went on. "You were a couple years behind us in school if I remember correctly. How's your sister?"

When I offered my hand, Sarah stripped off her buttery leather gloves. She clutched them in her left hand as she shook mine firmly with her right. "Charlene is fine," she told us. Her smile was wide and genuine. "She's in the Peace Corps, you know. In Ukraine. I don't see her or talk to her often, but we've been able to e-mail pretty regularly."

As I remembered, Charlene Whittaker was a quiet, studious girl, and in spite of Eve's glowing assurance, she and Sarah could not be mistaken as twins. Charlene was short and chunky, with a face rounder than Sarah's and skin that wasn't nearly as porcelain clear. Plain though she may have been, Charlene had a good head on her shoulders and a good grasp of politics. Back in school, she'd been involved in Greenpeace and Habitat for Humanity. I wasn't surprised to hear she was following through with her convictions.

"Sarah and I haven't seen each other for a couple months. Then we ran into each other at the grocery store last week. She lives right in Arlington, not far from you, Annie. I told her about this place, and she said she'd stop in. Isn't that just sweet? And you know, she's going to pooh-pooh this, but I'll mention it, anyway. She's no slouch herself." Eve provided the information and, as if on cue, Sarah blushed. "She's on the staff of Douglas Mercy. You know, the senator."

I knew, all right. Who didn't? Senator Mercy was being talked about as a vice presidential candidate in the next election.

"Being a staffer isn't as impressive as it sounds." Sarah slipped out of her coat. She was dressed to perfection in a dark suit and a white blouse, and though I was more the sales rack type myself, I knew expensive clothing when I saw it. Her blouse was silk, and I'd bet an entire carafe of coffee that the emerald-and-diamond ring on her right hand had not come from the costume jewelry counter. "Senators have lots of staffers."

"Especially senators with the chops of Douglas Mercy." Eve made herself right at home, flopping down in the chair next to Sarah's. I didn't object. She was Bellywasher's one and only hostess, sure, but it wasn't exactly like we had lines outside the door. "So, tell me, honey, is Douglas Mercy as gorgeous in person as he is on TV?"

Sarah tipped her head as if she'd never really considered the question. "Well, he is in his sixties, but I suppose he's nice-looking anyway." An idea occurred to her, and her eyes widened. "He's single, too, you know. A widower. What do you say, Eve, want me to arrange a blind date?"

"Dates! Men!" Eve tossed her golden girls. She didn't have to elaborate. I knew exactly what she meant. Eve wasn't thinking *men*. She was thinking *man*. One man. Tyler Cooper.

Tyler is an Arlington homicide detective and the thorn in Eve's romantic side. Here's the scoop:

Eve and Tyler were engaged once upon a time, but then, that's not unusual. Eve's been engaged—and unengaged—more times than I can count. What qualifies Tyler for Eve's special contempt is that before him, she was the one who ended every single one of the engagements. Yup, that's right. Tyler is the only man who ever broke up with Eve.

That in itself is nasty enough. Unfortunately, the nastiness swelled (past animosity and all the way to I-can't-stand-the-sight-of-him territory) when Eve and I found the body in the parking lot of the gourmet shop where we took our cooking lessons.

And our urgent call for help was answered by a patrol officer named Kaitlin Sands, Tyler's current fiancée.

Bad enough, yes? But wait! As they say in those hokey commercials, there's plenty more.

After it was determined that the man was murdered and didn't die of natural causes, Tyler himself—in all his egotistical glory—showed up at Très Bonne Cuisine and looked down his roman nose at us when Eve and I told him we thought we knew who'd done it.

Then there was the little matter of how he took it when he found out we'd been right (at least about some things) all along.

Do I need to point out that Tyler was not a happy camper when we solved a case he couldn't?

The fact that he held Eve and me in the highest possible professional disdain paled in comparison (at least in Eve's eyes) to the fact that throughout our investigation and the (unfortunate) amount of times we bumped into him because of it, Tyler never so much as gave Eve a second glance.

Hell hath no fury, and Eve wasn't just a woman scorned. She'd been rejected, spurned, and told right to her face that she wasn't as smart/pretty/young/clever as Kaitlin. That had to hurt. I knew it for a fact, because I'd been told pretty much the same thing about Mandy (or Mindy, I never could remember) by Peter.

It was certainly ammunition enough to account for the fact that Eve's top lip curled before she said any more about a date with Senator Mercy.

"Men," Eve said, "are disposable. Even rich, powerful, handsome men like that senator of yours. No thanks, sugar. I'm not interested."

Sarah didn't know Eve as well as I did. She took the statement at face value. I, who had been Eve's best friend since the day in first grade when we were assigned to be each other's bathroom buddy, knew that sooner or later, she'd change her mind and be back in the hunt.

I knew it would be sooner.

I prayed it would be later.

I already had six unreturnable matron of honor gowns—never worn—hanging in the deepest, darkest recesses of my closet. I didn't need another one.

"Well . . ." Sarah sat up a little straighter. She had eyes as brown as acorns, and they sparkled with excitement. "I'm glad I had a chance to stop in. I didn't have these pictures with me when I saw you at the grocery store the other day." She reached into her Coach bag and held a small stack of photos to her heart. "I have something really exciting to tell you about: Doctor Masakazu."

News of the romantic sort is usually greeted with interest by Eve. But this time, I watched as her brow furrowed. In a pretty way, of course.

"Doctor? What happened to that hunky news anchor you were dating? Dylan What's-His-Name? You know, the one with the great hair and the really white teeth? You didn't—"

"Break up with him? You bet I did. But this isn't about a new boyfriend." Sarah's grin was as bright as the sunshine that played hide-and-seek with the November clouds outside. "It's about him. Doctor Masakazu."

She flipped the photos around and proudly held them in our direction. Because Eve was still staring, widemouthed, I sat down and took the pictures from Sarah's hand.

"It's a dog," I said, stating the obvious since I was looking at a picture of a tiny puppy with a thin brown face and dark eyes. "This is Doctor Masa . . ."

"Doctor Masakazu." Sarah laughed. "I don't know what it means for sure, but it sounds right, doesn't it? His breed originated in Japan and it's a Japanese name, at least the Masakazu part. We had a trade delegation visit from Japan a couple months ago, and one of the men in it was named Masakazu. I put the *doctor* in front of it for no reason at all except that it sounds so cute. I got him from the breeder a week ago. Is he adorable, or what?"

Adorable? I wasn't so sure, though I was willing to go as far as *cute*. Not that I'm not an animal lover. Furry and cuddly are very good things. But the very good things that are furry and cuddly can also be very bad things, and they often do even worse things to furniture, not to mention carpeting. My hunger for predictability precluded me from ever letting a creature into my life. After all, I'd already had one cuddly thing to call my own—Peter—and at the same time he proved himself a dirty dog, he also proved that my theory was right. No matter how cute, no matter how cuddly, they can be unpredictable, uncontrolled, and unrepentant when they're bad.

Eve, on the other hand, had no such reservations. About men or animals. But then, Eve has a heart as big as a Texas ranch. "He's the sweetest little thing I've seen in a month of Sundays," she said, snatching the pictures out of my hands for a better look. "My goodness, Sarah, is that a diamond bracelet he's wearing for a collar?"

I leaned in close for a better look at the picture. The puppy was wearing what looked like diamonds, all right, two rows of them stacked one on top of each other and mounted on a thin band of black leather.

"Diamonds?" Sarah laughed like she was embarrassed, and I couldn't blame her. Leave it to Eve to think of pampering a pooch she'd never even met. "Don't be silly, Eve. Though believe me, if he wanted diamonds, I'd buy him diamonds. He's my little sweetie pie."

The last sentence was delivered in the kind of high-pitched, singsong voice women use when they're talking to babies. I didn't begrudge Sarah this eccentricity, but I have to admit, I didn't fully understand it. Not that I don't love babies. My biological clock was ticking as loud as any other mid-thirties single woman's. I guess I just found it hard to understand translating that kind of affection to a dog.

"Sorry!" As if Sarah could read my mind, she made a face. "I know I sound like a complete nutcase, but I'm head over heels in love with the little guy. I had to wait just about forever for him. The breeder had a waiting list a mile long. But now that I've got him . . ." Her bosom heaved beneath her silk blouse. "He's so tiny and so affectionate! He's my best buddy."

Eve patted her hand. "I think it's adorable. You'll have to bring him in to meet us one of these days real soon."

"I don't think so." I disabused her of the notion before she allowed it to take on a life of its own, as Eve's ideas often do.

"Something tells me the health department wouldn't be happy about us having a dog in here. Even a dog as cute as Doctor Masa . . ."

"Masakazu." Sarah grinned. "Don't worry about not remembering his name. It's my fault. I should have named him Rover or something easy to remember, but he's just so special, I wanted him to have a special name."

Heidi appeared, take-out bag with Sarah's order of orange and fennel salad in hand. After Sarah paid and left a generous tip, she slipped into her raincoat and popped out of her seat. "I'd better get moving. Like I said, I've got that meeting. I'll tell you what . . ." She pulled on her gloves. "Why don't you two come over and meet Doctor Masakazu sometime? I know the little darling would love company, and you just won't believe how adorable he is."

I was about to say no, for no other reason than I couldn't imagine where I'd find the time. But Eve, of course, had already said yes.

"How about Wednesday?" Eve suggested before I could blurt out the fact that I had a meeting at work on Thursday (my *other* work) and I knew I had to be at the bank early. When I knew I had to be up early, I never allowed myself to stay out late the night before. "We'll bring dessert. Jim makes a flourless chocolate cake with hazelnuts that is to die for."

We set a time, and Eve scratched Sarah's address on the back of one of the business cards we kept in a stack on a table near the front door.

She was ready for me even before she turned around after escorting Sarah to the door.

"You need to take an evening off sometime in this century," she said. "You're tired and stressed out. And don't tell me that's not true."

"It is true, but—"

"And you don't have to be here every minute when you're not at the bank, Annie. You can handle the business end of things and walk away. Jim knows what he's doing when it comes to everything else. The staff is great, and besides, Wednesday is my night off."

"I know that, but—"

"But nothing. It will be fun." The front door opened, and two men in suits walked in. "Come on, Annie," Eve said right before she went over to welcome them. "You could use a little R & R, and I can't wait to meet that sweet little dog. You're such a worrywart. What can possibly go wrong?"

It was the second time that day that I'd heard the question.

I tried not to think about it, but even as I did, I saw Heidi take another carafe of coffee over to Larry, Hank, and Charlie.

Three

✖

SARAH LIVED IN ARLINGTON. JUST LIKE I DID. TRUTH BE told, though, it wasn't exactly the same Arlington.

I live in a modest apartment in a building that was erected the same year I was born. Don't try to do the math. Let's just say it makes my apartment building older than I care to say.

Age aside, it's a nice place. My neighbors are (for the most part) quiet, the building is always clean, and the landscaping, though it isn't inspired, is neat, trimmed, and brightened with minimal displays of seasonal flowers and Santas/menorahs/Kwanzaa candles when appropriate.

But though it is where I live, my apartment will never really be home. Like millions of other little girls, I grew up dreaming of a house with a picket fence and a wide expanse of grass where my children (always clean, well-behaved, and—it goes without saying—in the gifted program at school) could play to their little hearts' content with their equally spotless friends.

For the first years of our marriage, it was Peter's dream, too. At least the part about the house and the yard. (He was a high school chemistry teacher, after all, and so, a little more down-to-earth when it came to the well-behaved and spotless parts.) Real estate prices in the D.C. area are out of this world, but Peter was determined. Or maybe he was just trying to humor me. We were actually looking at (very small) houses when he was overcome with dry cleaning fumes and the perfume of the girl behind the counter. That's when he came to the realization that my dreams weren't his dreams. None of them.

Our marriage wasn't the only thing split in two. So was our savings account. And there went any hopes I had of owning a home of my own. At least any time before I was so old, I couldn't make it up the front steps without help.

Still, dreams die hard. Some nights I lie in bed and imagine how I'll decorate my very own house, what shades of beige I'll use in each of the rooms, which flowers will edge the path that leads from the sidewalk to my front door.

Yes, it's a little delusional, but it is also fun, and call me crazy, but I know I'll go right on dreaming until I somehow make my dream come true. Nothing can shake me from my picket-fence fantasies.

Unless, perhaps, if I had Sarah's address.

The next Wednesday night, Eve and I stood side by side, our eyes wide and our mouths hanging open, in the lobby of Sarah Whittaker's apartment building. The fact that Eve was speechless should say a lot.

Sarah lived in Clarendon, the same Arlington neighborhood where Eve and I had taken our ill-fated cooking class at Très Bonne Cuisine. The neighborhood is a mixture of funky old and trendy new, and from the looks of things, this building was one of the newest of the new, so brand-spanking-new, in fact, that the carpeting smelled as if it had just been laid.

The architecture was, in a word, amazing. Clean lines, touches of chrome (or was it stainless steel?), and a lobby that featured a lofty ceiling and wide, high windows that during the day must have let in an amazing amount of light. It was airy and it was classy and it was spectacular. I tamped down a wave of lifestyle envy lest it get the better of me, and wished

I'd listened to my high school guidance counselor who always
said I should have attended college. Something told me a job
on a senator's staff paid more than I made at the bank.

Before the green-eyed monster could completely take
over, I shook myself back to reality. I left Eve checking out a
sleek sculpture of what looked like a vase of flowers (but
might have been a mother and child) and asked the doorman
to call and tell Sarah we were there.

There was no answer.

Convinced he'd called the wrong number, he tried again.

Still no answer.

I guess by this time, I looked a little confused and, by the
way, the doorman looked suspicious. When he left the lobby
desk to help an elderly lady with a boatload of packages, he
raised an eyebrow and gave us a look that pretty much said
we should get a move on. Eve came over to see what was up.

"You called Sarah, didn't you?" I asked her. "You said
you did."

She nodded. "I called yesterday. Just like I told her I
would. Sarah didn't answer, but I left a message. I reminded her we were coming tonight and that we were bringing dessert." As if to prove it, she lifted two bags. One of
them was from Bellywasher's, and I knew it contained three
larger-than-usual pieces of flourless chocolate cake. Though
Eve hadn't told me what was inside the other bag, I had my
suspicions the moment I saw that it came from an Old Town
boutique called the Pampered Pooch. "She's got to be home.
With all that traffic we ran into because of the water main
break over near the Pentagon yesterday that they were still
cleaning up, we're even a little late. She's had plenty of time
to get home from work. She wouldn't invite us over and then
not be here. She's dying for us to meet Doctor Masakazu."

"Well, you try." Since the doorman had disappeared with
the elderly woman, Eve leaned over the desk and grabbed
the phone. She punched in the numbers. She had no luck.

She replaced the receiver and harrumphed. "The buzzer
thingy is probably broken. Sarah gave me her cell number.

I have it with me. I think." She headed over to where a taste-ful grouping of leather furniture was nestled in front of a gas fireplace where flames sparkled in the grate. She set her bag on the couch, flopped down beside it, and started rum-maging.

I know Eve well. I know the kinds of things she carries in her purse, and I know how much she can jam into one bag.

I plunked down on a leather love seat for the duration, watching and waiting.

Eve pulled out three tubes of lipstick and set them on the couch. Next came a comb, a brush, and two of those round metal containers of breath mints. "I know my address book is in here somewhere." She was bent over her purse, and her voice was muffled. "That's where I wrote the number. Just give me a little while and . . ."

She continued to mutter and dig, and while she did, I tried to get comfortable. It should have been possible, con-sidering that sitting on the love seat was akin to riding on a cloud. I actually might have been able to enjoy the experi-ence if I didn't keep thinking that we'd been stood up and that I was sitting there doing nothing when I could have been over at Bellywasher's, checking inventory, paying bills, or doing one of the thousand other things that demanded my attention.

I was just about to tell Eve as much and ask her to drive me to the restaurant, so I could put in a couple hours in front of my unruly computer and hope I could get it to load my Quick Books program, when the glass doors that separated the entryway from the elevators swung open. A middle-aged man wearing gray work pants and a matching shirt walked out. The embroidery over his heart said his name was Foster.

"Excuse me. Do you work here?" I didn't want to look desperate, but I didn't want Foster to get away, either. I hopped off the love seat and closed in on him before he could make it to the front doors, and when he nodded, I breathed a sigh of relief. "We're trying to buzz a friend," I explained, "and she's not answering."

"Doorman didn't get through?"

"No, and he's gone now. We thought maybe—"

"No way the buzzer's not working." Foster was, apparently, not one to wait to hear all the details. "The system's brand-new, and we check it all the time. Tested it this morning, and it's working fine."

"Well, maybe, but—"

"Nobody buzzes you in, you can't get in."

"I know that. And I understand it. Security is important, but—"

"Your friend isn't home."

"But we called her. We left a message. She knew we were coming and—"

"Oh, Annie, don't be so insistent. This nice man is only doing his job." Sometime while I was trying to reason with Foster, Eve had joined us. She gave him her widest beauty queen smile and a little pat on the arm that told him she sympathized with his position. "Who would think a little thing like this"—She looked my way and yes, since she was wearing four-inch heels and I was in sneakers, and since at five-eleven she was far taller than my five-foot-two to begin with, I guess I did qualify as a *little thing*—"could be so pushy!" Eve giggled, and whether he knew it or not, Foster was caught in her tractor beam. He smiled back. "What my friend here doesn't understand . . ." she told Foster, leaning in close enough for him to get a whiff of Happy Heart and just the tiniest peek down the low-cut neckline of her pink cashmere sweater. "Is that there are rules about things like this. That's why beautiful and expensive apartment buildings have buzzers, Annie, honey. And conscientious employees like Foster here. So that not everyone can just go marching up, willy-nilly, anyplace they want. Unless they know someone, of course. Someone like our friend Foster."

She batted her eyelashes at him, and I knew exactly what was going to happen next. Poor Foster didn't stand a chance.

Little did Eve or I suspect that there were unplumbed depths to Foster's personality.

"Can't let you in," he said. Oh, he was still smiling when he said it. And he was still trying for a better look at Eve's cleavage. Only he wasn't budging an inch. "No one can let you in but one of our tenants. That's the rule, and if I don't follow it, I'm going to be up shit creek."

"Of course, I understand all that," Eve began, but Foster was already walking away.

"Maybe we're just not calling the right number." I chimed in again. If there was one thing I'd learned in the years I was married to Peter, it was that a lot of guys liked to think they knew things that women didn't. Even things like the right way to use a phone.

Foster, it seemed, was one of those guys.

He shrugged and walked over to the phone.

"Sarah Whittaker," I told him.

"Apartment 16A," Eve added.

"Sixteen A?" Foster stopped before he ever had a hand on the phone. "You sure?"

"About the apartment?" Eve dug into her purse again, but I didn't need her to find Sarah's address and phone number to be certain. I remembered what Sarah had written on the back of the Bellywasher's card.

"Yes, 16A," I told Foster. "Absolutely. Why, is there some problem?"

He scratched a finger behind his ear. "Had some calls today about that apartment. Complaints, you know. There's a dog up there—"

"Doctor Masakazu." Eve supplied the detail.

"Whatever." Foster rolled his eyes. "Don't know about no doctor. All's I know is that there's a dog up there and it's been barking all day long. This is an expensive place to live. People have certain . . . what do you call them? Expectations. The people up there on sixteen, they're getting mighty tired of hearing that barking. It was bad enough during the day when just about everybody was out at work. Now that it's dinnertime . . . well, if that mutt doesn't shut up soon, somebody's going to call the management company, and then my ass is going to be on the line. Pets are allowed here, see, but only if they're well-behaved. Sure as I'm standing here, I'm going to get blamed for not making sure that one is quiet."

"We could do it." I don't know why I thought so. After all, I had never met Doctor Masakazu, so I didn't know if the dog would respond to either me or Eve. I don't know why it seemed important to get upstairs, either, except for the fact that it struck me as odd that Sarah would invite us over and then not be there to let us in.

I pictured her sick.

I pictured her hurt.

I pictured my desk back at Bellywasher's and the stack of work that was waiting there for me, and I thought about how tired I was of running back and forth between the restaurant and the bank. I would never admit it—not to Jim, not to Eve, not even to myself—but I really wanted this night off. I needed it. Sarah had to be home so I could kick back, drink coffee, and eat flourless chocolate cake with a clear conscience.

"Doctor Masa . . ." The name was impossible. I didn't even try, just started again. "The dog knows us," I assured Foster. "He'll be thrilled to see us. We can feed him. Or take him for a walk. Whatever it takes to make him stop barking."

Foster wasn't convinced. "You're sure?"

"Sure?" Eve's silvery laugh rang through the soaring lobby. "Why, don't you know who this is? Annie Capshaw. *The* Annie Capshaw? If you read the *Post*, surely you've heard of her. You know horse whisperers? Annie here is a dog whisperer. The best in the business. Oh honey, her clientele is the Who's Who of Capitol Hill. Or at least the Who's Who's doggy friends. She'll quiet that critter up in no time flat."

Was Foster a sucker? Or just desperate?

Either way, he slid a key card through the keypad next to the front doors, and they swung open. "OK. But I'm coming with you," he said, and he led us to the elevators.

As soon as his back was turned, I shot a wide-eyed look in Eve's direction. "Dog whisperer?" I mouthed the words, but there was no mistaking my outrage.

Eve was still laughing about it when we stepped off the elevator on the sixteenth floor.

"Sixteen A is over that way," Foster said, pointing down a long hallway on our right.

He really didn't need to. Even from here, we could hear Doctor Masakazu. Foster had been kind when he said the dog was barking. What it was really doing was yapping. A lot. The high-pitched noise made my skin crawl and my teeth hurt. I pitied the poor people who had been listening to it all day.

"This is exactly the kind of case Annie specializes in," Eve told Foster. Leave it to her to milk a good story for all it was worth, even when we didn't need it to convince Foster to help us any longer. "You'll see. You'll be so grateful, you might want to keep her business cards. You know, to hand out to other people in the building who might be having the same sort of difficult canine problems."

Lucky for us, we arrived at Sarah's door, and Eve stopped talking. Foster knocked. Doctor Masakazu yapped even louder.

No one answered.

Foster pulled out his passkey and unlocked the door, rapping on it with his knuckles. He opened it, but not all the way. There was no sign of life. Except for the dog's yapping, of course.

"What did you say her name was?" Foster asked me, and when I supplied the information, he raised his voice. "Miss Whittaker? It's me, Foster. You know, the maintenance man. You got some visitors here. Can we come in, ma'am?"

Still no answer. This time, Foster pushed the door all the way open, and we had our first glimpse of the apartment.

The lifestyle envy came back with a vengeance.

Oh yeah, one step into Sarah's apartment, and already I knew I could learn to live like this. Champagne carpet, furniture in muted tones of sage and burgundy. The place was as neat as a pin and as beautiful as a showplace in a decorating magazine. Sarah had a killer view of Arlington, a collection of simple yet striking black-and-white photos on her walls, and a dining room table that was set with a china pot and cups. As if she was expecting company.

"Told you she knew we were coming," Eve said to Foster, pointing to the table, but though he nodded as if he was finally ready to admit we'd been right all along, he didn't take another step inside.

"You go look," he said from his spot near the door. He had to raise his voice to be heard above the dog's yapping, more plaintive than ever now that he knew he had company. "I don't feel right, you know, going through a tenant's place. If she's a friend of yours, she won't mind."

Eve didn't hesitate. There was a dog carrier in the living room next to the couch, and she hurried over to it, opened the door, and scooped Doctor Masakazu into her arms.

The dog couldn't have weighed more than a couple pounds. It had dark V-shaped ears that hung close to its head and an alert, clever expression on his face that seemed to say *Eureka! I knew if I yapped long enough, someone would come to play with me.* The attention was apparently all he wanted. He stopped barking.

"Isn't he just the most adorable!" I had never known Eve to be an animal lover, unless the animal in question was sable, mink, or fox. It didn't stop her from scratching a finger under the pup's rhinestone collar. Or from giving him a hug. As soon as she did, she wrinkled her nose and held him at arm's length. "Hey, aren't dogs supposed to not soil their crates? That's what I heard somebody say when I went to that doggy boutique today." She looked the dog in the eye, and I swear, there must have been some kind of canine mojo at work. Suddenly, she was talking in the same singsong voice Sarah had used back at the restaurant. "Doctor Masakazu, have you been a bad little puppy-wuppy?"

I didn't wait to find out. I peeked into the kitchen, a sleek and glossy room painted yellow ochre and filled with stainless steel that was reflected in the black granite countertops and hardwood floor. There was nothing out of place and no sign that anyone had been there recently, except for two wineglasses that were inverted on the dish drainer, washed and waiting to be put away.

The kitchen had two doors. One led back into the living room and dining room where I could hear Eve asking the dog (like she expected an answer?) where his leash was so she could take him out for some fresh air and where Sarah kept his food dish because—don't ask me how she decided this— she could tell from looking at his sweet little face (her words, not mine), that he was hungry-wungry. I decided not to go there, literally or figuratively, and headed in the other direction instead. The second door took me into a hallway where more photographs were displayed in simple black frames.

I felt a little funny checking out someone else's things. Still, I couldn't help looking. Or admiring what I saw.

Each photograph was black-and-white, and every one of them seemed to have been taken in the same setting. A park, I'd guess. The first was a picture of flowers. In spite of the lack of color, thanks to the clever use of light and shadow, they looked as if I could lean closer and sniff them. There was a picture of children on swings, their bodies blurred with movement but their smiles plain to see. There was another one of an empty park bench, icicles hanging from its seat, and still another that showed sunlight glimmering through the splashing water of a fountain.

I'm no connoisseur, especially when it comes to art, but I know good when I see it, and those photos were very good. I also saw that each one had Sarah's signature in the bottom right-hand corner.

I smiled, pleased to see that our new friend had such a special talent. Then I continued my search.

The first room I peeked into must have been Sarah's

bedroom. It was as pristine as the rest of the place, and as tastefully decorated. So was the office next to it where a computer sat on a desk next to a neat stack of mail. I recognized the logo on the envelope at the top of the pile; Sarah banked with us at Pioneer Savings and Loan. A third bedroom looked as if it was used as a guest room.

I may not be the brightest bulb in the box, but I was beginning to get the picture. Sarah wasn't home. If I wasn't so thorough (some people might say *anal*), I never would have looked into the bathroom. The way it was, it was at the end of the hallway, and I was right there. Besides, the door was closed, and I could see the glow of a light from under it.

Call me crazy, but that struck me as a bit strange, considering no one was around but the dog.

I knocked. Just in case. I didn't expect an answer, so I wasn't disappointed when I didn't get one. I turned the knob and walked inside.

I'm not the dramatic type, so I don't think I screamed when I saw the body in the bathtub. But I guess I must have made some kind of noise. Eve and Foster came running.

"Oh, my gosh!" Behind me, Eve's voice choked over a sob. I turned just long enough to see that she was still carrying the dog. She put her hand over his eyes as if to spare him the sight. "It's Sarah. Is she . . ." Eve couldn't make herself say the word.

I took a couple steps closer to the tub, but I really didn't have to. Even the not-brightest bulb in the box can recognize dead when she sees it, and Sarah Whittaker was definitely dead.

Her head was thrown back against the rim of the tub. Her eyes were open and staring. Her skin looked waxy and as pale as the white ceramic tile floor. As if it was some macabre, slow-motion dance, her body bobbed in the maroon-tinted water that filled the tub nearly to its brim.

The color struck me as odd. Until I saw the bloody knife on the floor next to the tub. And the hideous gashes that slit Sarah's wrists from one side to the other.

My own blood whooshed like a torrent inside my ears, but that didn't stop me from hearing Foster say something about calling 911. Or from hearing Eve's scream.

It was all Doctor Masakazu needed to decide that something was up, and that whatever it was, he didn't like being left out of it. He started yapping all over again.

Four

✖

THE POLICE ASSURED FOSTER THEY'D BE RIGHT OVER, and because there wasn't anything else we could do, we went to the living room to wait. Although Eve was reluctant to let him go, I thought it best if Doctor Masakazu went back in his carrier. I don't know if the site of a suicide is officially classified as a crime scene, but I suspected the cops wouldn't want anything to be touched, including the dog. Besides, Eve was hugging the little critter so tight, I was worried she would smother him. We already had enough on our plates.

I don't need to point out that Doctor Masakazu was not happy about my decision and for as long as I could stand it, I put up with the yapping. But let's face it, my nerves were stretched pretty thin. Yes, I may have been tampering with evidence, but I was willing to risk it for a little peace and quiet. After a few minutes, I put the carrier—and the dog in it—in the guest room and shut the door.

Distance and a closed door helped, but even the noise of the dog's incessant yapping couldn't drown out the sounds of Eve's quiet sobs. Or of Foster's breaths, quick and shallow. Staring straight ahead, he sat in a chair across from the couch where Eve and I sat side by side. His hands shook—I guessed he was a smoker. It was a nasty habit, one I never understood, but I sympathized. He needed a nicotine fix, and he needed it badly. Heck, I didn't smoke—never had, never will—but if someone offered me a cigarette then and there, I would have fired right up.

I was about to suggest that Foster step out on the balcony when two paramedics arrived along with a woman in a navy blue windbreaker who was carrying a camera. Foster had apparently told them enough for them to know what to expect; they weren't in any hurry. I led them to the bathroom, closed the front door they'd left open because the neighbors who'd caught wind of the commotion and were milling in the hallway made me feel ghoulish, and went back to the couch. There wasn't much we could tell the authorities and no question about what had happened to Sarah. Still, I knew they were going to want to talk to us.

I'm not sure how long we sat there. My hands clutched in my lap, I listened to the muffled voices of the people in the bathroom, punctuated by the rise and fall of the dog's mournful howls. I heard the swish and drip of water and wondered if they'd taken Sarah out of the tub. I hoped they remembered to clean up after themselves; she liked her apartment neat.

Really neat.

Something about the idea caught my attention and honestly, I was grateful. Studying the room was better than picturing the image burned in my brain: Sarah in the bathtub. Her wrists sliced. Her blood coloring the water.

I have been known to be a tad obsessive when it comes to orderliness, but as I looked around the living room, I realized that compared to Sarah, I was an amateur. The magazines on the coffee table in front of me were lined up by title and issue date. The books—mostly biographies, mostly of politicians—on the shelves across from where we sat were arranged alphabetically, not by title or author, but by subject. Reagan with Roosevelt down near the floor. Carter and Castro right next to Clinton (both him and her) on one of the higher shelves.

Talk about politics making strange bedfellows.

From there, I let my gaze wander to a narrow table against the wall just inside the front door where three exquisite porcelain vases of varying sizes were set out precisely: small, medium, large.

Admittedly, I was pretty shaken up, and in my state of mind, I didn't think any of this was odd or eccentric or even admirable. I didn't make any judgment at all. Apparently, like her spare and deft photographic style and her interest in politics, this was just another facet of Sarah's personality. If I thought anything about it at all, it was that, fussy or not, I was sorry I would never have the chance to get to know Sarah better.

I switched my gaze back to the bookshelf, reading each title over to myself. It was better than thinking about what had happened there in the apartment before we arrived and what darkness drove people to take their own lives. I was halfway through the *K*s (Kennedy, Khrushchev, King) when I realized the front door had opened, and someone new had come into the apartment.

This didn't concern me. Not as much as holding on to my tenuous composure. I moved on.

McCain, McCarthy, McGovern.

There were, apparently, no politicians whose names began with *L* who interested Sarah. Not even Lincoln. Quickly I scanned the shelves, wondering if Honest Abe had been misplaced. There was no sign of him or of any other *L* politico I could think of. Not Huey Long or Louis XIV or—

"Is there a reason I'm not surprised to find the two of you here?"

The question snapped me out of my thoughts. So did the fact that it came from a man who was standing in the doorway between the front entryway and the living room, his fists back just far enough on his hips to push his unbuttoned raincoat open and show off his shoulder holster and the gun in it.

I knew the exact moment Eve noticed him. I felt the couch shift as she sat up straight and tall. She hiccupped, pressed her lips together, and automatically combed her fingers through her hair. I forgave her the conceit. Tyler Cooper was like a poison. He was in her blood, and even if she wanted to, there was no way she could ignore him. The antidote had yet to be discovered.

I stood. I don't know why, except that sitting made me feel as if I had to make excuses, and the way I saw things, there was no reason for that. "Sarah Whittaker was a friend," I told Tyler. "She invited us over tonight."

"And then once you got here and she let you in, she just happened to kill herself?"

He was trying to get a rise out of us, so I knew better than to answer his question. Foster, however, did not.

"It ain't like that, Officer," the maintenance man said. As if he was cold, he rubbed his hands together. "She was already dead. When we walked in. I swear on my mother's grave. I let these ladies in and—"

With one withering look, Tyler stopped him right there. "You'll tell me all the details when I'm done with the deceased. And—" He cringed. "What the hell is that awful noise?"

"It's not an awful noise." Eve was on her feet in an instant. I don't think she'd planned the move. She was too upset for that. But she couldn't have designed it any better. Tyler was a smidgen under six feet tall. In her heels, Eve had to look down her nose to see him. "It's Doctor Masakazu you hear," she told him. "He's mourning the loss of his master, the poor little darling. And if you had one ounce of kindness in your stone-cold soul—"

Tyler turned around and headed down the hallway for the bathroom.

"Guess I told him," Eve grumbled.

I didn't point out that even if she had, he didn't stick around long enough to hear it.

Instead, I sat back down. Once she'd paced back and

forth to get rid of some of her nervous energy and put on a
fresh coat of lipstick, Eve joined me. That's where we were
when another team of paramedics came through the front
door with a stretcher. It's where we sat and watched, help-
less, silent, and holding each other's hands, as Sarah's body
was taken out of the apartment.

"So . . ." Tyler came back into the living room. The commotion he'd heard outside the guest room door made the dog
bark even louder, and Tyler had to raise his voice. "Somebody want to tell me what happened here?"

The answer was pretty obvious. Which didn't explain
why Tyler looked from Eve to me and back again. I knew
that an Eve versus Tyler smackdown wasn't going to get us
anywhere, so I answered his question before she could.

"I already told you," I said, and Tyler's neon blue gaze
swiveled my way. "Sarah invited us over tonight." I pointed
toward the Bellywasher's bag. "We brought dessert."

"And she let you into the apartment?"

"Of course not." He knew this, but I felt obligated to point
it out, anyway. "She was already dead."

"Then when she invited you over, she gave you a key?"

I fought to keep my voice even. "No. She didn't do that,
either. We called when we got here. From the phone in the
lobby. When she didn't buzz us up, we knew something was
wrong because she knew we were coming. That's when Foster came along and let us in."

Tyler pulled a small notepad from his pocket, clicked
open a pen, and scratched a note. "You supposed to do that,
Foster?" he asked the maintenance man.

Foster blanched. "I . . . um . . . I—"

"It's lucky he did," I said. Call me a sucker, but I hated to
see Tyler bully anyone. "Who knows when Sarah would
have been found if Foster wasn't around. He didn't do anything wrong. He was just trying to help Doctor Masa . . . the
dog."

"The dog." Tyler made another note. "How long has he
been carrying on like this?"

Foster shook his head. "Been getting calls all day. I knew I had to do something, and when these ladies said they'd help—"

"I'll just bet they did." Tyler did a quick turn around the room. He looked at the bookshelves, the magazines, the photos on the wall. He finally stopped with his back to the floor-to-ceiling French doors that led onto the balcony. Am I that small-minded? Or is it just that I know Tyler well? I was certain he'd chosen the spot because the glow of city lights accented his sandy hair, outlined his broad shoulders, and made him look more formidable than ever.

"If you came up here to shut the dog up, you did a hell of a bad job of it," Tyler said.

Eve's jaw clenched, but I had to give her credit. Tyler was behind her, and she didn't bother to turn around. "Doctor Masakazu was fine. Until we found Sarah." Her voice broke over a sob.

"The dog obviously hasn't been out for a while." I filled in the blanks for Tyler. "And I'll bet he hasn't eaten, either. Maybe not all day."

"Maybe not since yesterday." He walked around the couch and over to the bookshelves. "Crime scene techs say she's probably been dead that long, though it's hard to tell without an autopsy. The water's cold, and that kept the body cold, too." He glanced Eve's way. "Please don't tell me you called to confirm you'd be here today and that you talked to her when you did. That would mess up our whole timeline."

Eve's eyes flashed. "Are you more interested in your timeline or in finding out what happened to that poor girl?"

"What happened to that poor girl . . ." Tyler's words were edged with impatience. He reined it in and lowered his voice as much as he was able to and still be heard above the yapping. "What happened to that poor girl is that she poured a nice, hot bath, sat down in it, and cut her wrists. Any questions?"

It was one of those rhetorical questions, and I should

have left well enough alone. Fact is, though, I have never been known to accept things at face value. "Then why are you here?" I asked Tyler. "You're with homicide. If you knew this was a suicide—"

Tyler's sigh was monumental. "Yeah, I'm with homicide, and I just happened to be unlucky enough to be the closest one to the call. We check out all unexpected deaths. We'll close the books on this one in no time flat."

"You don't think it's suspicious?"

He shot me one of those cop looks, like the ones I remembered getting time and time again from the boys in blue the summer before when we were investigating Drago's murder. It walked the fine line between the politeness a public servant had to show the civilian population in general and the mind-your-own-business lecture I knew Tyler was tempted to give me.

"The only thing suspicious here," Tyler said, "is how you two keep showing up where there are dead bodies. You want to explain?"

I didn't, but I didn't feel as if I had a choice. "We told you. Sarah invited us. And Eve called yesterday to confirm."

"Time?" Tyler's pen was poised over his notepad.

Eve shrugged. "I don't know. Three, maybe. It doesn't really matter, because she didn't answer. I left a message."

Tyler looked around for a phone. I had seen one on the counter in the kitchen, and I had noticed the red message light on it was blinking. I didn't bother to point this out to him. Tyler Cooper might have been a coldhearted son of a gun, but he was also a good cop. He would check and find this out for himself.

"And the last time you saw Ms. Whittaker was . . . ?" This time, Tyler's icy gaze took in all of us.

Foster shrugged. "I dunno. Don't know if I ever met the lady. I been up here. You know, before she moved in. That couldn't have been more than two or three weeks ago. We vacuumed the hallways, did a last check on the heat and the lighting. You know, before the tenants started moving in. But before tonight . . ." His voice faded, and his eyes went blank. I knew he was reliving that first sight of Sarah's cold, pale body.

Because I didn't want to go there with Foster, I gave Tyler our side of the story. "Sarah stopped into Bellywasher's last week. It's a restaurant. In Alexandria."

Tyler made a note of this.

"And when she did, how did she seem? Was she upset about anything?"

Eve shook her head, but before she could answer, I remembered something Sarah had said. "She broke up with her boyfriend," I told Tyler. "Dylan. That's his name."

"A romance gone bad." Tyler wrote down the words and underlined them with a flourish. He flipped his notebook closed.

"But—"

I was not so easily put off. Not even by the look he flashed my way.

"But she didn't seem especially upset about it," I told Tyler. "Remember, Eve? She mentioned Doctor Masakazu. And you asked—"

"If she had a new man in her life." Eve scooted to the edge of the couch. "That's right. She said Dylan was history. But she didn't seem broken up about it."

"Oh, come on!" Tyler rolled his eyes. "You're telling me a woman gets dumped by her boyfriend one week, then slits her wrists the next, and one thing doesn't have anything to do with the other? What fairy-tale world are you two living in?"

"You think she killed herself because her boyfriend broke up with her?" Eve's voice dripped with contempt. "Oh, come on, Tyler, honey! There isn't a man in the world worth dying over."

His gaze met Eve's and never wavered. "Maybe you just never met the right man."

"Well, that's a fact." She rose to her feet. "So that's that? That's all you need to know?"

He didn't say yes or no, just pursed his lips. "Seems pretty straightforward," he said. "My work here is done."

"But what about—" I was thinking out loud and I didn't even realize it until the words were out of my mouth. Once I started, I figured I might as well keep going. "But why would she invite us over? Why ask us to stop by today if she was planning on killing herself yesterday?"

Tyler gave a noncommital shrug. "Who knows how people think when they get desperate. Maybe she forgot you were coming. Maybe she just didn't care anymore. Hell, maybe you were mean to her in seventh grade, and she wanted to get back at you, and she figured this would teach you a lesson. Maybe she wanted to make sure somebody found her. Suicide and clear thinking, they don't always go together."

"But if it wasn't—"

"Wasn't suicide?" This time, Tyler didn't even try to disguise the fact that he thought I was being woodenheaded. "You think just because you trip over one murder victim—"

"Two," Eve corrected him.

He ignored it. "You think because you got too close to a crime once—or twice," he added with a look at Eve because he knew she was going to interrupt again. "You think you know all there is to know about murder?"

"Of course not!" I didn't mind admitting it. "But it just doesn't make sense." I remembered something else I'd seen when I looked around the apartment. "You know, there are wineglasses in the kitchen."

Tyler shrugged. "So the lady liked a glass of wine now and then."

"Two wineglasses," I pointed out. "Washed and left on the sink to dry. She wouldn't have done that. She wouldn't have left them there."

His eyebrows did a slow slide up his forehead. "And you know this because . . . what, you knew this woman so well, you know about her dishwashing habits?"

"No, I hardly knew her at all, but—"

Tyler had heard enough. He turned to leave.

I tried a last-ditch effort to make him see that I wasn't buying his theory. "But it just doesn't make any sense."

The whole public-servant thing must have kicked in, because he stopped and turned back to me, even though it was clear that it was the last thing he wanted to do.

"It doesn't make any sense for Sarah to have us come over. Not if she was planning to kill herself. You think if she was, she would have—"

"Left a suicide note?" Tyler pulled a plastic bag out of his pocket. It contained a single piece of paper, written on with blue ink. The handwriting was flowing and feminine. He waved the plastic bag back and forth in front of us. "What do you think, ladies? This was on the dresser in the bedroom. Is it enough to convince you that you're seeing bogeymen where there aren't any? How about what Ms. Whittaker says in the note?"

He flattened the bag and read from the paper. " 'Not going to take it.' That's exactly what it says. 'Not satisfied, and I'm not going to take it.' "

"Not satisfied?" If you asked me, it was a mighty odd way to express heartbreak. "Not satisfied with what? With what Dylan did to her? What he left her?"

"Maybe she just wasn't satisfied with her life. Or heck, maybe he was a lousy lover. We're never going to know." Tyler's voice snapped, and I think his temper would have, too, if he didn't control it with an effort that was nearly palpable. "Look . . ." He drew in a breath, let it out slowly, and after he put the note back in his pocket, he scrubbed his hands over his face. "I know this can be tough. Finding a body is bad enough, but when it's someone you know . . . well, it's not easy. Believe me, I've seen this enough times to know. You're looking for answers, I'm not giving you any, and it's frustrating. But I'm not trying to stonewall you, and I'm not trying to give you a hard time, and I'm not trying to keep information from you, because there isn't anything that you don't already know. This is sad, and it's difficult, but it's as straightforward as it gets. Ms. Whittaker killed herself.

I know it's hard to make peace with something like that. Especially when it's a friend. But that's the end of the story. Wineglasses or no wineglasses."

Tyler was right, and I knew it. So did Eve. As much as she would have liked to argue with him, she pressed her lips together. I saw her shoulders rise and fall. We could spin this any way we wanted, but when our heads stopped whirling, we knew we had no choice but to face the truth.

I was about to tell Tyler this when Doctor Masakazu's howling grew louder and more insistent than ever.

The sound Tyler made from between clenched teeth was something like a growl. "Maybe she killed herself because she just couldn't stand living with that dog anymore," he said. "Maybe she wanted you here to make sure somebody found it before the neighbors stormed the door and tossed it out the window."

"Well, I never!" Eve marched forward and stood toe-to-toe with Tyler. "How you can be so insensitive at a time like this is a wonder to me. No, wait! It isn't a surprise at all. You were always a coldhearted bastard."

A tiny smile quirked the corner of Tyler's mouth. "That's not what Kaitlin says."

I had to give Eve credit—she didn't flinch at the mention of Tyler's current fiancée. "That poor little girl just doesn't know you well enough," she said. "She'll come to her senses. Sooner or later. And when she does—"

Doctor Masakazu's yaps rose to fever pitch, and Tyler threw his hands in the air. "Will somebody do something about that dog!"

I have a feeling the order was intended for the cops who were still in the bathroom, making their final notes about the scene, but Eve could move pretty fast when she wanted to. Even in four-inch heels.

She was in the guest room in a flash. Before I could remind her that what she was doing was making a commitment and that she was commitment-phobic, she was back, dog carrier and dog—quiet now that someone was paying attention to him—in hand.

"We'll take him," Eve told Tyler. "The poor thing is upset and hungry, and somebody needs to watch out for him until Sarah's sister can come and get him."

He snorted. "I can't let you do that."

"Would you rather listen to him?"

As if the dog understood Eve's question, he ratcheted up the noise, and Tyler gave in with a good-riddance wave of both hands. "It's that or I'm getting out my gun," he said.

Apparently, Eve wasn't willing to wait around and see if he was kidding. We hightailed it out of Sarah's apartment.

No sooner were we back in Eve's car than Doctor Masakazu was sound asleep.

Five

✖

WHEN I WALKED INTO THE KITCHEN OF BELLYWASHER'S the next evening, I found Eve on her break. She was sitting on a stool in a quiet corner between the walk-in cooler and the pantry where we kept the canned goods. At least she had the good sense to look embarrassed when I took one look at her and my mouth dropped open; she had Doctor Masakazu on her lap.

Red-faced or not, it didn't stop her from breaking off tiny bits of goat cheese and artichoke bruschetta and feeding them to the dog.

I hadn't had a chance to talk to Jim since I'd arrived; he was busy going from table to table (all three of them that were full), greeting our guests and making sure everything was to their liking. I knew there was no way he knew the dog was there—if he did, the dog would be gone. I looked over my shoulder to make sure he was still busy and made sure the door between the kitchen and the restaurant was firmly shut. Then I closed in on Eve. Suddenly, my heart was racing double time.

Just like my imagination.

In my mind's eye I saw teams of health inspectors in full

riot gear raiding the place. They all had health regulations code books in hand and pens poised over papers that said *violation* in big black letters at the top.

My voice was shrill, but I tried to keep it down. No use attracting any more attention from Marc or Damien, who were both busy at the grill. Besides, from the way they avoided looking at me, something told me they knew what was going on. No doubt, Eve had already worked a little of her mumbo jumbo guy magic. No way they were going to squeal on her.

I, however, was not so easily swayed. "Are you crazy?" I asked her, but I didn't wait for her to answer. "You can't bring an animal into a restaurant. It's against every health regulation there is. Does Jim know? He doesn't know, does he? No way would he be out there acting as if everything was normal if he knew. If he sees that dog, he's going to have a coronary."

There were windows in the swinging doors between the kitchen and the restaurant, and Eve sat up tall and craned her neck to confirm that Jim couldn't see us. Satisfied the coast was clear, she broke off another piece of bread and held it in front of the dog's nose. He sniffed appreciatively, licked his tiny chops, and gobbled it down.

"He's been here all day," Eve said. I knew the *him* she was talking about wasn't Jim. "Jim hasn't found out yet. That's because my little Doc is being a perfect angel. He's been asleep most of the day. In there." Eve looked toward where we stored the clean linens. Tucked between the shelf and the wall was a large purse I'd never seen before, fire-engine red and studded with rhinestones that matched the dog's sparkling collar. It was just about as big as the bathroom in my apartment. "He helped me pick it out this morning, and it's just perfect for him. He has his blanky in there and a chew toy and—"

"And it doesn't matter!"

Heidi banged through the door to pick up an order. I scurried out of her way, and Eve turned on the stool so that the waitress couldn't see the dog. I didn't open my mouth again until Heidi had headed back up front with a loaded tray of food.

"He's not allowed to be here," I reminded Eve. "Even if he is behaving. If somebody finds out and reports us—"

"Nobody's going to find out." Just as the little guy wolfed down the last of the bruschetta, Damien walked by with a tiny wedge of lemon pound cake. "Don't sweat it, Annie," he said. He tugged me away from Eve, clearly looking to keep me from freaking. "I'll show you how to make this pound cake. It's a killer of a recipe. You could serve it at a party and—"

"I could not serve it at a party," I said, and I didn't bother to add that not only did I not throw parties, but that if I did throw parties, I could never serve anything I made at them. Didn't Damien see the cook's equivalent of the surgeon general's warning over my head? The one that said I should avoid close contact with stoves at all costs?

I guess he wasn't into warnings. He breezed right on. "Give it a taste," he said, and before I could protest, he had a piece of the cake to my lips. "Come on, Annie, just a little bite."

What's a woman to do?

I bit.

It took no more than that for me to understand why Doctor Masakazu was sitting there with the doggy equivalent of a smile on his face. "It's heavenly," I said.

"You betcha. Come on." Another tug, and Damien succeeded at getting me even farther from Eve and the dog. "Marc's gonna whip up another pound cake. He has to. What he made earlier is almost gone. People are ordering it like crazy."

"It's the secret ingredient," Marc chimed in. "Not anything folks expect to find in pound cake. But see, here's the secret . . ." He had a small amount of butter melted in a saucepan, and he sprinkled a dried herb in it that looked and smelled like . . .

"Lavender?"

Marc met my question with a smile. He plopped a dollop of whipped cream on a dish. "I'll steep it in the butter for ten minutes, then strain and discard it. It gives the cake a great flavor, doesn't it?" he asked, and he took the plate over to the dog, who promptly licked it clean.

"Isn't he just the sweetest thing?" Eve wasn't referring to Marc. She was using that singsong voice again, and I rolled my eyes. She didn't notice. She was too busy making funny little squeaky noises at the dog. "He's my little honey bunch! My little sweetie pie! My little—"

"Your little ticket to the unemployment line." If Damien and Marc thought a little thing like lemon pound cake was going to distract me (even if it was incredible lemon pound cake), they were wrong. I unwound my arm from Damien's hold and hurried closer to Eve and the dog. Maybe if she looked at me, she could shake Doctor Masakazu's hypnotic spell. I waved my arms in the air. "Earth to Eve! They'll shut us down. Get it? Closed. No more Bellywasher's. Are you willing to risk that? For a dog?"

Eve's brows knit. She let the dog finish the pound cake, then brushed her hands together and scooped him into her arms. Nose to nose, she whispered something to him, retrieved the purse, and gently settled him inside. "I never thought of that," she said, and I knew it was true. More often than not, Eve's heart ruled her head.

As if she, too, could picture those hordes of health inspectors closing in on us, she darted a look at the back door. She gently nudged the purse farther into the corner. "You stay right there, sweet'ums," she instructed the dog before she turned back to me. "Honest, Annie, I never wanted to cause any trouble. I just didn't know what else to do with him. I've got a dog walker starting tomorrow. I'll take care of the mornings, then she'll come in on the days I work. Once after lunch, another time right before dinner, and a third time on the nights I'm here late. But that's tomorrow, and today . . ." She shrugged and glanced at the clock. "It's just a couple more hours. What could it hurt? Besides, I didn't have the heart to leave him alone today. He's been so down in the dumps. I think he really misses Sarah."

It was, of course, not the first time that day that I'd thought of Sarah Whittaker myself. Automatically, I checked the clock. Just a little more than twenty-four hours earlier, we'd stood in Sarah's bathroom, looking in horror at her dead body.

I shook the thought aside and congratulated myself. Though it wasn't easy, I'd worked hard on it all day, and I'd been able to compartmentalize everything I'd seen the night before. Little by little, I was coming to grips with the truth: Sarah had killed herself, and as much as we tried to fool ourselves into thinking we could have done something to stop it, it simply wasn't true. She was in charge of her own life. She'd made the ultimate decision.

Even before I saw the glimmer of tears in Eve's eyes, I knew she wasn't thinking the same way. It was the whole heart-over-head thing again.

"I know," I said. It was a lame bit of consolation and ineffectual as well, but it was all I could think to say. "I know it hurts. I've been thinking about Sarah, too. But I really don't think the dog—"

"He has such sad eyes!" Eve sniffed back her tears. "When I got home last night I walked him and fed him and he was so darling and so thankful, especially for the cheeseburger I got for him at the drive-through on the way home. But even so, I know he's feeling the loss.

"Maybe, but sad or not, a restaurant is no place—"

"If we hadn't gone over to Sarah's when we did, think of how miserable he would be right now." Eve sniffled. "He was so hungry and so lonely. If somebody hadn't come along, he might even have—" She gulped. "He could have died before anyone found him. Oh, my gosh, it just breaks my heart to think about it. And I was going to leave him home today. Honest! But just as I was leaving, he called out to me with a pitiful little bark. And I thought about how sad he is and about how lonesome he is and about how he could have starved to death if we didn't find him and get him away from Tyler who would have just left him there because he's a coldhearted son of a bitch. Tyler, that is, not my sweet little Doc," she added, as if I needed the clarification. "I thought about all that, and I tried to leave him home. I couldn't."

"I know, but—"

"And I know what you're going to say: that an animal can't know what's going on around him. That he can't be sad. But Doctor Masakazu does. He is. He's so grateful for all I've done for him. You should have seen him last night, curled up there in bed next to me. Why I—"

"You let the dog sleep with you?" I have already admitted that when it comes to cleanliness, I have something of a compulsion. OK, it's an obsession. Just the thought of a dog in Eve's—or anyone else's—bed gave me the heebie-jeebies. "You can't let a dog sleep in your bed!"

She raised her chin. "Why not? He's clean and cuddly and better behaved than any man who's ever been there! And he was just so sad."

Eve made a move back toward where Doctor Masakazu was tucked away. "Just take a look at his sweet little sad face, and you'll see. You'll understand why I did what I had to do."

"All right. All right." I gave in. It was better than letting her get the dog out of her purse so I could see that face. I didn't want to take a chance that Jim would find out what was going on. "But it never happens again," I told her.

"Cross my heart." Eve did.

"And you're sure he'll be quiet?"

She nodded. "I'll walk him on my next break. I promise. He'll sleep until then."

I glanced toward the linen rack. "And there's no chance he'll—"

"Get away?" Eve laughed. "Even if he does, he's too tiny to go far. And he's not going to even try," she added when that wasn't assurance enough for me. "His itty-bitty tummy is full, and he's a happy-wappy puppy! Except for being sad about Sarah, of course. And speaking of Sarah . . ."

I stopped Eve before she could get started. "Neither one

of us needs to deal with the emotional baggage of Sarah's death. Not now, Eve. Not when we have work to do. Let's put it aside for now and talk about it later."

Eve tapped her chin with her index finger. "But I'm not thinking emotionally. Not this time. I've been trying to work through the whole thing the way you always say I should. You know, logically. And I don't think it adds up. Remember, the linen guy was here."

Do I need to point out that I wasn't following her train of thought?

I guess my *huh?* expression said it all.

Eve pointed at the shelf of clean, neatly folded table-cloths and napkins. "The linen guy. He was here. The same day Sarah was."

"And—?"

"And he looks like a criminal type. And if he was following Sarah—"

I threw my hands in the air and turned my back, ready to head into my office.

"I knew that's how you were going to react," Eve said, darting in front of me to block the doorway. "I knew you weren't going to listen. That's why I did some research."

Eve and *research*. Two words I never thought I'd hear in the same sentence. Who could blame me if I stopped to listen?

"I looked on the Internet," she whispered, "for stuff about our linen supply company, Table Top Pros. The company is owned by Ivan Gystanovich."

I nodded. I knew this. Like I said, I'd done my homework before I contracted with the company.

"And Gregor, his last name is Gystanovich. That proba-bly means he's related to this Ivan guy."

I hadn't known Gregor's last name, but I nodded again anyway. There wasn't much else I could do.

Eve leaned closer and lowered her voice. "A couple of the articles I read said that Ivan has ties with the Russian mob."

This, of course, was news to me. Still . . .

"That's interesting," I told Eve. "Really, it is. But it doesn't mean a thing. Table Top Pros has a sterling reputation."

"But Gregor—"

"Wasn't doing anything but his job the day Sarah was here. Besides, I think he was already gone by the time Sarah arrived."

"But that doesn't mean he wasn't watching her. You know, from behind a potted plant or something. Maybe he was waiting outside for her."

"No, it doesn't mean he wasn't. But it sure doesn't mean he was. And why would he? There's no connection between them at all."

"No connection that we know of."

"And no reason to think that Gregor is dishonest."

"Like his shifty eyes don't mean anything?" Eve cocked her head, the better to try to bring what she saw as my irrational argument into focus. "I told you, Annie, there's something fishy about that guy."

It was hard to argue with that kind of logic, so I gave up without a fight. "OK, let's say this Gregor guy isn't on the up-and-up. That still doesn't mean he had anything to do with what happened to Sarah."

"But what if—"

I was done debating the issue. It was painful and it was hard, but it was time for Eve to face the facts. I put my hand on her arm. "I know, Eve, I know this hurts. Sarah was beautiful and smart and friendly. The last time we saw her . . ." The last time we saw Sarah, she was bobbing in a tub of bloody water. I decided on a different tack.

"As much as you might hate to admit it, this is one time that Tyler is right. You remember what he said. Sarah made a choice, and nobody's responsible for her death but her. Nobody could have stopped her, either. I know you wish you could have done more. I do, too, and I barely knew her. But you're doing all you can. You're taking care of the dog until her sister gets here."

Eve's eyes were red. She sniffed. "We're doing the funeral luncheon, too," she said. "Next Monday."

That was the first I'd heard of it. Then again, I'd been a little preoccupied with the whole oh-no-they're-going-to-close-us-down scenario since I walked in.

Eve understood this and nodded. "I got in touch with Sarah's sister, Charlene. I didn't have the number, but I remembered that Sarah and Charlene had a cousin in Baltimore. I went with them once to visit him. I called him and . . . and, anyway, he gave me a contact number, and I talked to Charlene. She's on her way back to the States. The memorial will be on Monday, and after, people will come back here for lunch."

I was grateful the next Monday was Veteran's Day and a holiday; the bank was closed. If we had a large group coming, Jim would need the help.

My mind already racing over the details, I hurried to my office to make a list. Like a lot of restaurants in the area, Bellywasher's was closed on Mondays. That meant I'd have to talk to everyone on staff ASAP to see who could work and who couldn't, and if we needed extra help, I'd need to find replacements. In addition, we'd need at least one extra person to take coats and pass drinks before lunch, and maybe some soft, soothing background music, too. There was a woman in my apartment building who played the harp. I knew I had her phone number somewhere.

I did a quick sweep of the restaurant before I stepped into my office. Tasteful flower arrangements on the tables would be a nice touch, too, I decided. They would add a hint of color and be a subtle way to help soothe those who attended the service.

Apparently, I wasn't the only one who'd had this last idea. When I walked into my office, I saw that there was a single white rose on my desk. Its petals were touched with pink, and it was about twelve inches long. Just the right size to be an accent without overpowering our small tables. Somewhere in the piles of papers that littered my office, I knew I'd seen a catalogue from a supplier who offered reasonably priced glass vases. I shuffled through the stacks on my guest chair. I wasn't even halfway through when Jim ducked into the office.

"This rose is perfect," I told him. "Did they say how much for a dozen?"

"They? Dozen?"

I didn't pay a lot of attention to Jim's questions. I was busy trying to excavate. "Yeah, I think we'll need at least that many, don't you? Even if we just put a couple in each vase, we'll want them on the tables and a few more on the bar. Did the people who sent them over say how much they'd be per dozen?"

"Annie, Eve told me what happened last night. I thought you'd be upset. I left the flower to make you feel better."

Jim's words sank in. My stomach went cold and my hands froze over the stack of papers. No easy feat, considering that my cheeks were suddenly flaming. "I'm so sorry!" I turned to find him looking at me like I was a stranger. "I just assumed—"

"That everything is business. Aye." He scraped a hand over his chin. "I'm beginning to get the picture."

"That's not what I meant."

"No, what you meant is that you're so busy thinking dollars and cents, you forgot that there are times when people just want to do something nice for you."

He was right, and realizing it only made me feel worse. As if to further prove the theory about how well I'd compartmentalized the facts of Sarah's death and my reaction to it, I burst into tears.

In a heartbeat, Jim had his arms around me. I buried my face against his chest, and he rubbed my back and whispered soothing words until my crying subsided. When it finally did, I refused to look at him. I am not a woman who cries prettily. Not like Eve. She can shed a swimming pool full of tears and still look as fresh as if she'd just walked out of a day spa.

I was not so lucky. I knew my eyes were red and swollen. My nose was red, too. It also needed blowing—badly—and I reached around Jim and grabbed a tissue from the box on my desk.

Even when I was done, Jim didn't let me go.

"I'm sorry," he said.

I sniffed and grabbed another tissue to wipe my eyes. "You? You're not the one who's supposed to be sorry."

"I snapped at you."

"I deserved to be snapped at."

"You've been under a lot of stress."

"And you haven't been?" A few more snuffles and sniffs, and I could almost make myself sound like I wasn't talking from the bottom of a lake. When Jim tugged me closer, I settled into his arms. "You're right," I said. "All I've been thinking about is money. I should have known—"

"I should have understood—"

"I shouldn't have jumped to conclusions."

"And I shouldn't have gotten defensive."

I felt a watery smile blossom and looked up at him. "Truce?"

He kissed me. "Truce," he said when he was done. "And believe me, I can understand why you're not thinking straight. Finding someone you know dead and knowing that she took her own life . . ." He pulled in a breath and let it out slowly. "I'm sorry," he said again even though he didn't have to. "I'm not usually so insensitive. I've been a wee bit on edge, I'm afraid."

No, I was the insensitive one not to have noticed.

Before I could tell him this, Jim explained.

"It's Michael O'Keefe," he said.

I may have been insensitive, but I was not unconscious. Even Annie Capshaw, a cooking calamity, had heard of O'Keefe. As food critic for *DC Nights*, a regional magazine, he had a powerful influence on the local restaurant scene. The tattoo that started up in my chest was all about nerves. "He's coming? To Bellywasher's? When? How do you know?"

"Well, I don't know. Not for sure. And not when. O'Keefe never announces his visits. Just shows up and expects to be treated like a king. If he loves your restaurant, you're an instant hit. If he hates it—"

"You go down the tubes."

Jim nodded. "Aye. Something like that. I have a friend who has a friend who works for the magazine. She said O'Keefe was making a list of new places to hit this month, and she heard our name mentioned. I found out just a few hours ago."

"That's wonderful!" It was, and no sooner had I realized it than my spirits plunged and my knees turned rubbery. "No, it's terrible."

Jim laughed and hugged me. "It's both. And we'll handle it as we've handled everything else." He unfolded his arms from around me. "It's all part of the business," he said. "We'll get by O'Keefe, right enough. I just need to get used to the idea of him pouncing on us unawares. You'll put up with me while I do?"

"You'll put up with me when my eyes are swollen and my nose is red?"

"I like your nose." He kissed the tip of it to prove it. "And now I'd better get back behind the bar." He stepped away, then thought better of it. "You'll be all right by yourself?"

"I'll be fine."

I was, too. I went over the day's receipts, balanced the charges and made out our daily deposit without further tears. By the time I was done, it was close to ten, but I had a few more things to clean up and a few more hours before I absolutely, positively had to be in bed or I'd be useless at the bank the next day. I ducked into the restaurant to get a cup of coffee.

There were six people at the bar. Larry, Hank, and Charlie were three of them, but at least tonight, they were sharing a pitcher of beer and a plate of Jim's incredible honey barbeque chicken wings. Only one table was occupied, by a man with the hood of his sweatshirt pulled up on his head. He was wearing sunglasses.

"What's his deal?" I asked Heidi when she whisked by.

"Dunno." She shrugged and reached for the Coke she'd left for herself at the end of the bar. She took a sip. "Came in half an hour ago and ordered a boatload of stuff. I mean, really. The crabcakes and the bisque and even the sweet potato pie. Asked a lot of questions, too. You know, like, what's in this? What's in that? I guess some people are just really picky when it comes to what they eat."

I guess she was right.

Except something about this picky eater struck me as awfully familiar.

As casually as I could, I strolled over toward his table. Not only was he persnickety, he was apparently a stickler for accuracy, too. With the tip of his fork, he picked apart Jim's crab cakes, then made notes on a pad next to the plate.

Michael O'Keefe?

My heart leapt into my throat, and I thought about running to the kitchen to warn everyone to be on their best behavior.

Until I heard our guest mumbling to himself.

"This is celery seed, yes?" He took a nibble of the crab cake, nodded to himself, and made a note. "And bread crumbs and—"

"Good evening, Monsieur Lavoie!" I pulled out a chair and sat down at the table with the owner of Très Bonne Cuisine. "It's good to see you. What brings you to Alexandria tonight?"

"Ah, Miss Capshaw!" Jacques Lavoie is a round little Frenchman with apple cheeks and an accent that would put Pepé Le Pew to shame. Aside from owning the gourmet shop where Eve and I took our cooking classes, he is the genius behind Vavoom! seasoning, a spice blend that's developed a cult following in the D.C. area. I used to be among the faithful until I found out Vavoom! wasn't all it was cracked up to be.

Something told me my knowledge of what was really inside a Vavoom! shaker wasn't why a flush of red stained

Monsieur's neck. I knew it for sure when he put an arm across his notepad to keep me from seeing it.

"But of course, I am here to support Jim," he said. A nervous smile came and went across his face. "It is the least I can do for an old friend."

"Which explains the sunglasses."

He cleared his throat and removed the glasses.

"And the hoodie? Is it cold in here? I can have Jim turn up the heat."

"That is not necessary, *chérie.*" He stripped off his hood, revealing a shock of salt-and-pepper hair.

"I think Jim's in the kitchen," I told him. "He'll be thrilled to see you."

When I made a move to get up, Lavoie stopped me, one hand on my arm. "No, no, no. You must not bother him. He is an artist, yes? An artist with food. We must not disturb him when he is creating."

Lucky for me, Lavoie had to move his arm to grab mine. I saw what he was writing on his notepad.

"Celery. Bread crumbs. Lemon. Monsieur!" I looked at him in wonder. "You're trying to steal Jim's recipes!"

"No, no, no!" He denied it instantly. What else did I expect? What I didn't expect was that Jim would walk out of the kitchen at that very moment. He caught sight of Lavoie and, don't ask me how, but I think he knew exactly what his old boss was doing there. Lavoie pushed his chair back from the table and sprang to his feet.

A little too fast.

He knocked over his water glass, which knocked over the bottle of wine he'd ordered, and I jumped up to avoid getting soaked. My chair fell over and crashed into the table behind us, sending it rocking. The chair smacked into one of the sandalwood screens, and it crashed to the floor.

Eve had been rolling silverware in napkins for the next day's lunch crowd. She came running. Heidi, Marc, and Damien dashed out of the kitchen. Afraid that I'd been hurt, Larry, Hank, and Charlie jumped off their barstools and offered to help. The other folks at the bar swung around to watch, their mouths open in wonder.

Perfect. It meant we were all there, all watching, when Doctor Masakazu lurched out of the kitchen.

He scampered into the center of the restaurant, burped loud enough to wake the dead, and promptly barfed all over our beautiful white ceramic tile floor.

Six

✖

"MY POOR ITTY-BITTY DOC. HE'S SO SICKY-WICKY. POOR little sweetie." Eve had the dog in her arms. She rubbed her nose against his. We were in the examining room at the local emergency pet clinic waiting our turn to see the vet, and I was so not in the mood. I paced between the examination table and a desk that was built into the wall.

"Maybe poor itty-bitty Doc is so sicky-wicky because you were feeding him cakey-wakey. Did you ever consider that?" I asked her.

Eve did not take criticism well. Or very seriously. I knew that, given the choice, she'd do it all again. In a heartbeat.

"The whipped cream must be bad," she said. "You really should call Jim and tell him. Before he serves it to somebody else."

"Calling Jim is probably not something either one of us wants to do right about now." I hugged my arms around myself, but even so, I shivered. *Angry* didn't begin to describe the conniption fit of a Scotsman who discovers a dog in his restaurant. Jim's last words still rang in my ears. The way I remember them, they started out with something about Eve and me being *aff* our *heids* and ended with *ye canna bring a dug inna a restaurant and ye best git him out now afore I take the little blighter and—*

I cringed one moment and smiled the next. Even Jim's anger hadn't been enough to stop him from looking up the address of the clinic for us. He called ahead and told them we were on our way, too.

All of which made me feel even more terrible: a bad situation could have been even worse.

"We're really lucky it was Monsieur Lavoie at that table and not Michael O'Keefe," I told Eve and reminded myself. "Can you imagine it, Eve? Can you even begin to think of the damage you could have done? That would have been the end of Bellywasher's for sure."

"I know." She hugged the dog, who burped, then settled into the crook of her arm. "I'm sorry. I really am. I told Jim before we left. I promised it would never happen again, and I swear, it won't. I'll send him a bottle of really expensive wine tomorrow to apologize. I just didn't think—"

"Exactly."

Eve nodded. "I deserve that. I know I do. And I'm willing to take responsibility. If Jim wants to fire me, I'll understand."

"You know he's too nice to do that."

She grinned. "I know. But it made me sound noble, didn't it?" Eve cuddled the dog. "I'm so worried about Doc, Annie. Something's wrong with his little tummy. What do you think they'll do for him?"

I didn't know, but fortunately, we didn't have to wait long to find out. A minute later a thirty-something man in a white lab coat came into the room. He introduced himself as Dr. Terry Novak, took the patient out of Eve's arms, and slipped off the blue and yellow argyle sweater Eve had put on Doc before we left the restaurant.

"What's his name?" the vet asked.

"Doctor Masakazu." Eve supplied the information. "Only I just call him Doc. It's easier, you know? And not nearly as pompous."

Dr. Novak put Doc on the examining table and looked into his eyes. He listened to his heartbeat. "The pompous part . . ." He smiled over at Eve. "Isn't that what a dog like this is all about?"

Of course, Eve got defensive. It didn't take a dog whisperer to see that she was already head over heels about Doc.

"If you're talking about his collar, it's just rhinestones," Eve said. "Not that he doesn't deserve the real thing, but—"

"I'll say." The vet looked into Doc's ears, felt his stomach, and cringed when the dog burped. "What have you been feeding this little guy?"

I kept my mouth shut.

Eve shrugged. "Just food."

"Dog food?"

"Food. You know, food that dogs eat."

Something told me the vet had heard this flimsy excuse before. But Dr. Novak was good-looking, and he wasn't wearing a wedding ring. I knew before we left the room, he was going to ask for Eve's phone number. He wasn't about to alienate her by coming on too strong with a lecture about proper nutrition.

Instead, he gave her a wink. "People food, right?"

She shrugged. "Some people food."

"People food that's too rich for dogs. Food with butter in it. And grease, maybe? My guess is hamburger."

Eve wrinkled her nose. "Cheeseburger," she admitted.

"And . . . ?"

The fact that she refused to look the vet in the eye proved that when it came to what she was feeding Doc, Eve had a conscience. She shrugged. "Maybe some bruschetta," she said. "And a little cake and whipped cream. And for breakfast this morning, ham and cheese omelet. With capers. And anchovies."

"Then it's no wonder he's sick." Dr. Novak rubbed Doc's head. "His system is far too fragile for that kind of food. Surely the breeder told you all about that."

Eve didn't answer, and I knew she was trying to come up

with a way to tell him about Sarah and the dog. Rather than get into it, I explained. "We're just watching him," I said. "For a friend. We really didn't know what to feed him, and we haven't had a chance to get to the pet store. Is regular dog food OK?"

"For this guy?" Dr. Novak lifted the dog from the table and handed him over to Eve. "You're kidding me, right?" When neither of us answered, he shook his head. "You're not kidding me. You have no idea what kind of dog this is. This, ladies, is a Japanese terrier. It's one of the rarest breeds there is."

Since I had assumed that Doctor Masakazu was a mutt, this was a surprise. "Rare? As in . . . ?"

Dr. Novak pursed his lips. "I'll bet there are no more than six or seven hundred of these little guys in the whole world. The friend you're watching him for didn't tell you that?"

"She didn't exactly have a chance," I told the vet.

"Then she probably also didn't mention how expensive they are."

Eve patted the dog.

"Thousands," Dr. Novak said. "The smaller they are, the more valuable they are, and from the looks of this guy, I'd say he's not going to get much bigger. His markings are perfect, too. Mainly white with a black-and-tan mask. Something tells me your friend is being modest. She must have paid a fortune for him. She's going to want you to make sure he's well taken care of." He went to the desk, sat down, and wrote on a pad. "Only kibble made with lamb and rice. All natural. No preservatives. No corn, there's no nutritional value in that." He ripped off a sheet of paper and handed it to me. "I've written down the names of a couple reputable brands that I know won't be a problem for his digestive system. But just so you know, none of it is cheap, and you can't find it just anywhere. You're going to need to look in one of the specialty pet stores. My guess is your friend is probably paying somewhere around sixty dollars for food."

"Sixty dollars?" I gulped. "That's for a year's worth, right?"

Dr. Novak laughed. "He's little. He doesn't eat much. A bag that size should last you a month or so. And if your friend isn't coming back anytime soon, I'd check to see what shots he's had and what he still needs. You don't want to take any chances. Not with a dog like this."

We promised we wouldn't, swore we'd get the right kind of food, and waited long enough for Eve to write down her phone number. (Was I good at predicting these things, or what?) It wasn't until Doc was bundled in his sweater and back in his carrier and we were all back in the car that Eve and I found our voices.

"Thousands!" Eve's eyes were wide. Even though we'd just put him in the car, she looked in the backseat to double-check that Doc was right where he was supposed to be. "Annie, I had no idea. I'm so nervous now. What if something happens to him?"

I did not point out that something had already happened to him, otherwise we wouldn't be sitting in the parking lot of the emergency vet clinic. "Nothing's going to happen to him," I said instead. "You're taking great care of him."

Eve's bottom lip trembled. "But I made him sick. I need to do better." She started the car and pulled out of the lot. "I wonder if there's a store around that's open this late where we can find that food."

"Food that pricey?" Yes, I believed in following rules. I made sure to chew my food thirty times before I swallowed, and I flossed every time I brushed. I looked both ways before I crossed the street, drank eight glasses of water every day, and checked *Consumer Reports* before I bought so much as a toaster.

I did not doubt that Dr. Novak was competent. I did not question the information he'd given us. I knew it was accurate, and I knew he was asking us to do what he thought was best for the dog.

But even I knew there were places where the line had to be drawn.

"There is no way I'm going to let you spend more than you can afford for a bag of dog food," I told Eve. "You don't have that kind of money, and besides, he's only a dog. How important can it be for him to eat only that certain kind of food?"

"You heard what Terry said." How Eve and Dr. Novak had ended up on a first-name basis after so little time together was a mystery I would ponder another time. "Doc needs this food."

"You need to eat, too. If you spend that kind of money on the dog—"

"He's worth it. Besides, Sarah loved him with all her heart. It's what she would want me to do."

Something about the comment sparked a thought deep in my brain, but at that point, my neurons weren't connecting. I was too tired, and besides, I knew if I didn't come up with a plan, Eve would spend the next who-knew-how-many hours searching for the magical dog food at a pet store that stayed open late. With me along for the ride.

"There must be the right kind of dog food back at Sarah's apartment," I said. "She had to feed him something. And she knew how expensive and rare he is."

"That's a good idea." Eve took a left at the next street and headed in the direction of Arlington.

There was one flaw in my plan, of course.

"Wait . . . there's no way we're going to talk Foster into letting us back into that apartment." I checked the clock on the dashboard. "It's late. There's no way he's even still in the building. It's a great idea, but it's not going to work."

"You mean it wouldn't work." Eve gave me a sidelong look and a big smile. "If I didn't have the key."

Eve laughed at my flabbergasted expression. "I didn't have a chance to tell you back at the restaurant. Sarah's cousin stopped to see me. Bill. Remember him? He's the one from Baltimore. The guy I called to get Charlene's number."

"And he gave you the key to Sarah's apartment?"

Did I sound skeptical? I didn't think so, but I must have. Otherwise, Eve wouldn't have made a sour face.

"It's not like I held him at gunpoint," she said. "Seems Bill had the key in case of an emergency. Charlene knew it, and she called him and asked him to stop at the apartment and get something for Sarah to wear. You know." Eve's voice faded. "For the viewing."

This was not something either one of us wanted to think about. Eve got rid of the thought with a shake of her head.

"Bill was creeped out by the whole thing. Not to mention the fact that the guy's a dock worker. What does he know about women's clothes? He stopped to see me at the restaurant early today, gave us a check for the deposit for the funeral luncheon, and dropped off the key. He asked me to pick out an outfit for Sarah and take it to the funeral home."

"So we're going to kill two birds with one stone."

"Oh, don't say that!" Eve shivered. "I can't stand thinking about Sarah and the word *kill* at the same time."

I knew what she meant. I couldn't, either.

Little did I know that in another hour or two, it was all I was going to be thinking about.

THE LAST TIME WE WERE AT SARAH'S APARTMENT, THE place was teeming with police, and Doc was barking up a storm in the guest room. Now it was as dark and as quiet as a—

Never mind!

Let's just settle for it was really quiet.

While Eve set the dog in his carrier in the living room, I skimmed my hand over the wall just inside the front door, searching for a switch. I found one, flicked on the light in the hallway, and breathed a little easier. I hurried into the living room and turned on a couple lamps there, too.

"What do you think?" I asked Eve. "I'd say the dog food is in the kitchen."

"Yeah." She nodded, but she didn't move an inch.

"And you're not going to get it because . . ."

"It just feels weird. You know, being here and knowing that just a couple days ago . . ." Her gaze drifted toward the hallway and the bathroom we both knew was at the end of it. I wondered if the police cleaned up after themselves before remembering that I'd read somewhere that they didn't. I vowed to avoid a trip to the bathroom.

"I just can't get the picture out of my head, that's all," Eve said. "You know, Sarah in the water. And all the blood."

I knew what she was talking about. Just like I knew it wouldn't do either of us any good to dwell on it.

I looped my arm through Eve's. "Let's pick out an outfit for Sarah first thing," I said, and my suggestion worked like a charm. Eve smiled and headed for the bedroom. There's nothing like the thought of fashion to get a girl's mind off death.

Like the rest of the apartment, the bedroom was orderly and nicely decorated. There was a walk-in closet on one wall, which Eve opened. A whoosh of surprise escaped her, along with an admiring, "Oh, my gosh!"

Sarah's closet would have done an obsessive/compulsive proud. Her clothes were arranged by season, fabric, and color. Skirts were organized on a bottom rack; jackets and blouses hung above them. Dresses over to the side (casual, work, formal) and next to them, pants and knockabout clothing. It was so pristine, so beautifully color-coordinated, my heart skipped a beat.

Until I realized that something was wrong.

I squinted at the jackets and blouses. "Check this out," I said, pointing. "The blues are with the blues. The grays are with the grays. The reds—"

"Are with the reds," Eve said. "Except . . ." She saw what I saw and pushed apart a cranberry-red silk kimono-style jacket and wool Christmas-red blazer. Between them hung a green linen suit jacket.

"Well, that's odd," I mumbled.

"It sure is. Red and green together is all well and good when it comes to kitschy Christmas decorations, but let's face it, it's against every rule of fashion there is."

"Not what I mean." I pointed. "Blues with blues. Grays with grays. And the greens . . ." I looked toward the far end of the closet. "The greens are all down there. What's this jacket doing out of place?"

Eve shook her head. "It just proves how upset Sarah must have been, poor darling. She wasn't thinking straight."

Maybe, but I wasn't so sure.

I tucked the thought away. While Eve took out outfit after outfit, held them at arm's length, and made a pile of possibilities on the bed, I looked around the room. There was a shopping bag from a pricey Georgetown boutique sitting on the floor near the dresser, and I peeked inside. "Cocktail dress," I told Eve, who was so busy trying to decide between navy linen and black silk, she wasn't paying a whole lot of attention.

"Now that would be tacky," she said. "A cocktail dress for a burial. I don't think so, Annie."

"Not for Sarah to wear. Here. This cocktail dress." I pulled it out of the bag. The dress was fire-engine red, a gorgeous combination of chiffon and sequins. Even before the receipt fluttered out of the bag, I knew it must have cost a fortune.

I checked the price and whistled low under my breath, before I carefully refolded the dress and got ready to set the receipt on top of it.

That's when the date of the transaction caught my eye.

"Eve! Take a look at this."

Holding the black silk dress, Eve came to my side.

I pointed. "Sarah bought this dress last Tuesday."

"Don't be silly." Eve rolled her eyes. "Nobody buys a dress that gorgeous and then comes home and kills herself. That's just crazy."

It was. That was exactly my point.

I didn't need to explain. After a minute of thinking about it, Eve's eyes got wide, and her mouth fell open.

"Annie!" She clutched my arm so tight, I expected I'd have a bruise by morning. "Annie, are you saying—"

"I'm not saying anything." I hadn't even realized how much the thought scared me until Eve was so ready to buy into it. Better minds than ours had already concluded that there was nothing sinister about Sarah's death. Who was I to contradict them? Besides, I'd had my fill of murder. Death was death, and suicide was bad enough. The thought that someone had taken Sarah's life . . .

My brain froze, and panic bubbled inside me like lava in a Hawaiian volcano. Cocktail dress or no cocktail dress, I refused to believe Sarah could have been murdered. To prove it, I dropped the receipt back in the bag and hightailed it out of Sarah's bedroom.

"But, Annie . . ." Eve was right behind me, black silk sheath clutched to her heart. "Annie Capshaw, you listen to me. Do you think this means that Sarah—"

"Kitchen," I said, though Eve could see exactly where I was going. "Let's get the dog food and get out of here."

Sarah's kitchen looked exactly as it had the last time I was in it except that the red message light on the phone wasn't blinking. I guessed that was because Tyler had picked up the message Eve left, the one reminding Sarah that we were coming over. The two washed wineglasses were still in the dish drainer. The countertops still gleamed in the glow of the lights we turned on. It was familiar and nonthreatening, and I stopped just inside the door, drew in a calming breath, and gave myself a good talking to.

I was letting my imagination run away with me, I told myself. Like Eve had been doing all summer. Just because I couldn't fathom what would make a woman as beautiful and as smart and as successful as Sarah take her own life, I was seeing mysteries where there were none. It was absurd. It was an insult to Sarah's memory. It had to stop.

Now.

I pulled in another breath, clearing my head. My heartbeat settled, and my blood stopped rushing in my ears. I had been so lost in thought, I didn't even realize Eve wasn't with me until she came into the kitchen a minute later. She didn't have the black silk dress with her, and I guessed she'd put it in the living room so we could take it with us.

She didn't say a word. She didn't have to—I knew she was thinking about what I'd said in the bedroom. But as I've mentioned before, Eve and I have been friends for a lot of years. I knew her well; she knew me just as well in return. In an uncharacteristic show of restraint, she knew pressing her case would get her nowhere.

And nowhere was exactly where I wanted to go with the idea that Sarah hadn't been responsible for her own death.

Eve followed my lead, and one by one, we went through the cupboards, searching for the dog's food. After what we'd seen in the bedroom, I wasn't surprised by what we found. Like her closet, Sarah's cupboards were arranged in painstaking detail.

"Even I'm not this meticulous," I grumbled, checking out the food that had been removed from its packaging and placed in Tupperware containers. "I guess it just goes to prove that you really can never tell what's going on inside a person."

I wasn't doing any more than thinking out loud, but Eve took it as a signal that the matter (and manner) of Sarah's death was now open for discussion.

"You'd think anybody who kills themselves must be pretty desperate," she said. "I don't know about you, but I don't think desperation looks like this."

I knew where she was going and attempted to head her off. Without a word, I looked in another cupboard and found the dog food. It, too, had been repackaged, but fortunately, Sarah had cut off the nutrition label and attached it to the container. Otherwise, I might have mistaken it for potpourri. Yeah, there was that much dried fruit in it.

Eve came up behind me. She pointed toward the price tag that was still attached to the dog food label. "Dr. Novak was right. This food is pricey. Why do you suppose someone would buy a really expensive dog . . . a dog she really, really loved . . . and pay that kind of money for dog food, and then . . . I don't know . . . kill herself?"

"Eve!" I sighed. Not like I was surrendering. More like I really didn't want to hear what she had to say.

But Eve had shown enough restraint for one evening. She pounced. "Oh, come on, Annie! You're trying to deny it, but you can't. Not with this kind of evidence staring us in the face. Remember what Terry said. He said Doc is a rare and expensive dog, right?"

I nodded. Reluctantly, but I nodded.

"So why would Sarah go through all the trouble of buying a rare and expensive dog and then kill herself?"

I couldn't answer. I didn't even try.

My reluctance to buy into the theory only made Eve more determined than ever to prove it. "Look around, Annie. Tell me if any of this adds up. Sarah's organized. OK, so she's compulsively organized, but she's organized. Not like she's never going to come back into her kitchen again. More like she knows she'll be back and she wants everything where she knows she can find it easily. And she bought a new cocktail dress. And she loves her dog. She paid thousands for him. It doesn't make any sense."

There was a stool next to the island in the center of the kitchen. I climbed up and plunked down. "You're right. But if all that's true, Eve, what we need to do is—"

"Prove it."

I was going to say, *Call Tyler and tell him what we think*, but Eve didn't give me a chance. Before I could open my mouth, she was already gone.

I made one last valiant attempt to talk her down. "We're not going to find anything," I called after her. "All we're doing is prying."

"We're investigating." Her voice came from down the hallway.

"We're being nosy," I reminded her.

"We're being detectives."

Ah, yes, being detectives. There was that.

I tried to stop myself—honest, I did. But even before I realized I was moving, I was out of the kitchen and searching for evidence.

Seven

✖

I WON'T BOTHER WITH A PLAY-BY-PLAY OF OUR NEXT day's visit to Tyler at the police station. It's an ugly tale and, in the great scheme of things, pointless.

Let's just suffice it to say that after a long tirade about minding our own business, leaving police work up to the real police and—I mention this reluctantly—a thankfully brief but nonetheless bruising remark about how he'd never had the bad fortune to meet two women who were more incredibly foolish, he didn't buy into our theory that Sarah had not taken her own life.

Not when we told him about the red cocktail dress.

Not when we explained about how rare and expensive Doc was.

Not even when we showed him the other crucial pieces of evidence we found when we looked through Sarah's apartment: a letter from the dog breeder in Japan that showed Sarah had been on a waiting list for a puppy for eighteen months and a ticket on a cruise ship scheduled to sail out of Fort Lauderdale just after Christmas.

To us, none of this spoke of a woman who was planning on killing herself.

To Tyler . . . well, like I said, I won't repeat his comments word for word. There are folks who are sensitive about that kind of language.

It should come as no big surprise that Eve was discouraged by his treatment of us. Personal feelings aside, I think Eve always had and always would think of Tyler as a kind of superhero with a badge, the good guy in blue who could swoop in on wrongdoers and fix the world's woes. This time, he refused to swoop. He stood by the ruling from the medical examiner. The one that said there was Valium in Sarah's system, and her wounds were self-inflicted.

I on the other hand, felt empowered. Yes, justice had to be served, but this time, it was more personal than that. Sarah's life was too precious to sweep under the rug. If any fixing was going to get done, I knew I was the one who would have to do it.

The good news is that I was aware from the start that I had options. The better news is that after a rallying speech, I convinced Eve that things weren't as bleak as they looked because (1) the cruise ticket we found was based on double occupancy, and that meant somebody could tell us more about Sarah's plans, and (2) the funeral luncheon was, after all, scheduled for Bellywasher's. If there were murder suspects to be interrogated, surely that would be the place to start.

This all sounds carefully thought out and enormously logical, I know. Believe me, it was. What I haven't bothered to mention, though, is that while I knew *what* I had to do, the *how* of it eluded me. I know, I know . . . Eve and I had solved a murder just a few months earlier. But that was then, and this was now, and as much as I would have liked to believe we'd acted professionally and competently in the matter of Drago's murder, I knew what we'd really been was just plain lucky. This time, I didn't have any idea what to say or where to start. And as always when I was pushing myself beyond my comfort zone, I was scared to death.

I guess that's what I was thinking about that morning as

I took one last look around the restaurant to make sure everything was ready when the crowd returned from the cemetery.
There weren't enough tables in Bellywasher's to accommo-
date the kind of crowd we expected, so with Charlene's approval, we'd decided on a buffet luncheon. I double-checked
the table set along the far wall where we would put the food,
made sure the vases with their single white roses were on
every table, and opened bottles of wine, both white and red. I
was so lost in thought, I jumped when Jim came up behind me.

"Look what I found!"

At the sound of his voice, I spun around, one hand—and
the corkscrew in it—pressed to my heart.

"Sorry." I knew he meant it, but he didn't exactly look re-
gretful. I think my first clue was his ear-to-ear grin.

I waved away his apology and looked at what he was carrying. Since he was still smiling, my guess is that he didn't notice that my top lip curled.

It was an old color-tinted photograph, a framed picture of a
tiny cottage surrounded by hills blanketed with heather. At
least I think that's what it was. It was kind of hard to tell, since
the glass that covered the picture was so dusty. The frame was
downright nasty, too, pitted and dirty and blanketed with spi-
derwebs. I was about to tell Jim to toss the picture back in the
Dumpster it came out of when he said, "It was my granny's."

He held the picture against the wall behind the bar and
nodded his approval. "I remember it from when I was a kid.
It was in the dining room of her home in Glasgow. Uncle
Angus must have brought it with him when he came to this
country. It was in the basement."

"Which is exactly where it belongs."

The fact that I did not appreciate what he obviously saw
as fine art bewildered Jim. The picture still against the wall,
he looked over his shoulder at me. "Are you saying—"

"I'm saying one word: *ambiance*. No, wait!" I held up a
hand to stop him when it looked as if he might argue with me.
"I'm saying two words: Michael O'Keefe. OK, more than
two words: Michael O'Keefe's review bringing in customers

who spend lots and lots of money and demand a little class in return."

"And you don't think this is—"

"It's charming." Without its coating of dirt, this may have been true, so I didn't feel bad saying it. "But remember, we worked hard to create an atmosphere here. A feeling. All summer, you talked about what you wanted. As I recall, you used words like understated and classy. You talked about chic. I hardly think a dingy old photograph—"

"A dingy old photograph that once belonged to my sainted granny."

"Who I'm sure was a delightful woman." I tried to find words that were firm without being harsh. "But that doesn't mean her taste is suitable to an upscale restaurant."

"No. Of course, you're right." Jim's smile faded, and he lowered the picture from the wall. Thank goodness.

That didn't mean he was done trying. He looked toward the wall next to the front door, bare and elegant in all its white-paint glory. "And you don't think—"

"Sure, if you want it to look like the Bellywasher's of old." I knew that deep down inside, Jim would react to this as if I'd asked him to cut off a finger. Or forget how to cook. I was right. He cringed.

He tucked the photo behind the bar, just in the nick of time. The next minute, the front door opened. The funeral service was over. Our guests had arrived.

Though I had tried plenty hard, I had found it impossible to hire the extra help we needed for the day, so I was taking over some of the front-of-the-house duties myself. For the next half hour, I didn't have time to worry about Granny's old photo; I was too busy taking coats, making folks comfortable, and getting them coffee or a glass of wine. The crowd was bigger than I expected, but then, that shouldn't have been a surprise. Sarah was young, employed in a hot-house of power and prestige, and from what I'd heard, active in her community, a book discussion group, and her church. She was bound to have plenty of friends.

They crowded into Bellywasher's, a mostly young, up-scale crowd of Capitol Hill up-and-comers who milled around in silence and spoke in hushed tones. Of course, the whole point of an after-funeral luncheon is to coax folks into relaxing. It took awhile, but it finally worked. Little by little, people got more talkative, and the noise level rose. Once or twice, I heard someone say something nice about the appetizers and about coming back for dinner. Before long, the welcome sounds of laughter rang through the room.

With everything under control, I took the opportunity to look around. Did one of these people know what really happened to Sarah? Had one of them killed her? It was a shocking thought, but I couldn't ignore it, not if I was going to get to the bottom of things. While I collected used napkins and dirty glasses, I tried to eavesdrop without looking too obvious.

". . . not how anyone thought she'd end up, that's for sure," a lady with red hair who was standing near the door said, and because I knew she was talking about Sarah, I moved nearer in an effort to hear more. "You'd think with the way she's been acting, it was more likely she would have been—"

"Ambition." The single word boomed out of a middle-aged man over on my left. The crowd was thick, and I'm short, so I couldn't tell who he was talking to, but I saw him nod in response to whatever his companion said. "She had plenty of it, that's for sure. You'd think a girl with those kinds of smarts would know better than to do stupid things. But then, I've never been a big believer in—"

"Suicide. Who would have believed it. It's so very sad." The emotion that edged this voice was real, and heartbreaking because of it. I looked to my right where a woman dressed head to toe in black touched a hankie to her eyes. "I can't stop crying. I can't help but think that maybe if we just listened to her a little more, if we paid attention to the things she was telling us, we might have been able to—"

"We're here."

I'd been so busy watching everything going on around me, I didn't see Eve approach. She arrived with Charlene.

I hugged them both, before giving Charlene my condolences and assuring her that everything was under control and the food would be out in a couple minutes. I was about to go into the kitchen to make sure that was true when Eve tugged on my sleeve.

"Oh my gosh! Can you believe it?" Her stinging whisper brought me spinning around. She pointed across the room. "That's Dylan. Dylan Monroe."

"The TV newsman?" I stood on tiptoe and craned my neck, but like I said, I was short, and the room was crowded. The only thing I could see of the man Eve pointed to was his left ear.

"I thought he was in Afghanistan or somewhere," Eve said. "I saw something on the news about it last night. He's preparing some sort of special hour-long show on the every-day life of a soldier. Can you believe he's got the nerve to show up here after he dumped Sarah? The creep." Eve shot daggers across the room. I don't know if Dylan got the message, since I couldn't see if he knew we were looking at him. She crossed her arms over her chest and stepped back. "Hey, you don't suppose he's the one who bumped her off, do you?"

With a look, I reminded Eve to keep her voice down. "If he's been out of the country, that seems pretty unlikely. Besides, we don't know anything about the man."

"We know he's a lowlife scum weasel who took Sarah's heart and ground it to smithereens under the heel of his expensive loafers."

I was not so sure we did know that, and I reminded Eve. "We'll talk to him. We'll talk to them all," I said. "For now . . ." I checked out the outfit she'd chosen to wear and realized that our minds were running in the same direction. Like Eve, I was wearing black pants, a black jacket, a white blouse. I looked like a nun. Eve looked like a million bucks.

"You'd better get an apron on and help with the salads," I told her. "That's the first thing Jim wants us to bring out; then we'll get the hot stuff on the buffet."

I was going to help, too, and I had just turned to head into the kitchen when the front door opened again. A hush fell over the crowd, and the people standing nearest the door parted like the Red Sea in front of Moses.

Senator Douglas Mercy had arrived.

Standing where I was, I had the perfect opportunity to check out the man, and I will say this: the pictures I'd seen of the senator did not do him justice. He was taller than I expected. Tanner, too. Though he must have been at least sixty, his skin was taut and wrinkle-free, except for around his eyes. There, a spider-work of creases attested to hours spent in the sun, and I knew from tabloid pictures and news reports that it was just as likely he'd whiled away that time skeet shooting or fishing as glad-handing constituents in his Southern home state.

The senator had neatly cropped, silver hair and eyes the color of the November sky outside the window. Iron gray and steel hard, they were the eyes of a man who held great power and relished every moment of it. His nose was well-shaped. His chin was square. In an instant, his gaze took in everything and everyone around him, and as if it was second nature, he didn't miss a beat—he started shaking hands.

"Thank you." The senator pumped the hand of the red-headed lady I'd noticed earlier. "Thank you so much for coming. You know this would have meant a great deal to Sarah. Thank you." He moved on to the next person, and the next one after that. "She always liked working with you, Renee," he told the woman in black who'd been talking about Sarah's suicide and crying softly. "She told me you were more than just the best administrative assistant we have on staff. She told me you were her friend."

Renee pulled out her hankie again, and when the senator moved on to the next guest, she sniffed and blew her nose.

Thinking I was one of the mourners, the senator shook my hand briefly and moved on to Eve. He held her hand a little longer. Tall, gorgeous blonde . . . Short, round brunette . . .

I guess it mattered, even in the political arena.

It wasn't until after the senator had passed that I saw that a man and a woman had walked into the restaurant behind him.

Unlike a lot of folks in the D.C. area, I am not a political junkie. But I didn't need to be on the Beltway grapevine to know that this man was related to the senator. He had the same square chin, the same gray eyes. He wasn't as tall or as thin, and he was years younger, but his taste in suits was every bit as expensive as the senator's, and he had the same talent for shaking hands, too. No way this wasn't Douglas Mercy's son.

"Dougy." Eve must have been reading my mind; she whispered in my ear. "Douglas Mercy IV officially, but Dougy was his nickname as a kid, and it stuck. He's not very happy about it, and who can blame him? It sounds like something straight out of Mayberry. He's the senator's chief of staff, and word has it that the senator's grooming him to take his seat in Congress once he becomes vice president."

I watched Dougy Mercy greet the people in the crowd as his father had done. When he stopped to chat with a man on my right, I let my gaze drift to the woman who walked at his side. She was dark-haired, dark-eyed, and petite, a wiry, athletic looking woman who in spite of the soft, appropriate-for-a-funeral smile pasted to her face, looked incredibly bored.

I didn't have to say a word. I looked at the woman. I looked at Eve. She knew what I was thinking.

"That's Lorraine, Dougy's wife," Eve whispered. "She's a mover and a shaker; has roots that go back to the Revolution and makes sure no one ever forgets it. Not that anybody holds it against her; she does too much good for that. In addition to throwing the best parties in town, she's a doctor. She runs some sleep clinic in Orange County, and when she's not doing all that or jetting off to Europe to ski, she organizes huge fund-raisers for all sorts of good causes. Of course, when it comes to asking for money, it helps to have a Christmas card list that reads like the Who's Who of Washington social life."

I didn't ask how Eve knew all this. I didn't need to. She'd spent the morning with these people and, funeral or not, she had a way of instantly turning folks from strangers into friends. Besides, I knew that if there was gossip to be had, Eve was the woman for the job. When it came to investigating, I was glad to have her on my side.

While the senator and his entourage made their way around the room, Eve and I made sure everyone knew they could move toward the salad buffet. After a while, everyone started eating. A hush fell over the restaurant. It was broken by the sound of a spoon clinking against a glass.

"Ladies and gentlemen . . ." Senator Mercy was seated at one of the tables near the front windows. He rose and stepped into the middle of the room, wineglass in hand.

"I'd like to propose a toast," the senator said, raising his glass. "To a young woman whose wit and intellect will be sorely missed."

While all eyes were on the senator, I took the opportunity to check out the crowd again.

Renee, the administrative assistant, wasn't high up enough on the office food chain to get a table or a seat. She was standing at the bar, her plate of food untouched in front of her. A single tear slipped down her cheek.

The senator went on. His voice was deep, his accent as thick as hominy. "Sarah Whittaker was more than just a coworker to many of us. She was an ally, a colleague. She had a razor-sharp mind and she knew . . . as you all do . . . that real transformation begins with the people of this country who have the courage to stand up for what they believe. People like you—people like Sarah—don't just talk about what has to change. People like you—people like Sarah— roll up their sleeves and get the job done."

"Bullshit!"

Since I was the only one who flinched, my guess was that no one else heard the comment. Even though it was no more than a whisper, it was the last sentiment I expected to hear at a moment like that. Especially when it was spoken with so much venom.

Naturally, I turned around to see who was standing close by.

Renee was just a few feet away, but I knew it wasn't her. She was crying too hard to have said anything. Call it a stereotype and my naive belief that little old ladies didn't curse, but I didn't think it was the white-haired, grandmotherly woman beside her, either. The only other people close enough for me to have overheard were a too-handsome-to-be-real man I recognized as Dylan Monroe and the redheaded woman I'd seen earlier.

Without looking too obvious, I couldn't take the chance of paying too much attention to either one of them. When the senator started talking again, I had no choice but to turn around.

"Here's to her beauty, to her talent, and to her life." The senator raised his glass a little higher. "Here's to Sarah Whittaker."

Everyone repeated, "To Sarah!" and drained their glasses.

Except for Dylan. Staring into the bloodred liquid, he rolled his wineglass between his palms—right before he banged the glass on the bar, pushed through the crowd, and slammed out the front door.

"He's feeling guilty." Eve saw what I saw. She looked toward the front windows. Out on the sidewalk, Dylan paced back and forth in front of the restaurant. "He's our guy, Annie."

Now that the toasting was over, the crowd waited for Charlene, Senator Mercy, Dougy, and Lorraine to start the line at the main dish table. Behind the buffet, Heidi served, and as I talked to Eve, I kept an eye out to see if anyone needed anything.

"Maybe," I said to her.

"Maybe?" She shook her head. "Does anybody other than Dylan have a motive?"

I didn't know. Wasn't that the whole point of investigating? Rather than stick around to debate the issue, I headed across the room. No, I wasn't after Dylan. When it came time to talk to him, he wouldn't be hard to find. It was the redheaded lady I was more concerned about. Was she a friend of Sarah's? A coworker? I didn't know. I didn't even know her name. I couldn't take the chance of letting her get away.

Lucky for me, the woman was finishing the last bite of her spinach salad, and I had the perfect excuse to approach her.

"May I take that for you?" I asked, pointing to her empty plate.

She answered with a dismissive sort of gesture that made me think she was used to being waited on, but even so, I took my time removing the plate.

"It's a shame, isn't it?" I said. "A funeral for a young person. It's always so sad. Did you know her well?"

The woman fished in her purse, brought out a tube of lipstick, and took her time applying it. "Worked with her," she said, checking her lips in a silver compact.

I nodded like this was news to me. "From what the senator said, she was quite a powerhouse. You'll probably miss having her around the office."

"Think so?" One of the woman's perfectly arched brows rose. She put the lipstick back in her purse and leaned closer to me. "If you ask me, the senator should have fired that little bitch months ago."

"Really?" I didn't have to pretend interest. I looked over my shoulder to make sure no one was listening to our conservation and bent my head closer to the woman's. "You mean she wasn't as great as the senator said?"

The woman laughed coldly. "She didn't give a damn about her work. Only cared about being the center of attention. For months, she's been screwing up everything she touched. Commerce reports, banking reports, voter reports. You name it, she made a mess of it. And who was left to pick up the pieces?"

I didn't have to be an insider to guess, so I wasn't going out on a limb when I said, "You, right?"

"Damned straight," she snarled. "Sarah was given all the plumb assignments. Then when it came time to present her findings, she'd turn in some half-assed report. A man of Senator Mercy's stature, he doesn't need that kind of bungled information. It's too important to his career. So of course, every time he asked . . ." She stood a little straighter. "Of course I told him I'd help. And I always did."

"Why not just have Sarah redo the work herself?"

"There's a good question, and believe me, you're not the first one to ask it." The woman shot a look across the room toward the senator, and when she realized he just happened to be looking our way, she pasted a smile on her face. "Missed my kid's last damn birthday party, thanks to Sarah," she said through clenched teeth. "Ended up staying late to clean up one of her messes."

"That's a shame." Truly, it was, but I made sure I slathered on the sympathy. It was the best way to keep her talking. "You think she was on the verge of getting fired?"

"It would explain why she killed herself, wouldn't it?"

It would. *If* Sarah had killed herself. I tried not to look too eager. "It sounds like you knew her pretty well."

"I knew she was useless."

"Then maybe you also know . . ." I didn't have to pretend to be embarrassed. Sticking my nose in other people's business did not come as second nature to me. Neither did lying. My cheeks were flaming, but I pressed on. "I've heard a lot about Sarah today," I said, easing into the change of subject. "You know, from the people here. I heard somebody say something about how much money she had. They said she bought a really expensive dog. And that she had really nice clothes. Somebody mentioned that she was going on a cruise. I know it's none of my business, but I hope you don't mind if I ask . . . I've been thinking about getting a new job, and if a position on a senator's staff pays that well . . ."

"If it paid all that well, believe me, honey, I'd be on a

tropical island somewhere. Sure would beat looking forward to another winter in this town. All that money Sarah had . . ." The woman sneered. "Just another example of how lucky she was."

I dunno, I'd never thought of a woman who ended up dead in a bathtub as lucky, but now was not the time to quibble. When the redhead crooked a finger to call me closer, I moved in.

"Her aunt Sadie," she said. "Rich widow with no children and no other relative in the world. Died just a few months ago and left every last cent to Sarah."

I had wondered how Sarah came by the wherewithal to support her lavish lifestyle, and I have to say, this news cheered me. It was enough to have to worry about Sarah's murder; I didn't need to throw the mystery of her finances into the mix.

"Isn't that just a kick in the butt?" While I'd been deep in thought, the redhead had kept right on going. "Woman leaves Sarah a chunk of change, and before she can go through even half of it, she up and does a hari-kari number on herself. Just goes to prove how much she craved the spotlight."

This time, I couldn't hide my disgust. "Really, if she wanted to be the center of attention—"

The redhead stopped me with a snarl. "Look around you, honey. We're all here, aren't we? And on a national holiday, too. What are we all talking about? Sarah, Sarah, Sarah. If you ask me, she got just what she wanted."

Investigation or no investigation, it was all I could take. With a polite (and very phony) smile, I whisked the woman's plate away. Even though I should have collected a few more of them and not wasted the trip, I headed for the kitchen, the better to put some distance between myself and the redhead's jaundiced view of the world.

I nudged the kitchen door open with my hip and nearly bumped into Charlene.

"I'm so sorry!" Charlene hadn't changed much since high school. She was still polite and concerned with other people. She held the door open and stepped back to allow me to get by. "I'm glad I found you," she continued. "I just told Jim . . ." She looked into the kitchen where Jim was putting the finishing touches on the plates of pastries that would be served for dessert. "But I wanted to tell you and Eve, too. This is perfect. Just perfect." She waited until I put the plate down, then grabbed my hand. "Thank you, Annie."

"I'm glad we could help." It felt good to be telling the truth again, and I smiled, then remembered what the redhead had told me. "And I'm so sorry about your loss," I said. "It must be especially difficult to lose two relatives so close together."

Charlene tipped her head. "Two?"

"Your aunt Sadie."

"My aunt? Sadie?" Charlene smiled. "I don't know where you got your information, but please, don't worry about me, Annie. Sarah and I, we never had an Aunt Sadie!"

Eight

✖

BY NATURE, I AM NOT A LIAR.
In everyday life, I believe this is a big plus. When investigating a murder . . . well, I hate to say it, but when it comes to getting to the bottom of a mystery, being honest falls into the not-so-good category. To uncover information—any information—it's sometimes necessary to bend the truth. I know this in my heart, but I still can't lie with a straight face or without my conscience prickling.

It goes without saying that because I don't lie, I assume other people don't, either.

Naive? I suppose. But, I always believe the best of people.

I suppose that was why it took me a couple moments to process Charlene's comment.

No Aunt Sadie?

I had a couple of reasons to believe this. Number one, it was coming from Charlene, and I knew that if anything, she was even more honest than me. Number two, why would Charlene want to/need to lie about a dead relative?

The night before, Eve and Charlene had met at Sarah's apartment, and Eve shared our theory about Sarah's death. Charlene wasn't ready to buy into it wholesale, but unlike

Tyler, she didn't completely dismiss it, either. Even murder offered a tad more comfort than the thought of suicide, and she was willing to consider the possibility and grateful that Eve and I had the knowledge and experience to look into the matter. (On this point, I think Eve might have bent the truth herself a tad and made us sound a lot more capable than we really were.) But, like us, Charlene was anxious to find out the truth.

In my book, all this meant that Charlene's word was golden. If she said there was no Aunt Sadie, I wasn't going to shake the family tree to try to prove otherwise.

That left me with two options:

Redheaded Woman had concocted the Aunt Sadie story.

Or Redheaded Woman was on the up-and-up, and Sarah was the one who made up the fib about Aunt Sadie.

Just like I don't lie, I don't jump to conclusions. But the latter conclusion seemed pretty obvious. Call me crazy, but I didn't think Redheaded Woman gave a damn. She had no reason to lie. That meant Sarah was our culprit.

"Why would Sarah tell someone you had an Aunt Sadie?" I asked Charlene. "She told her coworkers that's where she got all her money. She'd inherited it."

Charlene was not as attractive a woman as Sarah. She was short and stocky. Her mousy-brown hair was blunt cut, she didn't wear any makeup, and her clothes, while neat, were even more basic than mine. I suppose it came with the territory—she wouldn't have moved halfway around the world to teach people how to dig latrines if she was the type who worried about breaking a fingernail. I was grateful not to have to work past any pretensions and glad I didn't have to explain myself. Charlene knew exactly what I was thinking.

"This is about all that stuff in Sarah's apartment, isn't it?" It had been a long and difficult morning, and Charlene scrubbed her hands over her face. "I've been wondering how Sarah could have afforded it all, too. But believe me, the money didn't come from an inheritance. We don't have that many relatives, and the ones we have sure don't have any money. Why would Sarah make up a story like that? You think she was into something she shouldn't have been messing with, don't you?"

It was hard to deny the possibility, but I tried anyway. This was one conclusion I didn't want to jump to until I had more proof. More than none, anyway.

"Maybe it was a man," I suggested. This was an easier theory to swallow. "Could she have had a boyfriend who gave her all that expensive stuff?"

Charlene shrugged. "I've been in the Peace Corps for years," she said. "I've lived all over the world. Sarah and I . . . well, it's not like we didn't like each other or like we didn't write and call when we could. But it's hard to get personal when you've got three minutes to catch up on six months' worth of news. We only really saw each other once every couple years, and let's face it, our worlds didn't exactly overlap. Sarah worried about prestige, power, and designer clothing. Not exactly my thing. I'm ashamed to admit it, Annie, but I really didn't know her that well. I can't tell you about her personal life. The last guy she talked about was Dylan, but that was months ago, and according to Eve, they weren't seeing each other anymore. Some of the stuff I found around the apartment was obviously brand-new. If somebody bought it for her, it wasn't him."

Before I had time to process all this, Eve came by, and Charlene latched onto her arm. "You two are doing an amazing thing," she said, looking back and forth at Eve and me. "If it's true that Sarah didn't . . ." She cleared her throat. "If it's possible that she was . . ." She coughed again. "Look, I hate to ask for more, but . . ." Charlene's cheeks got pink.

"It's OK." Eve patted her arm. "Anything, Charlene. We'll help."

Charlene wiped away a tear. "You're already doing so much. But, well . . ." She sniffed. "I have to leave. Tomorrow. I won't have time to wrap everything up." She glanced at Eve, her expression imploring. "If I could sign over my power of attorney, you know, just in case there are things that come up that need to be handled."

"Of course." Eve put a hand on her arm.

"And if you could just . . ." It was clear Charlene wasn't used to asking for help. Her cheeks got red. "If you could clean out Sarah's apartment, I can't tell you how much I'd appreciate it. I picked up a couple little mementos when I was there last night, but there's nothing else I want or need. If there's anything that strikes your fancy, keep it. Donate what's left to a woman's shelter."

"And Doc?"

Do I need to point out that the question came from Eve? Or that while she waited for Charlene's answer, she held her breath?

"The dog?" It was obvious Charlene had not thought of this. She lifted one shoulder. "Maybe there's somebody who will—"

"I'll take him!" Like a kid in school, Eve raised her hand. "I promise I'll take good care of him. I'll walk him and feed him and love him and—"

"It's OK." Charlene laughed. "That would be great, Eve. I know you'll be good to him. And it would really help me out."

"Yes!" Like an Olympic gold medal winner, Eve punched one fist in the air. "Oh my gosh, he's going to be so happy that he gets to stay. I'm going to call him now and tell him."

Yes, Eve can be a little obtuse at times. But even she had her act together enough to realize Charlene and I were giving her blank stares.

Eve rolled her eyes. "No, I don't think he's going to answer the phone. But I can leave a message on my machine. He'll hear it. He's going to be thrilled."

She raced into my office to use the phone.

In the meantime, some of the guests had started to leave, and Charlene hurried to the door to thank them for coming. Left to my own devices, I wondered who I should talk to next. The matter was settled for me when an elderly woman walked out the door, and Dylan Monroe came back inside.

"Dylan!" I stopped him before he could reach for the raincoat that was draped over the back of one of the bar chairs. "Hi. I'm—"

"A big fan. Yeah, I get the message. I've heard it about a million times before. You do realize this isn't exactly the right time to ask for an autograph, don't you?"

Dylan's words were as cutting as the look he gave me. Startled, I stepped back. "I don't want an autograph," I said. "I'm Annie. Annie Capshaw. I was a friend of Sarah's. Eve and I, we're the ones who found her."

Dylan's handsome face went pale. He squeezed his eyes shut. Something told me that when he opened them again, he hoped that I'd be gone.

No such luck. Now that I had his attention, I wasn't about to let him get away. Not until I had some answers.

"I'm sorry," Dylan said when he saw that I hadn't moved an inch. "Honest, I am. Now you know the truth. I can be an insensitive jerk."

I wasn't about to argue with that. Of course, telling Dylan as much wouldn't have gotten me anywhere. Instead, I gave him a brief smile. "I just wanted to give you my condolences," I said. "I understand that you and Sarah were dating."

Dylan made a sour face. "*Were* being the operative word." He plunked down on one of the barstools. "I'm sorry. Again," he said, and he tried to prove it by pointing to the empty seat next to him. I shook my head, declining the offer. There was no use calling any more attention to what I was doing.

"I'm a little on edge," Dylan admitted. "Attending the service this morning, then the burial . . ." A shiver snaked over his broad shoulders. "I feel awful about this whole thing."

"About not dating Sarah anymore? Or about Sarah dying?"

"Both." He ran a hand through his hair, and I wondered what magic TV news reporters had. When he was done, his hair looked as good as it had before he touched it. "If I knew she was going to take it this badly, I never would have dumped her. I just never thought . . ." He let out a shaky breath.

"I've been in Afghanistan," he said. "Working on a major report. I've been gone for months, and I tried, I mean I really tried to keep in touch with Sarah. We e-mailed. We talked just about every day. But I knew what was happening. Every time we talked, I could tell. We were growing apart. We just didn't have anything in common anymore."

"But you came to her funeral."

Like he didn't understand it himself, he propped his elbows on the bar and steepled his fingers, tapping his index fingers on his chin. "I just got back yesterday. I heard the news and . . . Damn! It's my fault. The world has lost a beautiful person. And it's all my fault."

It's not like I didn't believe him. I was, after all, the honest person who saw the good in everyone else. But I felt our conversation coming to an end. And I hadn't found out anything useful. I knew I had to dig a little deeper. "You don't really think she would take a breakup that hard, do you?" I asked Dylan. "After all—"

"What?" His macho image questioned, Dylan got to his feet and looked at me down his perfectly shaped nose. "Maybe you don't understand because you've never been dumped, honey, but let me tell you—"

"Don't bother!" A spurt of anger shot through me. No need to ask where it came from. This was Peter-induced fury, pure and simple. Even I was surprised that I was prepared to take it out on a perfect stranger. "Believe me, when it comes to breaking up, I'm an expert. My husband ran off with the girl from the dry cleaner's. How's that for real-life experience?"

"And when it happened, tell me you didn't feel like ending your own life."

The very idea shook me to the core. I glared into Dylan Monroe's perfect brown eyes at the same time I looked into the depths of my own soul. "Never," I told him and reminded myself. "I felt like hell, sure, but I never once thought suicide was the answer."

"Then maybe you're just a stronger person than Sarah."

"Or maybe Sarah didn't kill herself."

I hadn't meant to let the words slip, but like I said, I was angry. Once they were past my lips, there was nothing I could do but hold my ground and wait to gauge Dylan's reaction.

I didn't have to wait long. By the time he slipped on his coat, he was shaking his head. "Women," he said. "You can't accept the fact that you're not as tough as men. You're always looking for touchy-feely excuses to explain everything."

"I wouldn't exactly call murder touchy-feely."

"And I wouldn't call suicide murder just to make myself believe that my friend was a stronger person than she really was. That's what it was, you know. Suicide. And as much as I hate to admit it, I know it was my fault. From what I've heard, everything else was going well in Sarah's life. I was the only bump in the road, and our relationship was the only thing that had changed lately. Do the math. Oh, wait! Women aren't good at math, either, are they? Then get over it and face the facts. Sarah killed herself. Now, if you'll excuse me . . ."

He didn't wait for me to say I would or I wouldn't. Dylan Monroe walked away. As soon as my temper had a chance to calm down, I thought about what he'd said.

Their relationship, he'd told me, was the only thing that had changed in Sarah's life recently.

Except it wasn't.

According to Redheaded Woman, Sarah's work had suffered as of late. Big time. So much so that there was talk around the office of Sarah losing her job.

And according to what I'd seen in the apartment with my own two eyes, Sarah suddenly had a whole lot of money to spend, too.

Changes?

No doubt of that. My only question now was who would be willing to talk about them?

I didn't have to wonder long. No sooner had I watched Dylan stomp out of the restaurant than I decided to look around for dishes and glasses that needed to be picked up.

All set to do just that, I turned away from the bar—and ran smack into Senator Douglas Mercy.

"I am so sorry!" My nose put an indentation in the senator's tie. Automatically, I reached to smooth it, then realized I was being much too forward. I slapped my hand against my side. "For running into you, Senator. And for trying to act like your mom and fix your tie. Force of habit, I'm afraid."

The senator smiled. "That must mean you're a mom."

"No, afraid not. Someday, maybe. But I am a person who likes to fix things. And I'm the business manager here at Bellywasher's." I introduced myself, and the senator shook my hand and assured me that the food was excellent and the service above par.

"I'll be back for dinner one of these nights," he said, but I really didn't believe it. Something told me senators were too busy and way too used to five-star to hang out on the wrong side of the Alexandria tracks. Still, it was nice of him to compliment us, and I told him so. Right before I forced myself into nosy mode.

"That was a wonderful toast you gave," I told the senator. "After you were finished, I felt as if I knew Sarah better."

"Yes. It's a shame about Sarah, isn't it? So much promise. And all of it wasted."

"You mean because of her suicide. Or were you talking about the way the quality of her work has declined lately?"

If the senator was surprised by how blunt I was, he didn't say anything. He did look at me with renewed interest, though. "You've been talking to Jennifer," he said, and he looked toward the door where Redheaded Woman was just slipping on her coat and getting ready to leave. "She should know better than to air our dirty laundry on an occasion as solemn as this."

"She's bitter, and I can't blame her. Sounds like thanks to Sarah, she's been carrying a lot of the office load."

"I'll remember that when it comes time for employee reviews." The senator backed up a step. I knew he was about to walk away.

"I found her, you know." What a ghoulish thing to say! I was embarrassed, but I pressed on. Just like I hoped, the words stopped Douglas Mercy in his tracks.

"You? And another woman, right? I heard it was that tall blonde." He glanced around, and I knew he was looking for Eve. Someone must have pointed her out to the senator earlier.

"Eve DeCateur. That's right. We were the ones who stopped at Sarah's apartment the other night."

"That must have been horrible." The senator was honestly upset, and I was sorry I'd brought up the subject.

"It wasn't so bad." OK, so I was getting better at this lying thing. How could I say anything else? I'd already upset one of the most powerful men in the country. And I was a habitual fixer-upper. I couldn't stand the thought of not trying to make him feel better. "But even so, I can't help but wonder why. I'm sure you understand. Why would a woman as talented and smart as Sarah—"

"It was Dylan, of course." The senator looked toward the door, but Dylan was long gone. "Ever since their relationship ended, Sarah's been down in the dumps. And yes, Jennifer was right. Sarah's work had suffered. Terribly. It wasn't fair to the rest of my staff to make them pick up the slack, but honestly, what was I supposed to do? I wanted to hang in there with Sarah, to give her time and some space so she could put her life back together again. I thought that sooner or later, she'd come around. I never expected this. I should have listened when she wanted to talk. I should have—" His voice broke, and he turned away. When he turned back to me again, there was a sheen of tears in the senator's eyes.

"You'll have to forgive me," he said. "It's going to take me a while to get used to the fact that she's gone. Now, if you'll excuse me, I need to get to work."

I didn't remind him that it was a national holiday. Instead, I watched Douglas Mercy say something to his son and daughter-in-law before he put on his coat and left.

Since Dougy Mercy was the next interviewee on my list,

I was grateful when he stopped on his way out. Before he started talking, he looked over his shoulder to see where his wife was. I wondered if it was because he wanted her to hear what he had to tell me. Or because he didn't.

"My father tells me you asked about Sarah, about her work." Dougy was wearing cologne that smelled expensive. He had his father's charming smile and a bit of a twitch in his left eye. "I can't help you much. She was a lower-level staffer, and we didn't work together very often. I must say, though, your sources are right on. Sarah's work had suffered lately. It's a shame." He shook his head. "A terrible shame."

He was still shaking his head when he walked away.

Lorraine Mercy followed him out of the restaurant, but she didn't stop or say a word. She did give me a long, assessing look when she came by, though, and when Eve scrambled out of my office and stood at my side, Lorraine looked her over, too.

Eve gave her a look back.

"Can you believe a woman of her stature doesn't pay more attention to how she dresses?"

I could, because as far as I could see, Lorraine was as impeccably dressed and as well turned out as any woman I'd ever seen.

Of course, I didn't have Eve's eye for fashion. She clicked her tongue. "Annie, didn't you notice? Maybe not. I didn't. Not when she came in. But the light, it's a little different now. It shows off the colors better."

Curious, I gave Lorraine Mercy another once-over.

And finally saw what Eve was talking about.

"Her skirt and her jacket . . ." Eve's words echoed my thoughts. "They're both navy blue, but not the same shade of navy blue. It's a fashion faux pas of the first order." She shivered. "Think she realizes it?"

I didn't, and I wondered what it meant.

It was possible that Mrs. Mercy was upset about attending a funeral and hadn't dressed with her usual care.

It was possible she was in a hurry and hadn't looked

carefully to make sure that the jacket she grabbed matched the skirt she was wearing.

It was possible she just didn't care all that much about colors, which made me think about our visit to Sarah's apartment.

And the mixed-up red and green jackets in Sarah's closet.

Nine

✖

WHEN I GOT TO BELLYWASHER'S THE NEXT EVENING, I thought somebody had died. Somebody other than Sarah, that is.

That's how quiet the place was.

I had come in through the back door and directly into the kitchen, and I shrugged out of my coat, pulled off my scarf, and stopped cold. What happened to all the usual noises? The slap of knives against cutting boards? The clink of the metal spatula against the grill? Running water? People talking?

Curious, I looked around and found our cooks, Marc and Damien, standing side by side near the walk-in cooler. Damien was far taller than Marc, and he craned his neck and looked out the window in the door that led into the restaurant. Like the folks who provided the play-by-play on the all-golf channel, his voice was a reverent whisper. "He's chewing. He's swallowing. Now he's picking up his wineglass to take a sip of the wine. No, wait. He's putting down the wineglass. He's taking a forkful of the confit and another bite of chicken."

"He who?"

I spoke in a normal tone, but in the quiet, my words came out like thunder.

"Shhhhh!" Marc was a heavyset, easygoing kid who had the bewildering habit of coloring his hair whenever the mood struck him. Which was usually a couple times a week. At the funeral luncheon, it was neon orange. That night, his hair was the color of eggplant. It took me a moment to orient myself to the change.

He silenced me, one finger to his lips. "We're waiting to see what's going to happen," he whispered.

"With who?" I had learned my lesson—I kept my voice down. I was shorter than both Damien and Marc, and when I went to stand next to them, I couldn't see a thing. "Come on, guys. Don't keep me in suspense. What's going on here?"

Damien was a young man with dark hair that he wore in a ponytail. He had a ring in his nose, another one in his eyebrow, and a series of tattoos up each arm that I found compelling and creepy all at the same time. I knew from his initial job interview that he had an encyclopedic knowledge of food and dreams of someday becoming as skilled a chef as Jim. Thanks to a series of stupid mistakes as a teenager, he also had a prison record.

He slanted me a look that was akin to coming right out and saying that if I had cooking oil in my veins like he and Marc and Jim did, I wouldn't have had to ask stupid questions.

Damien pointed toward the door and the restaurant beyond. He mouthed the words, "Michael O'Keefe."

"Oh?" Awareness flooded through me, hot one second, icy cold the next. "Oh!" I stood on tiptoe, hoping for a glimpse of the famous and influential food critic. Maybe it was the change of altitude that triggered my thought process. In one moment of blinding, panic-filled epiphany, I realized that our future as a restaurant hung in the balance and in every bite that went into Michael O'Keefe's mouth.

"Oh." My knees wobbled enough for Marc to see me stagger. He grabbed on to my arm, ushered me over to a chair in the corner, and plopped me down.

"Breathe, Annie," he said. It would have been a caring gesture if not for the fact that the whole time he rubbed my back, he was still trying to see what was happening out in the restaurant.

I pulled in a breath. "How long as he been here?"

Marc didn't need to look at the clock. "Long enough to order dinner," he said. "Celery root soup with bacon and green apple. Then the chicken with black pepper maple sauce, grilled asparagus, and polenta with red pepper confit."

"And?"

He knew what I meant. "The dude's like a robot. Bites and chews and swallows and doesn't say a word." Marc shrugged. "No expression on his face, either. Ain't no way we can figure out what he thinks of the food."

Of course I couldn't see anything from where I was sitting, but I still burned with interest. I had to try again. I sat up tall and stretched even taller (which, let's face it, wasn't very tall). Even so, my view was limited to a square of the restaurant's ceiling. I gave up with a sigh, and my spine accordioned back into place. "How's Jim holding out?" I asked.

Marc and Damien exchanged looks.

"What?" I was out of my chair in an instant. "He didn't say anything to offend O'Keefe, did he?" I asked, even though I knew there was no way possible. Jim was a born restaurateur. He was friendly, warm, and charming, as at home behind the bar regaling the likes of Larry, Hank, and Charlie with stories about Scotland as he was going from table to table to chat up the more tony clients and make sure everything met their expectations. I had never seen Jim angry (well, except for the time Doc barfed all over the restaurant), and I'd never heard him speak a rude word.

I knew this in my head and in my heart.

None of which calmed my fears or stifled my imagination. In my mind's eye, I pictured every disaster possible. I even checked the corner near the linen storage shelves for the purse Eve used to carry Doc. It wasn't there—thank goodness—and for this bit of luck, I was grateful.

"All right. I know." I got hold of myself and stemmed Damien and Marc's comments, which I was pretty sure were going to be in the ballpark of *Are you crazy?* "Jim has been the perfect host. So why the strange looks between you two?"

"It's nothing. Really." Damien poked his hands under his white apron and into the pockets of his jeans. "We was just talking, is all. About Jim. When we heard O'Keefe was here, me and Marc, we just about freaked. But Jim, he's as cool as a frozen margarita. Didn't even want to cook the dude's stuff. Not even when I begged him and told him I was too nervous to do it. Said we were capable and we should just do our jobs. Now he's out at the bar and—"

"And he's acting like it's no big deal," Marc chimed in. "He hasn't even been over to the table to talk to the guy."

None of this came as much of a surprise. Like I said, Jim was a born restaurateur. He knew better than to push or to pry. He didn't care who a customer was, he wasn't going to suck up.

I knew this was wise. It was also professional and logical. But I was afraid that in the case of the most influential restaurant critic in D.C. wise, professional, and logical might be a mistake. It couldn't hurt to suck up. Just a little.

I pulled my brown blazer into place, picked a piece of lint off my khakis, lifted my chin, and headed for the bar.

"Annie! Good to see you." Jim was pouring a beer for Larry who, for reasons I could not fathom, was actually there without Charlie and Hank. Larry waved, and I smiled a hello.

"How was your day at the bank?" Jim asked me.

I darted a look toward the table where Michael O'Keefe was finishing up the last of his polenta. He wasn't smiling. But he wasn't frowning, either. In fact, there was no expression at all on his face. I wondered what was going on inside his head and how he was rating the food and the service. Terror filled me head-to-toe along with an image of a sign on the front door that said, Closed Due to Critical Ennui.

Just in case O'Keefe happened to notice me, I put a smile

on my face. "How can you think about my day at the bank at a time like this?" I asked Jim.

"A time like . . . what?" There was a clock on the wall behind the bar, and Jim looked at it. "A time like six forty-five? I always wonder about your day around this time. It's when you leave the bank and come here. And I always look forward to seeing you."

It was considerate and sweet—in a way that made me think Jim was having some sort of panic-induced psychotic break.

I knew it was my duty to bring him back to reality. "Have you been over to talk to him yet?" I asked with another look at O'Keefe.

"Not yet." Jim smiled. Before I knew it was coming, he latched onto my hand and pulled me out from behind the bar. "I've been waiting for you. Come on, let's go over and say hello."

"Oh, no. Not me. You're the owner. You're the host. You're the one who should do all the PR." I locked my knees and refused to budge a step, but there really was no question about me going along with Jim. A lifetime of chopping vegetables, boning chicken, and fileting fish had apparently developed muscles nonchefs never dreamed existed. When Jim tugged, I followed.

He waited until O'Keefe paid his bill before he introduced himself and me.

The critic nodded, but he didn't smile. He was a middle-aged man with saggy cheeks and a paunch that suggested he spent a lot of his time in restaurants.

"I hope you found everything satisfactory," Jim said.

O'Keefe didn't smile. But he nodded.

"We're so glad you made time in your schedule to stop in." Was that my voice? I sounded as breathy as an *American Idol* contestant. I turned my smile up a notch. "You picked the most popular items on the menu. Jim's celery root soup is famous."

O'Keefe grunted. He pushed back from the table and stood. "Familiar without being trite," he said, and without another word, he walked out.

The sound of the door closing behind him was apparently the signal everyone had been waiting for.

Marc and Damien were out of the kitchen in a flash. They were both talking at once while they checked O'Keefe's plate to see what he'd finished completely and what he left behind. They didn't have to worry in that department. He'd eaten every last bite.

Heidi beamed over the twenty dollar tip the critic left her. Eve had apparently been hiding out in my office watching O'Keefe's every move, and she came running, mumbling something about his taste in clothes. Larry joined the group. He sipped his beer and shook his head sadly, looking at the front door. "Seen livelier folks in funeral parlors," he said.

And Jim?

Through it all, he didn't say a thing, which was unfortunate. I was a banker, and banks and restaurants didn't speak the same language. I needed someone to translate what had just happened into words I could understand.

Instead, Jim just picked up O'Keefe's plates and carried them back into the kitchen.

Which left me standing in the middle of Bellywasher's, more mystified than ever by the restaurant business. My too-wide-to-be-real smile faded. "Familiar without being trite?" I asked no one in particular. "Would someone please tell me what the hell that means!"

I FOUND OUT SOON ENOUGH.
In the world of restaurant reviews, "familiar without being trite" is apparently a good thing. O'Keefe's review (which included those exact words) ran the following Friday. By that night, we had a waiting list and a line out the door.

In a kind of an I-dream-of-profits euphoria, I watched the crowds come and go. They were a well-dressed bunch who asked intelligent questions about the wine list, knew how to pronounce words like *arugula*, and spoke in hushed and refined tones about things like watercress vichyssoise and poached salmon.

This was all good, I told myself. It was all very good.

That night, I finished up the paperwork that was waiting for me when I arrived from the bank, waved a quick good-bye to Jim (who was too busy hobnobbing with a congress-man from Arizona to do any more than wave back), and by the time I drifted off to sleep that night, I was still smiling. The next day, I had a rare Saturday off from the bank and a million things on my to-do list. But believe it or not—and I hardly believed it myself—when Eve called and asked me to come with her when she dropped Doc off at the groomer, I didn't say a word about the cleaning and laundry I had to take care of or about the personal bills that were stacking up now that I spent so many hours at the restaurant I didn't have time to pay, much less file them.

I guess for the first time, I realized how much the extra re-sponsibilities of my job and worries about Bellywasher's profitability had weighed me down. Not to mention the nag-ging questions about Sarah's death. But now that I saw that all our hard work at the restaurant was finally starting to pay off, I felt as light as a feather and as happy as the proverbial clam (though what clams have to be happy about is a mys-tery to me).

I couldn't say no to Eve. In fact, I suggested that after we dropped off Doc, we cut loose and treat ourselves to lunch at some place where neither one of us was responsible for seat-ing anyone or balancing the books.

When she pulled into the parking lot of my apartment building, I was waiting for her. I waved, and when she stopped, I slid into the passenger seat and glanced into the backseat where the dog carrier was strapped in and the dog's tiny black nose was pressed against the door.

"Good morning, Doc," I said.

Eve pulled out of the lot and swung out into traffic. Both

her hands were on the wheel. Her knuckles were white. "He's a little nervous," she said, though since the dog looked the way he always looked, I wondered how she knew. We stopped at a red light, and she drummed her hot-pink nails against the steering wheel. Her voice was breathy. "He's never been to the groomer before."

"And except for when you're working, you haven't been away from Doc all day since you got him." I patted Eve's arm. "Don't worry. You said you checked out the groomer. You got recommendations. These folks know what they're doing. They'll take great care of Doc."

They did. From the moment we walked into Salon de Chien, Doc was treated like a furry little king. The woman behind the reception desk scooped him out of his carrier and cooed about how cute he was.

Eve's rough breathing calmed.

The high school–aged girl in pink scrubs who took Doc out of the receptionist's arms and escorted us back to Doc's private "spa room" made little squeaky noises in the dog's ear.

Eve beamed.

By the time we were settled in and waiting for Doc's "personal stylist and masseuse," Eve was actually looking forward to lunch. Before we could decide where we'd eat, a stick-thin, middle-aged woman with a store-bought tan and a huge diamond on the ring finger of her left hand came in and introduced herself as Minette.

"He doesn't need much." Minette was short, her skin was leathery. Her hair was spiked and unnaturally blond. She looked Doc over and nodded. "We don't see many of these Japanese terriers. I'm thrilled to have the chance to work with one." She unfastened Doc's collar. "You really like this little guy, don't you?"

"He's the cutest little thing on the planet." Eve accepted the collar when Minette handed it to her.

The groomer laughed. "I know he's cute. That's not what I'm talking about. I mean that." With her chin, she indicated the sparkling collar. "Usually, I ask folks to leave the dog's collar here so we can put it right back on when the session is done. No way I'm going to take responsibility for that one. We don't have that kind of insurance."

Eve looked confused. And who could blame her? Because she didn't know what to say, I stepped forward. I plucked the collar out of her hands. "Why would you need insurance for rhinestones?"

Minette winked. "If that's what you want to call them, honey, I understand. I wouldn't want word to get around that my dog's collar was worth ten or twenty grand, either."

"Ten?"

"Twenty?"

Both our voices broke, and Eve and I exchanged looks. Her eyes were wide, and her mouth opened and closed over words that refused to come out. Knowing that I had to take over, I shook aside my surprise and skimmed my finger over the collar. It was less than an inch wide and completely covered with the small, sparkling stones.

"You don't think these are real, do you?" I asked Minette.

"You don't think they aren't?" She tipped her head, considering the possibility, then dismissed it with a wave of one hand. "Come on, you two. Stop putting me on! Let me tell you something. I'm older than both of you, and I've learned a couple things from three husbands . . . no, wait, it's four now. Anyway, I've learned a whole lot about diamonds." She held up her left hand and turned it back and forth, and the overhead florescents sparked against her ring. "Believe me, I know the real thing when I see it. You can be sure I checked to see if this one was real before I accepted it."

I knew right then and there why diamonds were sometimes called *ice*, because that's exactly the sensation that shot through me. Icy water rushed through my veins and hardened in my stomach. I swear, it felt as big as the burg that did in the *Titanic*. While I tried to come to grips with what Minette had to say, I turned the collar over in my hands and saw Doc's initials inside it.

"But . . ." While I was still thinking through everything

Minette said, Eve found her voice. "But if the diamonds are real, that means Sarah—"

I didn't let her get any further. Before she could say another word, I latched on to her arm and dragged her toward the door. The collar clutched in my hand, I told Minette we'd be back for Doc by three and hurried Eve out of Salon de Chien and into the car.

I looked all around to make sure no one was watching before I handed the collar over to Eve. I made sure the car doors were locked.

"You don't think she was right, do you?" Eve asked. I looked where she was looking, at the collar she held in a death grip. In the sunshine, it sparkled like a million supernovas. "I mean, if she is—"

"If she is, we've got another reason to believe that Sarah didn't commit suicide."

"Because nobody who has that kind of money can possibly be depressed?"

It was one theory, but I didn't think it was the right one. "Because somebody who has that kind of money has to get it from somewhere."

"Which means—"

I sighed. I hated when I didn't have all the pieces to a puzzle, and this one was definitely minus a few. "I don't know what it means," I confessed. "And I'm sorry I dragged you out of there like that, but I didn't think we could risk the chance of talking about Sarah and where the money might have come from. Not in front of strangers."

Eve gave me one of her *gotcha!* looks. "I get it. Until we know what really happened—"

"Lips sealed." I trusted Eve. Honest, I did. But I knew her well enough to know that it wouldn't hurt to remind her that we might be dealing with murder. "We can't tell anyone. Not about the collar and not about where Sarah got the money."

"We couldn't even if we wanted to, Annie. We don't know where Sarah got all the money."

"No, we don't. But we're going to find out. Remember

that old saying: follow the money. Well, that's exactly what we're going to do."

Eve didn't dispute this. But as she started up the car, she did ask the logical question. "How?"

"Remember that day we were at Sarah's? The night we found the body?" Like I had to ask. Like either of us would ever forget. "Well, I saw a letter in her office. A letter from my bank. If she had an account with us, I just might be able to do a little sleuthing."

A slow smile inched up the corners of Eve's mouth. She didn't have to ask any more questions. She pulled into traffic.

Ten

LET'S FACE IT, I'M FAR TOO PRACTICAL TO HAVE BAGGED the idea of lunch completely. We might be women on a mission, but we weren't completely without priorities. And we *were* hungry.

First things first. We went through the drive-through at the local greasy burger joint and discussed what we'd discovered and what it might mean over French fries, double cheeseburgers, and so-thick-you-could-eat-them-with-a-spoon chocolate shakes. By the time we were done slurping up the last of our milk shakes, we had a plan all worked out.

We had a couple hours before we had to pick up Doc, and we planned to use part of that time to hit the bank. Before that, though, we took a quick detour around Arlington and headed back in the direction of Bellywasher's and Old Town Alexandria.

As I might have mentioned before, Arlington, where I live, is a mix of old neighborhoods and new, funky and fabulous, ordinary and out-of-this-world. Old Town Alexandria, where Bellywasher's is located, is something else altogether. The area was first settled way back before the American Revolution, and the streets are narrow and lined with skinny buildings that stand slap up against each other. Once upon a long time ago, they were the shops and homes of the early settlers. Today, they house everything from fusion restaurants to antique galleries, wig shops to clothing stores.

King Street is the main thoroughfare through the heart of Old Town, and Bellywashers's is located on the not-so-fashionable end of it. In the other direction, closer to the river, the real estate is pricier, the shops are more exclusive, and the clientele is a mixture of tourists and the area's upper crust.

As is true of the entire region, parking in Alexandria is horrendous even on good days. On Saturdays, horrendous morphs straight into impossible.

Which is why I sat up, surprised, when Eve found an empty space not far from where we were headed. Within minutes, we were parked and walking toward an unassuming shop with a plain-Jane facade, a nondescript display window, and prices that I knew for a fact were beyond the reach of ordinary mortals.

This was the shop where not one, but two of Eve's former fiancés had bought her engagement rings. Edgar, the clerk behind the long glass counter, knew Eve on sight, and since I had accompanied her on a couple of buy-gifts-for-the-bridal-party jaunts, he probably recognized me, too. The moment we came through the door, his eyes brightened and, believe me, I knew it had nothing to do with the way I looked. Or with Eve's outfit, for that matter.

Aside from the fact that I was clad in black pants and bundled in my winter coat and that Eve was wearing a thigh-high pink dress and a fake fur that I knew cost nearly as much as the real thing, ol' Edgar immediately pictured another happily-ever-after. Yup, his ear-to-ear smile could mean only one thing: he was thinking of the commission check that would result from the too-expensive ring he knew Eve was about to choose.

I hated to burst Edgar's bubble, and I told him so.

Right before I showed him Doc's collar.

I guess the fact that he practically dropped his teeth proved that when it came to diamonds, Minette knew what she was talking about.

The good news was that they had a safe at the store, and after filling out the proper paperwork and getting a receipt, we left the collar with Edgar for safekeeping.

The bad news?

What with stopping to eat and driving all the way to Alexandria, we didn't have much time left before we had to collect Doc, drop him at Eve's apartment, and get back to Bellywasher's for what we hoped would be a blockbuster Saturday night crowd. I took full responsibility and blamed it on the milk shakes. Eve, as befits her beauty queen background, wasn't one to point fingers. She accepted her part of the responsibility and drove like a bat out of hell all the way back to Arlington. She got us to Pioneer Savings just before closing.

I rushed through the front door and waved a quick hello to Cheryl Starks, the part-timer who filled in on weekends, and because I didn't want to have to explain what I was doing there on my day off, I headed right for the employee break room and the computer that sat in one corner.

A couple minutes later, I was back in the car, where Eve was waiting for me.

"Well?" She looked at me expectantly, and when she saw that I wasn't carrying anything, her expression fell. "Don't tell me you were wrong? Sarah didn't bank here?"

"Sarah banked here, all right. Not this branch. The one over in Clarendon." I glanced around at the cars parked on either side of us and the bank at the other end of the parking lot. "That's all I'm willing to say. At least while I'm sitting where my branch manager can see me."

Eve got the message.

It wasn't until we were back in the lot at Salon de Chien that I pulled out the computer printout I had folded and tucked under my gray sweater.

I skimmed my finger down the columns of numbers that

laid Sarah's financial history out before us. "Regular deposits, twice a month," I told Eve. Even though she was looking over my shoulder at the numbers, I knew she wasn't understanding them the way I was. "The first and the fifteenth. Those have to be her paychecks. And her paychecks . . ." I glanced at Eve, just to make sure she was paying attention. "They're not nearly big enough to account for Sarah's lifestyle. They're sure not big enough for her to be able to afford a diamond collar for Doc."

"So someone had to be buying her all those fancy things: the expensive cocktail dress and the apartment and the collar and the rest of it."

"Or giving her the money to buy those things herself. Look. Here." I pointed at another set of numbers. "A deposit. Once a month. Nine thousand nine hundred dollars. Just enough to squeak under the radar."

"From who?"

Did I care that Eve's grammar was off? At a time like this, *who* and *whom* weren't nearly as important as *why* and *how were we ever going to find out.*

I checked the report again. "Cash deposits," I told Eve. "Every one of them. No way to trace where they came from."

Eve checked her watch. It was time to get Doc, and I knew she wouldn't wait an extra minute. She opened the car door and got out, leaning down to look at me right before she closed the door. "All this means we're at another dead end, right?"

She didn't wait for me to answer, and it was just as well. At that particular moment, I didn't have an answer.

By the time Eve came back with Doc in the carrier, though, I was feeling a little more sure of myself. I waited for her to stow Doc in the backseat and slide behind the wheel. I noticed he had a new collar, and I suspected it came from the extravaganza of doggy attire elegantly displayed across from the receptionist's desk. More sparkles, but this time, I could breathe easy. I knew they weren't real.

"It does tell us something," I said and caught Eve up on

my thought processes. "I mean, the cash payments to Sarah every month. They tell us that someone was supporting her. Pretty lavishly, too. Did anyone we talked to at the funeral luncheon mention anything like that?"

Eve shook her head. "I'd remember that for sure. Some of her coworkers complained about the quality of Sarah's work. And some people, like Senator Mercy, talked about her like she was Mother Teresa with a Coach bag and an MBA. But nobody mentioned a boyfriend."

"Nobody had to mention Dylan. He was right there."

We drove along in silence, each of us considering the implications of what I'd said.

"Dylan was in Afghanistan the day Sarah died." I knew this, of course, but I let Eve go right on talking. Hearing it helped solidify everything we'd discovered. "He didn't get back until the day before the funeral. Isn't that what he told you at the luncheon? There's no way he could have killed her. And besides, he said they broke up, remember. He dumped her. So why would he be mad enough to kill her?"

"Unless the reason he dumped her was why he was mad in the first place."

We went back and forth like this all the way to Eve's apartment, where she left Doc in the care of the dog walker. We were both on the Bellywasher's schedule that night, and though I would have preferred a night at home in front of mindless DVDs, I knew it was just as well. If the crowds the night before were any indication, it was going to be a mob scene at the restaurant that night.

And that, I reminded myself, was a very good thing.

"NO, NO. IT'S BAD! IT'S A VERY BAD THING."
Something told me those weren't the first words Jim expected to hear come out of my mouth. He was behind the bar checking out our liquor inventory, and he looked at me from between the bottle of tequila he held in one hand and the fifth of vodka he balanced in the other.

"Tequila and vodka? Of course, they're bad together." He set the bottles down. "Don't worry, I'm not developing some crazy new drink."

"I'm not talking about drinks. I'm talking about that."

My eyes remained fixed on the object that had attracted my attention the moment I walked into the restaurant.

Granny's picture. The one of the Scottish cottage. In all its glory.

It was hanging on the wall behind the bar.

"Oh, that!" Jim had the kind of grin that was infectious. Unless the person who should have been infected was too busy being horrified.

Which I was.

Horrified.

"I hung it this afternoon," Jim said, his smile wider than ever. "As a sort of celebration. You know, in honor of the good review."

"Isn't the review what you're supposed to hang?"

"Oh, did that, as well." Jim motioned over to the copy of Michael O'Keefe's review that had been cut out of the latest copy of *DC Nights*, framed, and hung on the wall near the door. "People will notice the review when they come in, and that's all well and good. But this . . ." He turned around and looked at Granny's picture, and I swear, his face glowed. "A few of the regulars were in this afternoon," he said. "You know, Larry, Hank, Charlie, and the rest of them. They were thrilled to see the picture. Says it shows we're a restaurant with heart."

Whatever. Big points for me. I thought it, but I didn't say it.

What good would it have done me, anyway? There was nothing I could say that didn't start with *Are you nuts?* and end with *Get that thing off the wall before someone notices.*

Who was it that said discretion was the better part of valor? I'm not exactly sure it applied in this situation, but I understood exactly what it meant. Rather than point out the obvious and risk hurting Jim's feelings and defiling the sacred memory of Granny, I headed into my office and closed the door. It was nearly dinnertime, and with any luck, in another few minutes, I'd hear the sounds of the crowds gathering. With just a little more luck, maybe our high-flying customers wouldn't notice the picture.

I shuffled through the charge receipts that had accumulated since the day before, but I didn't fill out the bank deposit as usual. I couldn't concentrate. Every time I tried, I got sidetracked by thoughts of Sarah's bank transactions.

The monthly cash payments she'd deposited into her account had started four months before, about the same time, so we heard, that Dylan had broken up with Sarah. Who had given her nearly ten thousand dollars in cash each month? And why?

Something told me that when we discovered that information, we'd be a lot further along with trying to figure out what had really happened to her.

I was thinking just that when my office door popped open, and Eve scampered in.

"Look!" She was holding a newspaper, and she waved it in the air. "This proves it. It proves everything, Annie. It's just like I said."

What was exactly like she said was a little hard to determine. At least until I was able to snatch the newspaper out of her hands. She had the page folded in half, then folded again. Looking up at me was a picture of Ivan Gystanovich, or at least that's what the caption below the picture said the fellow's name was. He was a heavyset guy in his sixties, with a wide nose and eyes that were too small for his face. The photographer had captured him just as he brought both his hands up to his chest, and the pose emphasized the sheer physical power of the man. He had hands like hams and fingers as fat as pork sausages. The line of print below his name said Gystanovich was the head of the Russian Mafia in northern Virginia.

"See?" Eve stabbed a bright pink fingernail into Gystanovich's stomach. "It's just like I said."

"Just like you said . . . what?"

Eve heaved a monumental sigh. She plucked the newspaper out of my hands. "Don't you see the resemblance?" She held the newspaper in front of my nose. "Come on, Annie, who does this guy look like?"

Considering the picture was close enough for me to see two Gystanovichs, it was a little hard to say.

I inched my chair back. "Jabba the Hutt?"

Eve rolled her eyes.

"Bad Santa minus the beard?"

She made a face.

"OK, OK." Whatever she was up to, she was taking it seriously, and I owed it to her to at least not make fun of her. I wiped the smile off my face. "He looks like . . ."

I tried. Honest. For a couple whole minutes. But even though I thought and thought and thought some more, it didn't help. I threw my hands in the air.

"Honestly, Eve, I don't have a clue what you're getting at."

"Gregor! The linen guy." Eve tapped her finger against Gystanovich's nose. "Admit it, Annie, they could practically be twins."

"Sure, except that Gystanovich is about forty years older than Gregor, twice as fat, and has half as much hair."

"Which doesn't mean they're not related."

"And even if it's true, it doesn't mean a thing!" I was tired of looking at Ivan Gystanovich up close and personal, and I popped out of my desk chair. "We've been through all this before," I reminded Eve. "You're suspicious of the linen guy for no reason. He hasn't done a thing."

"He hasn't done a thing that we know about yet." Eve thought she was correcting me. She didn't realize that I wasn't listening. "OK, we have talked about it," she admitted. "But we owe it to ourselves to go through it all again. We owe it to Sarah. Isn't that what real detectives do?"

Good thing Heidi tapped on the door to let Eve know that there were customers waiting to be seated. It saved me from mentioning that, though I agreed with Eve about what real detectives do, and though I was all for the bit about how we owed it to Sarah, I wasn't so sure one had anything to do with another.

"We're not real detectives," I mumbled to myself. Once Eve was gone, of course. I spun my chair away from the door, dropped into it, and turned back to the charge receipts. I dragged my calculator closer, but even as I did, I recognized that I was wasting my time. With a sigh, I shoved aside the receipts and took out the copies of Sarah's bank transactions that I had tucked in my top desk drawer.

"We're not real detectives," I reminded myself again right before I went back over the information, line by line, and wondered what we were looking at but not seeing.

IF MY LIFE WAS LIKE THE DETECTIVE SHOWS I SOME-times watched on TV, I know exactly what would have happened next. With a shout of "Aha" I would have jumped out of my chair and hurried into the restaurant to tell Eve that I'd figured the whole thing out.

But this wasn't TV.

And I didn't see anything different than I'd seen before.

Lines of deposits. Some of them obviously paychecks, others that tantalizing nine thousand plus. But no matter which way I looked at them or how I tried to spin the information, none of it made any more sense the second time through than it had back at the bank.

By the time ten o'clock rolled around and the crowds out in the dining room had thinned, I was no further along in figuring out how we could find out where Sarah got her money.

Dead end.

The words echoed through my head, taunting me.

If this was TV, something spectacular would happen and lead us in a new direction.

I sat back in my chair and waited.

Nothing spectacular happened.

In fact, nothing happened at all.

With a sigh, I dragged myself out into the restaurant. The bulk of the Saturday night crowd was gone, but there were still four tables filled with diners. Jim moved smoothly between them. I heard the low burr of his voice as he explained the difference between Shiraz and Cabernet to a lady with big hair and a too-white smile. There were people seated at the bar, too, but I saw right away that none of them were Larry, Hank, or Charlie. Not unless they'd gotten a big dose of fashion sense. Where once our barstools were filled with guys in camouflage jackets, now Brooks Brothers reigned.

Provided I didn't look at Granny's picture, it was enough to make me smile. I was still smiling when I turned and realized that one of our tables was occupied by a man in a very bad blond wig and a phony-looking mustache.

"Good evening, Monsieur Lavoie." I smiled and waved. I had to give Lavoie credit—with a good-natured and very Gallic shrug, he stripped off the mustache and raised his wineglass in my direction.

"Annie!" Eve poked her head out of the swinging kitchen door. In keeping with our new, upscale ambiance, she kept her voice down. "Psst! Annie, get in here."

I hurried into the kitchen.

There was a TV in one corner, and I knew when Marc and Damien weren't busy, they sometimes watched professional wrestling, NASCAR, or that show that follows the lives of the tattoo parlor workers. Jim knew this, too, but as long as the food was cooked right and came out hot and on time, he was cool with it. That night, there were no muscle-bound cretins whopping on each other, no cars speeding around the track. The picture Eve pointed to showed none other than Dylan Monroe, looking like a million bucks in a three-piece suit and a red silk tie. It was time for the local news, and obvious at first glance that this was a promo for that special report Dylan had told us about.

"*A Soldier's Life* airs tomorrow at six," Dylan said. "Join me. I promise you, you'll have a new appreciation for the men and women in our armed services." Patriotic-sounding music rose in the background. The camera panned out. When it did, I realized for the first time that Dylan was standing in front of the Pentagon. In the background, a group of workers from the utilities department was busy with a street repair. Their bright yellow jackets were reflected in what looked to be a couple inches of water that filled the street from one curb to the other.

"See that!" Eve pointed at the water. "I noticed it when the commercial started. That's what I wanted you to see."

"The water main leak. Near the Pentagon." I tipped my head, thinking through what we'd just seen. "Hasn't that been repaired?"

"Sure has." Damien chimed in. "I got to come through that way every single day. Believe me, I'd know if it was still a problem. Had traffic tied up for friggin' ever for a couple nights."

"It was fixed—"

"Just a day or so after it happened." Damien nodded, sure of himself. "Bad going home one night. Coming in the next day, too. Then the next day, it was gone." He snapped his fingers. "Like that."

"Which means . . ."

I looked at Eve.

Eve looked at me.

Neither of us was willing to say what we were thinking. Not in front of Damien and Marc, anyway. But it went pretty much like this:

Aha!

Because just when I least expected it, something spectacular had happened. All thanks to a broken water main.

I grabbed on to Eve's arm and tugged her into a corner of the kitchen where we could talk without being overheard.

"The main was fixed the night we went to Sarah's," I reminded her. "Remember. It broke the day before."

"Exactly." She nodded. Her blue eyes glistened with excitement. "And now the main is fixed."

"Which means that Dylan's commercial was taped long before he said he was back in the country."

"Which means he was in town the night Sarah died."

"And not in Afghanistan like he said."

Eleven

✳

THERE WERE A COUPLE OF THINGS WE KNEW FOR SURE about Dylan. The next day, as we sat around Belly-washer's and wondered if he'd show up in response to the invitation we'd left on his voice mail, Eve and I made a list.

"Number one, he said he was in Afghanistan the night Sarah was killed." Eve tapped the tip of her pen against the legal pad in front of us where, like real detectives, we'd noted our ideas in neat, logical order. "But he couldn't have been out of the country, because we saw the commercial, and the commercial proves Dylan was in town that night."

"Number two . . ." I eyed the list warily. Eve's handwriting was full of loops and curliques. No big surprise there. It was always hard to read, but that morning, the job of deciphering was even tougher. Before we left my office to grab coffee and sit in the empty restaurant, she'd slipped a yellow legal pad off the pile on my desk. The pink Sharpie, needless to say, was her own. I squinted. "Number two, we figure Sarah wouldn't have hesitated to let Dylan into her apartment."

"Especially if she was desperate to get back together with him." Eve put a star next to that item on the list. "This is important. Remember, he dumped her. If he called, say, and said he'd made a mistake and he wanted her back, she would have been vulnerable. She wouldn't have suspected Dylan. She would have been at ease with him."

"And . . ." I slid the pad out from under her hand, grabbed the Sharpie, and added an idea that had just occurred to me. "He probably knew she took Valium. You said they'd been dating for a while, right? There's no reason he wouldn't have known what kinds of medications she was taking. Tyler told us that Sarah had Valium in her system the night she died. My guess is that Dylan waited until she took it. That would have made her groggy so that she couldn't fight back. That's when he attacked her. He probably dumped her in the bathtub, put the knife in her hand, held his own hand over it and—"

Both Eve and I shivered. The scenario was too awful to consider. Rather than thinking about it, we went right on.

"Or Dylan might not have wanted to take any chances," she said. "He could have slipped her a little extra Valium."

"Like in the wine."

When Eve raised her eyebrows, I explained. "There were two wineglasses," I said, thinking back to the night we found Sarah's body. "They were drying in the rack on the kitchen sink. They'd been washed, but they hadn't been put away. You saw what I saw in that apartment, Eve. Sarah was compulsive about everything, her clothes, her food, even the books on her bookshelf. I don't think she's the type who would have washed wineglasses and not put them where they belonged. But if someone else washed the glasses, that someone else might not have thought of putting them away."

Eve sat up straight and grinned. "Which means there might be fingerprints on them!"

"Except they were washed."

Her smile faded. "He wouldn't be that dumb, anyway, would he?" she asked, and I didn't bother to answer. We both knew Dylan Monroe was way too smart to make stupid mistakes.

How smart, though, remained to be seen, and lucky for

us, we didn't have to wait long. A few minutes later, Dylan sauntered into the restaurant. It was Sunday, and he was dressed more casually than we'd seen at either the funeral luncheon or in the commercial that aired the night before. In butt-hugging jeans and a deep green sweater that brought out the flecks of emerald in his sapphire eyes, Dylan Monroe looked yummier than ever.

Call me crazy, suspicious, and maybe a little paranoid, but I thought he looked a little wary, too.

"Ladies." Dylan nodded a greeting and just as he got close to the table, I realized the legal pad was still in plain sight. I flipped it over so he couldn't see what we'd written. He flicked a look from the pad to me and dropped down in the chair across from Eve's. "Hope you don't mind that I didn't return your call. I'm a little busy today. My report airs tonight."

"We know." I was the one who answered him. That was because Eve, being Eve, was busy looking Dylan over. Since I'd already seen the way his eyes brightened with appreciation when he caught sight of her in her champagne-colored cashmere sweater and the too-short brown suede skirt he could see because her chair was pushed back and her legs were crossed, I wondered how long it would be before he asked her out.

I also wondered if I should try to encourage it. With Eve on the inside (so to speak), we might learn some valuable information.

And if we learned Dylan was a murderer?

The very thought sent a bolt of fear straight through me. No way I was going to let Eve get close to this guy. Rather than even consider the idea of Eve as a spy, I got myself back on track.

"Your report," I said to Dylan. "That's kind of what we wanted to talk to you about."

"Funny, that's not what you said in your phone message."

Thinking it was more likely he'd respond to Eve's sultry tones than my unremarkable voice, I had Eve call and leave the message for Dylan, telling him that because he was so upset at the funeral luncheon, we were concerned about him. We wondered how he was doing. At least that's what Eve was supposed to say. Now, watching the way he was looking at her, I wondered exactly what she'd said instead and jumped right in. Just in case damage control was necessary.

"What we meant—"

"I'm pretty sure I know exactly what you meant." Dylan sat back. "The trailer aired last night, and my guess is that you saw it. So now you know the truth. You know I left Afghanistan earlier than I said I did. Yes, I was in town the night Sarah died. You don't think I had anything to do with her death, do you?"

"Did you?"

Do I have to say that it was Eve who blurted out the question, not me? I was, remember, the one who looked (two or three times) before I so much as even thought about leaping. Eve, on the other hand, was always rarin' to go.

Dylan didn't hold it against her. In fact, he gave her, then me, the same smile that looked out at millions of people each night on the national news. It was calming and reassuring. Touched with empathy. Not too cheerful.

I wasn't fooled.

Dylan might be gorgeous, but he wasn't dumb. And he was a reporter through and through. Something told me that he was as curious as we were.

Why, remained to be seen.

"What makes you think the police are wrong?" he asked. "The medical examiner's ruling is official, remember. Sarah committed suicide."

"We don't agree." I took over before Eve could say anything else even slightly out of line. I didn't want Dylan to walk out on us before we learned anything useful. "We think there's enough evidence to prove that Sarah wouldn't have done that."

He propped his elbows on the table and steepled his fingers. "Like?"

"Like Doc, for one thing," Eve chimed in. "She waited a long time for him. And she paid a fortune for him, too."

Luckily, Eve didn't mention the diamond collar. That was a good thing. I didn't want to give away the farm. Not this early in our questioning.

"Sarah had a lot to live for," I said. "We don't think she would have killed herself."

"So you're investigating?" I had to hand it to Dylan, he could have made the question sound even more skeptical. "And you've come to the conclusion that I had something to do with Sarah's death." He pursed his lips and cocked his head. "It's an original theory. There's only one flaw in it. Well, actually two or three. And they're big ones."

He didn't wait for me to ask.

Dylan leaned forward. "If I did kill Sarah, you don't think I'd admit it to you two, do you?"

"Then why did you lie?" This time, I was the one who asked the question. "Why did you tell us you were in Afghanistan the night Sarah died?"

"Why do you care?"

"Because we cared about Sarah."

"And you're way off base." Dylan waved a dismissive hand in our direction. "In case you haven't noticed, I didn't have any reason to kill her."

Eve's eyes flashed in defense of Sarah. "You broke up with her."

"Exactly." He waited for the message to sink in. "*I* broke up with *her*. That's how civilized people end a relationship. They might get angry, and someone's bound to get hurt. But they don't kill. Look . . ." He let go a long sigh. "I know your hearts are in the right place, but let me give you girls a piece of advice. Mind your own business."

I took offense to the fact that Dylan wasn't taking us seriously. Not to mention the bit about calling us *girls*. But I knew Eve's feelings ran deeper. Sarah was a friend, and Eve was as loyal as they came. She was so incensed, she clutched the edge of the table to hang on to her temper.

She shot Dylan a look. "This is our business. Sarah is our business. And no one will listen to us when we try to tell them what we think really happened."

"That's because you're talking nonsense."

"It's because the authorities don't want to hear what we have to say." Eve thumped her fist against the table. "Once we show the cops our evidence—"

"Provided you have any that isn't so full of holes that—"

"That won't make any difference. Once the police know you lied—"

"And you can prove that, how?"

"Because we saw your commercial, of course."

"And you think that proves anything?" Dylan laughed. But not like it was funny. "You don't know much about slander, do you? You think I had something to do with Sarah's death? Think again. You want to suspect somebody, how about the person she was going on that cruise with?"

Was it my imagination? Maybe, but I had the distinct feeling that Dylan wasn't happy he'd let this slip. He crossed his arms over his chest and shifted in his seat.

Eve, of course, was not about to ignore it. She looked Dylan in the eye. "Oh yeah? And how do we know the guy she was going on the cruise with wasn't you?"

"How do you know the person she was going on the cruise with was a guy? As a matter of fact, how do you know anything? You two are acting like this is some sort of game. Colonel Mustard. In the conservatory. With a candlestick. There isn't any evidence to support what you think, and even if there was—"

"Hold on! Hold on!" I knew I had to jump in before things got even more out of hand. I stood. I didn't expect my not-so-commanding height to intimidate anyone, but I figured it would get their attention.

My strategy worked. Eve gulped down whatever she was going to say. Dylan, his face red, slumped back in his chair and glared at me.

"No one meant for this to turn into a shouting match," I

told Dylan and reminded Eve. "All we wanted to do was get some information."

"Information, huh?" Dylan scraped his chair back and rose. "If that's what you're looking for, then you weren't paying attention. I already gave you the most important piece of advice you're ever going to get. I told you to mind your own business. This isn't a game. It isn't for amateurs." He marched to the door.

"If you're smart," he said, "you'll back off before somebody else gets hurt."

WAS IT A FRIENDLY WARNING?
Or a not-so-friendly threat?

I spent the rest of the day wondering, and all of the next morning working through the problem in my mind. Good guy or bad guy, Dylan was right about a couple things. If he had a motive to want Sarah dead, we sure didn't know what it was. That didn't mean it didn't exist, just that we didn't know enough to figure out what made Dylan tick.

He was right about another thing, too. The cruise. Like I said, I might be crazy, suspicious, and maybe a little paranoid, but something told me that he wasn't happy he'd spilled the beans about the cruise, figuratively speaking.

It was a clue that had been in front of us the whole time, and we'd failed to follow it up.

What was that I said about being a real detective? Maybe *real detective in training* was more like it.

With that in mind, I approached this new avenue of investigation as analytically as I could. Logic told me the place to start was the cruise line. Of course, if they were anything like hospitals, airlines, and the hundreds of other businesses that were more cautious than ever lately about giving out personal information about their clientele, I wouldn't get very far.

But remember, we had an ace in the hole: Eve had power of attorney.

First thing Monday morning, she'd be placing a call.

*   *   *

I TOLD EVE TO STOP BY DURING MY LUNCH HOUR— Bellywasher's was closed, but I was on duty at the bank. Munching on the peanut butter and raspberry jelly sandwich I'd brought for lunch, I sat at her side while she made the phone call, just to be sure she asked all the right questions. Before she punched in the phone number of the cruise line, we decided that the information we wanted to draw out might involve a little sweet-talking. Bless her! Eve knew exactly what to do.

I didn't have to hear the voice of the person on the other end of the phone to know it was a man. As soon as he answered, Eve went into full Southern belle mode. When she explained her predicament, her accent was as thick as honey and twice as sugary.

She waited to hear what the man on the other end had to say before she responded.

"A complete refund? My goodness! You don't say." The phone receiver to her ear, Eve looked at me and raised her eyebrows. "No, I didn't know that. And aren't you just the sweetest thing to tell me. I never would have guessed that you could get a full refund if you're dead." Her cheeks shot through with color. "I mean, *you* can't get a refund if you're dead. Because obviously, sugar, you're not dead. What I mean is that the person who bought the ticket can get a refund." Her golden brows dipped. She crinkled her nose. "But the person really can't, you know? I mean, that person's dead so even if she could—"

Apparently, the man on the other end of the phone (who obviously was not dead), had had enough of Eve's own peculiar brand of logic and interrupted her. Lips pursed, Eve listened.

"Yes," she said, nodding. "Of course I can send you the proper paperwork. And yes, you can mail the refund check directly to me." She gave the cruise line representative her address and spelled her name for him. "I'll make sure Miss

Whittaker's sister receives the money. She can use it where she is."

Again, Eve listened. She rolled her eyes. "Is Miss Whittaker canceling? Of course you have to ask. Just to be official. I understand. Why, yes, she most certainly is canceling. But what I was really wondering—"

She stopped to listen, and my half-eaten sandwich in one hand, I leaned forward. We were getting to the meat of the phone call, and my blood thrummed inside me to the rhythm of every nervous heartbeat. Another piece of the puzzle was about to fall into place, and I couldn't wait to see what it was going to be. Would it be one of those flat-edged border pieces that made it easier to fit everything else together? Or some formless blob of nothing that would only confuse us more?

I held my breath. Which wasn't very hard—my lips were sticky with peanut butter.

"No, no." Eve laughed the silvery little laugh that so often put people at ease. "It's not the massage Sarah had scheduled that I was going to ask about, though now that you mention it, if you could send a refund for that, too, it would be just the dearest thing. No, what I was really wondering about . . ." She looked at me, just to make sure she had her story straight, and peanut butter notwithstanding, I let go the breath I was holding.

"What I was really wondering is if y'all are going to notify Miss Whittaker's companion of the fact that she won't be traveling on that cruise? And if he's canceled, too?" She stopped and listened. "Yes, of course I understand, he wouldn't get a refund, too, since he's not dead. But she did have a double occupancy cabin reserved, and you see, I'm not really sure if the person she was going with knows of Miss Whittaker's passing. I know you understand how awkward it could be for me, sugar. I mean, if I'm the one who has to break the news, well . . ."

Eve paused.

"He hasn't canceled? You will call him?" She smiled as

brightly as she would have if she was looking at the cruise agent across a ticket counter. "That is just the nicest thing in the world, and I am so very grateful. You see . . ." Another look at me. I nodded. She had laid the groundwork well. It was time to close in for the kill.

"I mean, I do feel so silly admitting this." Just to prove it, Eve laughed. "But, well, you see, I just can't seem to locate his name and number. Isn't that the silliest thing you've ever heard? I mean, leave it to me to be such an airhead. But after all, I am a blonde. Natural, of course." Her voice was breathy with embarrassment.

"I mean, I should call him, don't you think? That is, after you tell him about the unfortunate circumstances and that Miss Whittaker's portion of the cruise has been canceled. I should extend my condolences. After all, if he and Sarah knew each other well enough to be traveling together . . . well, you can see what I'm getting at here, sugar. It's an embarrassing situation for me not knowing who to call and all. And if I don't call . . . Well, that could be just as bad. Imagine making that kind of social faux pas!"

Apparently, the man on the other end of the phone could imagine it quite well. He put Eve on hold and she gave me the thumbs-up.

"He's gonna get the name." She mouthed the words, and before I had a chance to respond with an appropriate *hip-hip-hooray*, he was back on the line.

"You have the name for me?" She made it sound like he'd gone far above and beyond, which, now that I thought about it, he actually had. "You are just the best ever. Now, before you tell me who her traveling companion was, you make sure you refresh my memory. What was your name again?"

The man responded, and Eve nodded. "Grady Kovach. I'm writing it down here, sugar, because I am going to let your supervisor know that you were just the most helpful, the sweetest thing ever." She paused, and I have to give her credit, she really did write Grady's name down. I knew Eve

was as good as her word. The man's supervisor would be
hearing from her.

Eve was pretty proud of herself. And rightly so. Her eyes
glistened with excitement. "Now what's that you were saying, Grady, honey? About Miss Whittaker's companion. You
said his name was—"

Listening to the man on the other end of the phone, Eve
sucked in a breath. Her face went as white as the linen tablecloth and her eyes widened. When Grady was done speaking, her voice didn't sparkle nearly as much.

"Thank you," she said, and I wondered if Grady even
heard her. She was already hanging up the phone. "Thank
you very much."

Eve sat with her hand on the receiver. Her expression was
blank. Her face was still pale.

And me? I couldn't stand it anymore.

"Well?" I jumped out of my chair. When Eve didn't answer me fast enough, I bent down and looked her in the eye.
"Eve! What did Grady say?"

"He told me who Sarah was traveling with." Her voice
was hollow. "But, Annie, I'm not sure it makes any sense. I
mean, I thought he'd say it was Dylan and that would prove
he was lying about the whole thing. Then we'd know for sure
that he was guilty. But Annie . . ." She shifted her gaze to
look at me.

"It's not Dylan. It's Douglas Mercy."

Twelve

✼

"DOUGLAS MERCY KNEW THE QUALITY OF SARAH'S work wasn't up to snuff lately. But Douglas Mercy didn't."

For a change, it was *my* train of thought that Eve wasn't following. She looked at me in wonder. And who could blame her? Thanks to what we'd learned from Grady at the cruise line the day before, we were both still in a state of shock. I pulled in a deep breath and prepared myself to once again try to explain.

Anxious to continue the investigation, I'd left the bank precisely at five o'clock and, thanks to traffic that wasn't nearly as bad as usual, I made it to Bellywasher's in record time. It was a little early for our fashionably late dinner crowd, so there was no one in the restaurant except for Marc and Damien back in the kitchen and Jim, who had breezed through a few minutes earlier and promptly disappeared into the basement. Still, I wasn't taking any chances. We were talking about important and prominent people, after all, and I made sure I bent my head close to Eve's and kept my voice down.

"Senator Douglas Mercy," I said. "When I talked to him

at the funeral luncheon, he knew that Jennifer at the office had been picking up the slack on Sarah's work. He said that when it came time for employee reviews, he wouldn't forget all Jennifer had done. He told me that he knew Sarah's work had suffered because she was down in the dumps over her breakup with Dylan. Doesn't that seem a little odd?"

"That she'd be down in the dumps because of Dylan? Not in my book." Eve was so sure of herself, her spine went rigid. "Sure, he's full of himself, but he's got every right, don't you think? Dylan Monroe is the handsomest—"

"That's not what I meant." I knew I had to stop Eve before she got started, or we'd never get around to talking about the case. "I meant that I think it's strange that the senator would be so familiar with Sarah's work when his son—the other Douglas Mercy—isn't. When I talked to him, to Dougy, the day of the funeral, he told me Sarah was a lower-level staffer and that they weren't in contact much."

"And he's the senator's chief of staff."

I nodded. "Exactly. Seems, funny, don't you think, that the guy on top of the food chain knows what the underlings are up to when the guy who's supposed to supervise them doesn't?"

As soon as I'd walked in that evening, we had started another list. Or at least, we'd tried. So far, there wasn't anything written on the page except "What We Know About Sarah and Douglas Mercy." The way things were going, it looked like the page might remain blank for a long time.

Now, I tapped the pink Sharpie against the empty page. "We need to find out which Douglas Mercy was headed out on that cruise with Sarah," I said.

"And how are we going to do that?"

I already had something of a plan, but before I could run it past Eve to see if it made as much sense to her as it did to me, we were interrupted by a horrendous clunking sound from the direction of the basement stairs. The next moment, the door swung open, and Jim stomped into the restaurant. He had an armful of framed pictures stacked so high he could barely see over the top, and he staggered under the weight. On top of the pile was a long piece of wood that looked as if it had come out of some dark and dank corner of the alley in back of the restaurant.

Sensing disaster, I shot out of my seat and hurried over to help. I grabbed the piece of wood. From the other side of the mountain of pictures, I saw Jim's eyes light up when he smiled.

"Appreciate the help," he said. "I knew I'd grabbed one thing too many, but I could'na let *that* sit down in the basement. Not once I realized what it was."

I looked at the piece of wood in my hands. What it was, as far as I could see, was a—

"Walking stick." Jim must have been reading my mind. While he carefully set the pictures down on the bar and arranged them so that they wouldn't tip or get knocked over, he filled in the blanks. "Family legend says it once belonged to my great grandfather. Look." He pointed to a series of small, uneven marks near the bottom of the stick.

"Grandpa Bannerman owned a terrier. Or so the story goes. Seems the little fellow was fond of chewing wood. And look at this!" Jim took the stick out of my hands and turned it over to show me the two tiny gold loops that had been screwed into the back of it. "Uncle Angus must have intended to display it and just never had the chance. That's why it wasn't hanging with the rest of his stuff. Good thing I was down in the basement looking around, or I might never have found it."

"And you were down there looking around because . . ." I really didn't have to ask. Something told me I knew exactly what Jim was up to. I eyed him carefully. I'll say this much for the man: at least he had the good sense to look embarrassed.

"It's not what you think," he said.

"Good. Because I think we just took all this stuff downstairs for a reason. A good reason. Remember? Ambiance? And now, I think you're bringing it all back up again."

"Not all of it."

I glanced over to the picture at the top of the stack. It was black-and-white and so grainy, I doubted if anyone could attest to what the little brass plaque at the bottom of the picture said it was: the Loch Ness monster. At least not without a few beers first.

"Tell me you're not going to hang this stuff back up."

"OK." As affable as always, Jim nodded. "I won't tell you. Except I was hoping to get your opinion. You know, about where to put everything."

My sigh said it all.

Jim, however, said nothing. Humming what I could only imagine was some old Scottish tune, he took the walking stick over to the wall and held it up to see where it would look best.

I wasn't in the mood for a fight, and let's face it, I really did have more important things to worry about. I left Jim to it and crooked my finger at Eve. We ducked into my office and closed the door.

"Here's what I think we have to do," I told her, and ignoring the sounds of a hammer banging against the wall out in the restaurant, I laid out my plan.

BY THE NEXT DAY, I WAS ITCHING TO PUT MY PLAN into action.

Except I had one little problem: my real job got in the way.

So did the fact that the people who ran our federal government didn't return their phone messages.

It wasn't until the next day, a Thursday, that I was able to collect the information I needed. Don't ask me what was happening in Alexandria that night, but there wasn't a single place to park anywhere near Bellywasher's. I left my car in the only space I could find, a few blocks over, and walked in the front door, more anxious than ever to talk to Eve and tell her everything I'd learned.

Ignoring Grandpa Bannerman's walking stick (now ensconced in a place of honor right over Michael O'Keefe's framed review) and the photo of Nessie (hung closer to the bar), I scanned the room and found Eve busy placating a group of elderly ladies in fur coats who were too cold when she seated them near the door and too hot when she moved them to a table closer to the kitchen. I left her to it, waved hello to Heidi, who rolled her eyes, poked a finger toward a table where three men were eating the day's special, lobster bisque, and mouthed the words, "Picky. Pickier. Pickiest."

I greeted Jim, but he didn't have a chance to so much as look my way. The bar was packed with a just-come-from-work crowd, and from the looks of them, the work they'd just come from were jobs that paid well and demanded that they dress for success. They were demanding, too, and Jim was busy. A man at one end of the bar was in the middle of saying that Jim's idea of a perfect martini did not jibe with his and was demanding another drink. A woman at the other end was talking too loudly on her cell phone. Always the perfect host, Jim didn't fuss or fight. He ignored the loud woman, tossed out the not-so-perfect martini, and mixed another.

With no hopes of cornering Eve any time soon, I pushed through the swinging kitchen door in search of a cup of coffee.

"Boy, am I glad to see you." Damien rushed over, and for a second, I thought he was going to hug me. Instead, he looped an apron around my neck. "We're slammed."

"It didn't look like it." I glanced back toward the restaurant, but I don't know why I even tried. All I could see was Damien, who had scooted behind me to tie the apron around my waist. "Four ladies who may take all night to order if they can't find a table that's not too hot and not too cold. The people at the bar who seem to be more interested in drinking than eating. Three guys who already ordered—"

"And a party of seven with reservations for eight fifteen." Damien grabbed my arm and dragged me toward the grill. "You're going to have to help."

"Help? Cook?" My blood ran cold. My knees locked. My breath caught behind the sudden ball of panic in my throat. "You don't know what you're asking. I've been known to burn water."

"Yeah, so I've been told." There was a counter next to the grill and a huge bowl of vegetables on it. Damien slid the veggies in my direction and held out a knife. "Believe me, after the stories I heard from Jim, I'm not thrilled about this, either. But we don't have any choice. Marc colored his hair again yesterday, and Marc and green dye . . . well, it looks like they don't exactly get along. He's got a rash just about everywhere, and I do mean everywhere." Just thinking about it made Damien squirm. "He says it itches like a son of a bitch. He's home soaking in an oatmeal bath."

"But—"

"Ain't no buts. Jim's orders."

To Damien, Jim walked on water, so of course he didn't imagine that I would dispute this.

Little did he know that nothing could strike terror in my heart like cooking did.

I scrambled out of the kitchen and behind the bar, prepared to state my case. Since Jim was my cooking instructor at Très Bonne Cuisine, and since my days at Très Bonne Cuisine were (in a word) a complete disaster (I guess that's two words), I knew in my heart of hearts that he would not be willing to risk his reputation, not to mention his customers' health, on my questionable culinary skills.

"Jim—" I began.

But Jim was in the middle of explaining the difference between rye and potato vodka to a young woman who didn't look as interested in liquor as she did in the bartender. She batted her eyelashes at Jim. Jim ignored her and went right on to the advantages of Polish vodka over the stuff made in Russia.

I wasn't usually the pushy type, but I knew a crisis when I saw one. The fact that Damien had poked his head out of the kitchen and was watching me with an eagle eye and a look that said he wasn't going to let me slide on this, was, in my book, a crisis of the first order.

"Jim, excuse me, we have something of an emergency in the kitchen and—"

"Not the only place you people have an emergency." Martini man slammed his empty glass against the bar. "Good but not perfect," he said. "Try again."

"Jim—"

When he finally turned to me, Jim's teeth were clenched around a smile. His voice was calm, but I wasn't fooled. The spark in his eyes told me that between cooks who called out because of bad hair color and demanding customers, he'd just about had enough. "What?" he asked.

The front door opened. The party of seven had arrived. They were early. And they brought three friends.

"Never mind," I said. My stomach reeling, I retreated into the kitchen to throw myself on the mercy of the cooking gods.

"MASCARPONE? IS HE ANY RELATION TO AL CAPONE?"
Damien didn't get the joke. I could hardly blame him, since it wasn't very funny. What it was, was my attempt at stalling the inevitable.

"I can't cook," I said. Again. Just like I had the second I walked into the kitchen. "Didn't Jim tell you?"

"He did, and you know what, Annie, right about now, I really don't care." Damien had said that before, too. This time, though, when he saw that I was staring in horror at the recipe on the countertop in front of me, wringing my hands, he took pity on me. "Look . . ." Damien had salmon steaks on the grill, so he couldn't talk for long. "All you have to do is follow the directions. You can do that, can't you? Jim's very careful when it comes to writing out his recipes. No way you can make a mistake if you do exactly what it says."

"*You* could do exactly what it says."

"I could." A timer rang, and he took off in answer to it.

"But I don't have time. And besides, Marc handles the desserts. I wouldn't know what to do, anyway."

"And I do?" But by that time, I was talking to myself. Damien was busy doing whatever it was that chefs who knew what they were doing did, and I was left on my own.

As if it would somehow change things, I squinted at the recipe. Looked like I was officially in charge of a fresh fig tart with rosemary cornmeal crust and the infamous—at least in my book—mascarpone cream.

There was a handwritten note attached to the recipe that explained that the two patrons who were coming in tonight to celebrate their twenty-fifth anniversary had specifically requested the desssert, since they'd had it in Paris on their honeymoon. I did not in any way, shape, or form want to be responsible for ruining such an important occasion. Lucky for me (and the happy couple), the tart crust was already made and waiting for me on the counter. One look at the crust that was flour, cornmeal and rosemary perfection, and I knew Jim had baked it. No one could make such simple (not to mention disparate) ingredients look so good.

I was in charge of the filling. "Sour cream, mascarpone, sugar, grated lemon zest," I read over the recipe, grumbling the ingredients under my breath. It was longer than my Christmas card list. "Why would anyone bother to mess with a recipe this complicated?" I asked Damien. He was too busy putting the flawlessly cooked salmon steaks onto their plates to answer. Seeing no help from that quarter, I pressed on, following Damien's advice. I did exactly what the recipe told me to do.

By the time I'd whisked the sour cream, mascarpone, sugar, and lemon zest in a bowl along with some salt, my heartbeat had settled. So far, so good.

But I should have known that nothing is that easy, especially when it comes to cooking. What's that saying about pride coming before a fall?

The next step was heating red currant jelly with honey. I didn't have to check the recipe to know that by the time

I was done, it wasn't supposed to be the consistency of rubber cement.

I tossed the concoction—along with the saucepan that was so black at the bottom, I determined I had burned it beyond its usefulness—and started again.

This time, I stirred the jelly and honey mixture until it was melted and watched it like a hawk. I turned off the stove to allow it to cool and prepared myself for the next step: taking the tart crust out of the pan.

I know, I know . . . sounds like a piece of cake (or in this case, a piece of pie). But honestly, is anything in the world of the culinary arts ever that easy?

Fortunately, the tart pan had removable sides, so I accomplished the actual removal with ease. It was when I had to spread the mascarpone mixture into the shell that things went awry.

They also went amiss, wonky, and a little kerflooey.

Not to worry. Much to my amazement, I discovered that mascarpone cream filling does the trick when it comes to sticking pieces of broken tart shell together.

Satisfied the tart would pass muster (at least if the lights in the restaurant were low), I cut the figs and arranged them as artistically as I was able on top, then drizzled the glaze over all.

I had just decided that maybe I had a talent for baking after all, when Damien called out to me, "You get those green beans off the burner?"

"Beans?" I looked over to the stove where a pot was boiling away merrily. "I didn't know about the beans."

Damien took a look. "They're mush. Clean a couple more pounds."

I turned toward the cooler where we kept the veggies.

"And while you're at it," he added, "the people at table three want another appetizer. I'm going to slice the melon. You get the prosciuto."

I swung toward the walk-in cooler where we stored the meat.

"And table ten has asked for blueberry cobbler, table one is still waiting for the sweet potato pie, and table six . . ." On his way by with a melon in one hand, Damien studied my glassy-eyed stare. "You OK, Annie?" he asked. "You need any help?"

My head was spinning so fast, I didn't even bother to answer. But then, Damien probably wouldn't have believed me, anway, if I told him that I'd already asked for help.

Looked like the culinary gods weren't taking any requests.

BY THE TIME IT WAS ALL OVER, IT WAS NEARLY ELEVEN, and to my credit, I had set off the smoke alarm only twice. Who knew that pasta could get so crispy? Or that left to their own devices, veal patties could turn into a substitute for hockey pucks.

"Here. Something tells me you need this." Our customers were gone, and I was sitting at the bar, my head in my hands. Jim slid a glass of white wine under my nose. "You worked hard tonight."

"I worked hard at nearly getting us closed down." I squeezed my eyes shut, remembering one of the fur-coat ladies and how she'd gagged at the first taste of my chicken Florentine. "Sorry."

"Not your fault." Jim had poured himself a chocolatey-looking beer. He sat down on the stool next to mine and took a drink. There was thick foam on his lips, and he licked it away. "You came through in a pinch. That's what counts."

"You're being kind."

"I knew what I was getting when I hired you."

"You didn't think you'd ever have to let me near the kitchen."

He grinned. "Not going to argue with you there! Don't worry, lass." He slid an arm around my shoulders and gave me a quick hug. "It isn't the end of the world. And everyone left happy."

"Because you promised them all free meals the next time

they came. And you told them you'd make sure I stayed in my office where I belonged."

"A brilliant strategy on my part, yes?" Jim wiggled his eyebrows. "Cheer up. The worst they can say is that the kitchen wasn't up to snuff tonight. And hey . . ." He leaned in close and kissed the tip of my nose. "There's always a silver lining. You didn't poison anyone."

I groaned. I was too tired to agree, too tired to disagree, and too, too tired to remind Jim that I had tried to warn him and that he wouldn't listen. There was no good to be had from letting Annie Capshaw within an arm's length of a stove. Any stove. Maybe from then on, he'd remember and believe.

I leaned my back against his shoulder and closed my eyes. "Hire another cook," I told him.

"Marc will be back tomorrow. I talked to him not ten minutes ago. The swelling is down, and the itching is mostly gone. He says he's never going to color his hair again."

"Right." I didn't want to budge an inch, but that glass of white wine was calling to me. The only way to take a drink was to sit up, so I did. "I'll believe that when I see it."

Jim chuckled. "Aye. And I'll—"

"Hey, Jim, come have a taste of this. It's awesome!" Damien called from inside the kitchen. Like I may have mentioned, when it comes to food, Damien is obsessed. It was late and nearly time to close up and go home, but he had insisted on trying out a new recipe for a white sauce he claimed would taste great with seafood. "I think you're going to love it," he shouted again.

I knew that when it came to food, Jim was just as obsessed. I gave him a nudge. "Go on. The kid worships the ground you walk on. He won't sleep tonight if he doesn't find out what you think of his new creation."

Left to my own devices, I would have liked nothing better than to close my eyes and go right to sleep. My back ached from hours of standing at the grill. I smelled like fish and olive oil. I'd chopped about a million vegetables, and my right wrist ached.

None of which stopped me from calling Eve over when I saw that she was done rolling silverware in napkins for the next day.

"I've been trying to talk to you all night," I told her.

She took the seat Jim had just vacated. "You found out? About the cruise? Which one is it? I've got a theory, see. It's got to be the senator, and if it is, it's no big deal. He's not married, and Sarah wasn't married and—"

"I don't know if it's the senator," I said.

"Then Dougy?" As if she found the very thought repulsive, Eve shivered. "He's not Sarah's type. And he's married."

"I don't know if it's Dougy, either."

Now I had to explain myself. A process that had seemed simple hours ago when I walked in. Right about then, it was nothing short of a monumental effort.

I stretched my back and worked a kink out of my neck. "I called the senator's office, just like I said I was going to do. I told the woman who answered the phone that I was with a local women's group and that we'd just found out the person who was going to speak at our next meeting had to cancel. I asked if Senator Mercy could come instead, and I told the secretary we needed him to speak on February 1, a date right smack in the middle of the cruise."

"And?"

"And she told me that as honored as he would be to speak to us, Senator Douglas Mercy would have to decline. You see, he's going to be gone. On vacation."

"But that's terrific!" When I didn't agree instantly, Eve eyed me carefully. "Isn't it terrific? Why not? It tells us that the senator's the one going on the cruise, right? His vacation and Sarah's vacation, they're set for the same time. That means—"

"Nothing. Because then I asked if the senator's son could fill in. And guess what? Dougy's scheduled for vacation that week, too."

"Oh." Eve chewed her lower lip. "So we don't know much more than we knew when we started, right?"

"Well, we know that the senator has a fund-raiser scheduled for this Friday. We're invited. And not because the secretary thought I was anyone special. I think they invite everyone who calls. No stone gets left unturned when it comes to raising campaign money."

"I hear you talking about politics, but something tells me"—Jim had come out of the kitchen, and he closed in on us— "that you're not organizing the latest neighborhood watch."

I knew better than to answer. Jim wasn't overbearing, but he could be overprotective. He had proved it time and again when we investigated Drago's murder. If he knew we were on the trail of another killer—

"Don't be silly," Eve said before I could send her a warning look to remind her to keep her mouth shut. "It's not politics, exactly, it's the senator. You know, Senator Mercy. We think maybe he killed Sarah."

Of course that wasn't even remotely true, but it hardly mattered. Jim propped his fists on his hips, and as soon as I heard the words "Dunna tell me" leave his lips, I knew we were in for it. When Jim was worried, his accent thickened almost beyond comprehension.

"You're sticking your nose where it dunna belong."

This, I understood, along with the finger Jim pointed in the direction of my nose.

"No good will come of it."

"We're being careful." I slid off the barstool. "And what Eve said about Mercy isn't precisely true. We're not accusing him of anything."

"Nor are you gonna. D'ye have any idea how powerful the man is? Ye could be getting yourself in a passel of trouble."

"We do. We're not." I had tossed my coat in my office— it seemed like days ago—and I retrieved it and slipped it on. "All we're doing is following a couple leads. We just think it's odd that Sarah would have killed herself. She had too much going for her."

Jim followed Eve and me to the front door so he could

lock it behind us. Eve walked out first, and after she did, Jim put a hand on my shoulder. "You canna know the way a person's mind works," he said, and this time, it wasn't anger that glimmered in his eyes, just honest concern. "Ye must learn to accept the fact that everything can't be fixed. Sarah made her choice."

"I know. And Eve knows it, too. But that doesn't change the facts. There's just something that doesn't feel right about this whole thing."

"Aye. That would be you sticking your nose—"

"Aye, I know." I laughed. "Where it doesn't belong."

"You'd best be careful no one pokes it to keep you in your place. Back off, Annie. Guilty or not, a man of Mercy's standing can't afford somebody minding his business. I don't want to see you get hurt."

I gave Jim a quick peck on the cheek. It seemed a better way to end a long evening than arguing with him.

Still thinking about what Jim said and how much it sounded like the warning from Dylan, I walked outside. I didn't pay much attention when a car cruised by. I set my purse on the sidewalk so that I could button my coat. When I was done, I bent to pick it up.

Good thing.

That meant when the shots rang out and the first bullets hit the front of Bellywasher's, I didn't have far to go to fall facedown on the ground.

Thirteen

✖

IT WAS OVER IN A FLASH—SO FAST, IN FACT, THAT I
still can't say exactly what happened. I remember the
first burst of gunfire and seeing Eve duck into the alley between Bellywasher's and the ceramics studio next door. I
clearly recall hearing the squeal of car tires and realized in a
slap-my-forehead instant that I'd been looking right at the
car—and the shooter inside it—as I walked out of the restaurant. Had I paid any attention? Male or female driver? Make,
model, color of the car? My mind was a complete blank. But
then, at the time, I didn't know that the person behind the
wheel was going to take potshots at us.

When it was all over, there was one moment of complete
silence, and in that instant, I took a quick inventory. I wasn't
hit, and nothing had been injured except for my nose, which
had been scraped when I hit the pavement. It stung like hell.
Wincing, I vaulted to my feet just in time to see the last of a
dark-colored sedan as it took the corner at Saint Alphath's
on two wheels. I might actually have been able to run and
maybe even catch a glimpse of the license plate, if Eve
hadn't thrown herself at me.

"Annie! Are you all right? Oh my gosh! Oh my gosh!" For

a willowy woman, Eve had a grip like a limpet. She wrapped me in a hug. A moment later, she grabbed my shoulders and pushed me back to get a better look at me, so fast I wobbled like a bobble-head doll. "You didn't get hit, did you?"

"If I did, you wouldn't be doing me much good." I disentangled myself from her grasp. After I looked Eve over and made sure she hadn't been hit either, I brushed off my coat and the knees of my pants and picked up my purse to sling it over my shoulder. Mundane motions and definitely not the proper response to just having nearly been killed.

Or maybe it was.

By the time Jim came running at breakneck speed from the back alley where he parked his motorcycle, and the people who lived in the apartment above the ceramics studio threw open their window and told us not to worry, they'd already called the police, I was ready for them.

"What the hell?" Big points for Jim. He could have taken a look at the cracked front window of Bellywasher's or the pockmark of bullets around the front door and lost his cool. Instead, he concentrated on Eve and me. It was me he clasped to his chest, though.

"You're all right? You're not hurt? You didn't get shot?" Like Eve had done, Jim held me tight one moment and pushed me far enough back to take a good look at me the next. I bobbled some more.

Jim's hands skimmed my head and my shoulders and my hips. The next second, he pressed me into a hug again, so tight I had to fight for breath. "You're OK!"

"I'm OK." My voice was muffled and tinged with discomfort, thanks to my scraped nose pressed flat against Jim's chest. I came up for air. "Eve and I are both OK. We just walked outside and—"

"He tried to kill us!" Eve wailed and hurled herself at both Jim and me. Jim on one side and Eve on the other, and I was pressed between them like a burger on a bun. I ducked and squirmed and broke up the lovefest before my nose could sustain any further damage.

"Nobody tried to kill us," I said. This was, of course, the most logical explanation for the whole thing. "Not us specifically. It was a drive-by. Random."

"Who? Who tried to kill you?" So much for logic. Ignoring me, Jim glommed onto Eve's statement. His eyes flashed, and I had the distinct feeling that if Grandpa's walking stick had been within easy reach, he would have grabbed it and gone after the shooter himself. "Did you see who it was?"

Eve's eyes were wide with fear. Her face was ashen. She shook her head. "I didn't need to see. The senator, or the Russian mob, or Dylan Monroe, or—"

"Eve!" I warned her with a look and hoped she was paying attention. We'd attracted a crowd, of course, and the people who'd come running from the apartments across the street and from the coffee place a little farther down King Street didn't need to hear any of Eve's crazy theories.

When I turned to Jim, I made sure I kept my voice down. "It was random. It had to be."

"Why, because you're treating Sarah's death as if it's a suicide?"

It was not exactly the warm and fuzzy response I'd been expecting. The spark in Jim's eyes intensified. With the shooter long gone, it was aimed right at me.

Who could blame me for getting defensive?

I pulled myself up to my full height. All right, all right . . . so it's not so high. But at least with my chin up and my shoulders back, I felt commanding, even if I didn't look it.

"Are you telling me this is my fault?" I asked him.

I saw a muscle twitch at the base of his jaw. "Aye." He didn't look happy to be admitting it. "If you'd mind your own business—"

"Walking out of the place I work *is* minding my own business," I shot back. "And maybe if my place of business wasn't on the seedy side of town—"

"Seedy?" It was Jim's turn to stand up straight and tall. He had the height advantage, but I didn't back down.

My fists were on my hips before I even realized it, and

though I knew it was far too aggressive a stance, I was beyond caring. It wasn't like me to react emotionally instead of rationally, but hey, I was allowed. Somebody had just tried to turn me into Swiss cheese. At a time like that, any response was the right response.

If Jim cared about me, wouldn't he have known that?

My stomach tightened, more painful than it had been when I was facedown on the pavement with bullets flying all around. I felt as if I'd been kicked in the chest. Logic be damned! I went on the defensive.

I glared at Jim. "Nobody asks to be shot at."

"Unless that person is sticking her cute little nose—"

I screeched my frustration. It wasn't Jim's criticism that grated on my last nerve as much as it was his use of the word *cute*. I hate being called cute, and you'd think a man who I'd dated before I decided that dating was dangerous to my self-composure and my heart would know that. *Cute* is guy code for "I want to be your friend, but no way could I ever fall in love with you." It's patronizing and not the least bit comforting.

I'm cute. OK, so I admit it.

Did Jim have to rub it in?

"It's none of your business where I stick my nose," I told him.

"Really?" He stepped back and crossed his arms over his chest. In its own way, the pose was just as assertive as mine. "If that's the way you feel—"

"That's the way I feel."

"Then maybe you should have told me—"

"I'm telling you now."

"Annie! Jim!" Eve's quiet prodding interrupted us, but it wasn't until I had a couple seconds to allow my temper to throttle back that I realized we had company—a police officer who had a notebook out and a pen poised above the page. He looked from me to Jim.

"You ready to make statements?" the officer asked. "Or

should I just back off and let you two duke it out and see who's left standing when it's all over?"

"YOU SURE YOU WANT TO DO THIS?"
          Eve was standing behind me. Over my shoulder, she looked at my reflection in the mirror and the fresh bandage that I'd just stuck on my nose. She didn't have to say it, I knew what she was thinking: I looked like a freak.

"We could always back out," she said.

"I want to go," I told Eve. "We have to go. You don't think I'm going to let something like a shooting scare me off from the investigation, do you?"

The look Eve tossed my way brought me spinning around. "What?"

"What?" She leaned toward the mirror and checked her lipstick. She fluffed a hand through her hair. "Last night, you swore to Jim that it was random. You said the shooting didn't have anything to do with Sarah's death."

"Yeah. Well. It was the most logical explanation, wasn't it? Of course it's the first thing I thought of. And it could have been random," I added, scrambling as I had all day to find something that pointed to the fact that Eve and I had been innocent bystanders, not intended targets.

"But I don't know." I thought back to the moment, the instant between when we'd stepped out onto the sidewalk and when the shooting started. "I think he was close by, waiting for us. The car didn't speed past Bellywasher's, it cruised. Slowly. Like he was just waiting for the right moment." This was too disturbing for words, and rather than consider what it meant, I turned back around and checked my reflection.

Gingerly, I touched a finger to my nose. "Aren't bandages supposed to be flesh-colored?" I asked.

What could Eve say? While she thought about it, I turned my head, studying the square of gauze and plastic and wondering exactly whose flesh those well-intentioned bandage manufacturers were talking about. I don't have a peaches-and-cream complexion like Eve, and I'm not olive-toned, either. I'm some bland shade right in the middle, and even on me, the bandage stuck out like a sore thumb.

Or in this instance, a sore nose.

"I'm not self-conscious at all, so don't worry about me. And I'm not worried about looking weird, either," I said, because I figured if I reminded myself enough times, I might start to believe it. I stared at my reflection. The bandage *did* look weird. "It doesn't matter if anyone notices, and besides, if they ask, I'm used to explaining. I spent all day at the bank talking about it. First to everyone who works there, then to each of my customers."

"What, you told them that your nose was scraped because you were down on the sidewalk while someone was shooting at you?"

"I told them I slipped and fell and hit the pavement. It's not exactly a lie." The black evening bag I'd bought for a prom Peter and I had once chaperoned was on my dresser, and I grabbed it and double-checked to make sure there were a couple more fresh bandages inside, just in case. While I was at it, I automatically checked for my cell phone and my lipstick, too. Satisfied I had everything I needed, I snapped the purse shut. "Besides, nobody's going to notice me and ask about my nose anyway. Not once you walk in."

In the mirror, I checked out Eve's shrimp-pink, thigh-high dress with its plunging neckline and compared it to the little black dress I had bought for that same, long-ago prom. At the time, I'd thought my dress with its spaghetti straps, nipped-in waist, and handkerchief hem was the ultimate in sexy. The way I remembered, Peter agreed.

I shook off the memory and looked over Eve again. Next to her, my sexy faded straight into stodgy.

The bandage on my nose didn't help.

"Oh, forget it!" I plucked it off and peered in the mirror. Aside from the fact that the skin on my nose was rosy and raw, it didn't look half bad. At least it didn't look as bad as it did with a bandage on.

"I'm ready," I said, spinning away from the mirror. "Let's get out of here before I change my mind."

Eve chuckled. "You're not going to change your mind. You never do. Not about anything. You're more dependable than . . ." Her forehead creased. "Well, I don't know what you're more dependable than, but I know you are. If there's one thing you're not, Annie, it's full of surprises."

"Oh yeah?" I guess the fact that it was less than twenty-four hours since someone tried to pump us full of lead accounted for my adrenaline still running high. I had been feeling feisty all day. "Then what would you say if I told you I called and told Jim I wouldn't be coming in to work tonight?"

Her mouth fell open.

"Well . . ." I was honest to a fault. I squirmed. "I didn't exactly tell him. I called and left a message. But I would have told him. If he picked up the phone."

"He picked up my call when I phoned it to tell him I'd be a little late." Eve gave me a penetrating look. "You're not going to quit, are you?"

"The restaurant?" I didn't tell Eve, but I had considered it. All of the night before as I replayed the fight with Jim. All that day at work. But just as I didn't jump into things quickly, I didn't jump out of them on a whim, either. "I'm still mad at him," I said. "I know it's childish, but that's why I'm not going in tonight. I hate being treated like a kid. I hate it that Jim doesn't believe we can conduct an investigation and not be so obvious about it that someone wants to kill us."

"But isn't that exactly what happened?"

"I guess so, and I hate that, too." I grabbed my coat and stepped aside so Eve could walk out of the apartment first, and I could lock the door behind us. "I hate that we don't have the answers. I hate that more than anything, Eve. If the shooting wasn't random, it means that somebody sees us as a threat. And I hate it that we don't know who or what we've done. Then, on top of it all, to have Jim throw it in our faces . . . He practically came right out and called us amateurs. You heard him."

"He was upset. Because he cares about you, Annie."

We were out in the hallway, and even though I knew it was locked, I checked the door one more time, just to be sure. "I know he does," I told Eve. "At least I used to know that he liked me. These days . . . well, I haven't exactly been kind to him. After all, I'm the one who freaked and put the kibosh on our dating. If he changed his mind and decided to find someone else, I'd understand."

Just as I hoped, Eve didn't jump in and tell me she knew for a fact that Jim had finally thrown in the towel.

The realization should have made me feel better instead of just making me feel more guilty for the way I'd treated him. "Then there are times like last night . . ." I sighed again. "Honestly, Eve, sometimes I just don't know what the man is thinking."

Eve laughed and looped her arm through mine. "Isn't that the whole idea! They don't know what we're thinking. We don't know what they're thinking. Come on, Annie, it's what makes the whole thing so much fun."

FUN WAS NOT THE WORD I WOULD HAVE USED TO describe the fund-raiser for Senator Douglas Mercy.

A tiny plate of appetizers I was too nervous to eat in one hand, a glass of sparkling water in the other, I stood beside a showy display of chrysanthemums in a sweep of fall colors that had been arranged under a bigger-than-life picture of the senator. When it came to mingling, I really was an amateur. While I waited for Eve to come back from the ladies' room where she had gone for one last makeup check with the promise that she'd be back in a twinkling, I tried my best to look inconspicuous. It wasn't hard. All around me, serious-faced men in suits and women in dresses that put mine to

shame talked in hushed tones about things like the trade
deficit and global warming and how Senator Mercy, should
he be chosen to run for vice president, was sure to make the
world a better place.

I saw Renee and Jennifer, two of the women who had
worked with Sarah and had come to the funeral luncheon,
walking toward me. I tensed, but of course, I had no need to
worry. They weren't expecting to run into any of the help
from Bellywasher's mixing with the movers and the shakers.
They walked by, looked at me and through me, and kept
right on going.

Which, as far as I was concerned, was all well and good.

If one of them stopped and asked what I was doing there,
what would I have said?

*Oh, I just dropped in to talk to your boss. I was wonder-
ing, see, if he might have been having an affair with Sarah
and if he was going on a cruise with her and if he might have
killed her, too.*

Just thinking the words caused heat to shoot through my
cheeks. When a man standing close by happened to turn and
look my way, I took a drink, hiding behind my glass of water.

"Any luck yet?" Eve had sneaked up behind me. "Any
sign of our perp?"

"We don't know he's our perp."

"No, but he might be. Any sign of him?"

"He's over there." I looked across the room to where Senator Mercy was talking to a TV reporter. "He's kind of busy."

"He going to be busy all night. That's how these things
work. People are going to hound him until he walks out."

"So maybe we should leave. Maybe this was a bad idea
after all."

"Annie!" Eve plucked the plate of food out of my hand,
deposited it on a nearby table, and snatched the water glass
away, too. So that Eve wouldn't be too late getting to work,
we had arrived at the fund-raiser just as it started, and there
was a crush of people between us and the senator. She
slipped behind me and poked her hand into the small of my

back, propelling me forward. "You said this was our best opportunity," she reminded me.

"It is our best opportunity." It was slow going, but with each step, we got closer to Douglas Mercy. I saw him wrap up his conversation with the reporter. No sooner was he done than a group of well-wishers surrounded him.

I held back. "I just can't believe I'm going to walk up to a senator and ask him if he was going on a cruise with Sarah."

"Then you don't have to." Eve gave me another poke. "I'll do all the talking."

Like that was supposed to make me feel better?

Another shove from Eve. It was perfectly timed—I ended up smack-dab in front of Senator Mercy just as the group of people he'd been talking to wished him their best and walked away. Unfortunately, at the same moment, a group of the senator's supporters squeezed between me and Eve.

I was on my own.

"Good evening." The senator gave me his campaign smile and automatically stuck out his hand. "Good of you to come."

I had no choice but to shake his hand. That, and wonder how I was going to ease into the conversation. I knew there wasn't much time. Out of the corner of my eye, I saw another group forming. They'd give me a minute or two, tops, before they moved in for their audience with the senator.

"You probably don't remember me, Senator," I said. "We've met before."

Douglas Mercy was, after all, a politician. Though I could see the wheels turning, he never missed a beat. "Of course," he said, but I knew that, try as he might, there was no way he could place me.

I sensed a movement behind me, and Eve stepped up to my side.

"Of course!" The senator beamed a smile in Eve's direction. He extended his hand. "Miss DeCateur. From the luncheon in Sarah's honor. It's lovely to see you again. And you, too," he said, almost as an afterthought, shifting his gaze back to me. "I'm surprised to see you here."

"Well you surely shouldn't be." Eve's smile was bright enough for the campaign trail. "We know a good cause when we see one."

The senator was still holding on to Eve's hand. "And I know beauty when I see it," he said.

"And there is something we need to tell you." I jumped in, because behind me, I could already hear the anxious shuffle of feet as the next group waited to take our place. I couldn't take the chance of leaving things up to Eve. I had the floor, and I wasn't going to get another chance.

"Actually, we just wanted you to let you know that we were able to get a refund," I said. "For that cruise Sarah was scheduled to go on."

Mercy gave me a blank stare.

"So it's all taken care of, and you don't have to worry about it." I tried for a smile. "But I'm sorry that you'll be traveling alone."

His gaze never wavered. I never hoped more that the floor would open and swallow me whole.

Because one look at the senator's blank and slightly confused expression, and I knew that we had the wrong man. It wasn't Senator Douglas Mercy who was headed out on that cruise with Sarah.

And I had just made myself look like a complete idiot in front of the next vice president of the United States.

Mortified, I excused myself and hurried to the other side of the room. I didn't even realize Eve hadn't followed me until I'd pushed through the crowd and into the ladies' room. There, I leaned against the wall. The cold tile felt good on my nose.

My stomach roiled, and it had nothing to do with the appetizers. The only way to keep from being sick was to keep my mind off how goofy I must have looked as I practically came out and accused the senator of having an affair with one of his aides, and the only way to do that was to remind myself of everything we'd learned about the cruise.

Sarah was traveling double occupancy.

The other occupant was named Douglas Mercy.

Both Douglas Mercy the senator and Douglas Mercy, his son, were scheduled to be on vacation that week.

And the senator didn't look like he had any idea what I was talking about.

The conclusion was obvious: Sarah was traveling with Dougy. But proving it . . . That was another thing altogether.

There was still no sign of Eve, so when an idea finally occurred to me, I couldn't run it by her. Instead, I reached into my bag for my phone and dialed information to ask for the number of the sleep clinic run by Lorraine Mercy, Dougy's wife.

"THERE YOU ARE!"

By the time I stepped out of the ladies' room, Eve was waiting for me. She was all smiles. "Where'd you go? What did you find out?"

I was smiling, too. But then, I was feeling pretty satisfied with myself, not to mention pretty smart.

"I called the sleep clinic in Orange County," I explained. "You know, the one Dougy's wife runs."

Eve moved in closer. "And?"

"And I've got an appointment to see her. At the beginning of February."

Eve's blue eyes clouded. "I didn't know you have trouble sleeping."

I sighed. "I don't. But don't you see what this means? That's the week of the cruise, and Dougy is scheduled for vacation."

"But his wife isn't!" Eve's eyes went wide. "Which means—"

"Along with the fact that Senator Mercy didn't seem to have a clue what we were talking about, I'd say it means Dougy is our man. He's the one who was going on the cruise with Sarah. And that might mean he knows something about her death."

"Oh, I'm so glad." Eve grabbed my arm with both her hands. "I was so worried. I mean, I wouldn't want to date a killer."

It was my turn to be confused, but Eve cleared that up fast enough. She laughed, so excited she just about jumped up and down.

"It's the senator," she said. "We're having dinner together next week."

Fourteen

✖

BY THE TIME I ARRIVED AT BELLYWASHER'S, THE LINE of Sunday diners snaked out the door, onto the sidewalk, and down King Street.

Logic dictated that word of Michael O'Keefe's review was spreading, but I knew better. The drive-by shooting had added a weird sort of notoriety to the place, especially since last I heard, the police had yet to find out a thing about who the culprits were and why. Questions abounded, and questions left people to find their own answers. I'd already heard a rumor that Bellywasher's was mobbed up, and another that said (believe it or not) that there was pirate treasure buried in the basement and factions warring to find it. In my mind, this sort of reputation would naturally be bad for business. Apparently, I didn't think like other people.

If I needed proof, it came as I walked toward the alley that would take me to the back door. As one group of customers left and before another group walked inside, each and every person checked out the bullet holes in our front door.

Still thinking about how odd this was, I stepped into the kitchen, took off my coat, and stopped cold.

I'd just naturally assumed that Jim would be out at the bar.
Wrong.

He was at the counter near the stove chopping parsley,
and when he heard me walk in, he glanced over his shoulder.

He didn't smile, but then, what did I expect? It was the
first we'd seen each other since our spat outside after the
shooting. If Jim didn't know then that I was miffed, he'd
probably figured it out since. I'd called out both Friday and
Saturday. "Good afternoon," he said.

"Hello." Unlike Eve, whose life is full of passion and
grand emotion, mine has always been on a pretty even keel.
I do not like uncontrolled feelings, mostly because I don't
know what to do with them, at least not without looking like
a complete idiot. If I needed proof, I had only to recall the
way my marriage disappeared in a *poof* of smoke. Now, remembering the last, angry words Jim and I had, my stomach
bunched.

Don't worry. I handled the situation like a grown-up. I
held my head high and walked out of the kitchen.

The restaurant was a mob scene, but Heidi and Eve
looked like they were taking it all in stride. I can't say the
same for myself when I saw that in the two days I'd been
gone, a sort of transformation had taken place. More of Uncle Angus's stuff was up on the walls. A (very bad) oil paint-
ing of the queen had joined Granny's cottage, Grandpa's
walking stick, and the autographed photo of Mel Gibson in
blue face paint. One of our beautiful sandalwood screens
was nearly lost under the green and white tartan kilt that had
been thrown over it. There was a yellow flag emblazoned
with a red lion hung in a place of honor on the opposite wall.

"It's a thing of beauty, you know?"

I hadn't realized Larry, Hank, and Charlie were squeezed
together at the far end of the bar until Larry spoke.

I turned to him. "You're not talking about our decorating
scheme, are you?" I asked.

"Sure." Hank finished the last of his beer and slid off his
barstool. The people waiting at the door sensed there would

be open seats soon, and the crowd surged forward. "Good to see Jim hasn't completely abandoned his roots," he said. "There's hope yet for the boy. Now all he has to do is get rid of this snooty crowd so there's more time for us to visit."

"And get the old menu back," Charlie piped up. "When you gonna add a hot dog special of the day?"

More big points for me. Like the grown-up I am, I did not say, *When hell freezes over.* Instead, I scooted out of the way so Larry, Hank, and Charlie could leave and scooted even farther back when three ladies with big jewelry, big fur coats, and big attitudes nearly knocked me over in the effort to take their places before anyone else could.

Once they were finally settled, I had a clear path to my office, but before I could get there, Jim walked out of the kitchen.

Remember all that talk about being a grown-up? My maturity flew out of the window the moment I saw what he had in his hand. It was a potted thistle plant. Faux silk, of course, and all the more ugly for it. He plopped it down behind the bar and turned to me, an unspoken challenge glinting in his eyes.

Can I be blamed for taking up the gauntlet?

"What are you doing?" I made sure to keep my voice down. "Why are you ruining our decorating scheme?"

"Arugula," he said, and while I stood there, baffled and trying to translate what he meant, he disappeared into the kitchen.

I was still mulling over this curious turn of events when Eve motioned to me from the other side of the restaurant.

"Annie, look who's here." She was standing near a table by the window, and she gestured to the woman seated there. It was Renee, one of Sarah's coworkers. I said hello and asked how she was doing. I didn't mention that I'd seen her just recently at the senator's fund-raiser, but I did remember how upset she'd been at the funeral luncheon.

Renee had a mouthful of cheese and grilled vegetable omelet, so Eve answered for her. "Renee stopped by to see us," she explained. "She wants to talk. About Sarah."

We decided that after Renee finished eating, she would come to my office. Until then, I grabbed hold of Eve's arm. Once we were inside the office, I shut the door.

"No way is this a coincidence," I said.

"You mean Renee? Of course not." Eve looked as pretty as a picture in black skirt and a gold silk blouse, but she was fiddling with her string of gold, black, and pumpkin-orange beads. "I called Renee and asked her to come by. Remember what Doug said at the luncheon," she added, and before I could ask how she and the senator were suddenly so friendly, she went right on. "He said that Sarah considered Renee a friend. I was thinking about it last night, and I decided that's exactly who we needed to talk to, one of Sarah's friends. A friend is going to know way more than anyone else about Sarah's personal life."

I had to admit it, Eve was right. "And let me guess," I said. "You lured Renee here by promising her a free meal." Eve didn't answer. She didn't have to. And honestly, I didn't mind footing the bill. Not if it meant we might get some information in return.

With that in mind, I shooed Eve back out into the restaurant and plunked down in my desk chair. A lot of paperwork had accumulated in the days since I'd last been there, but I wasn't worried. Oh, a few short weeks earlier with my old, mind-of-its-own computer, it would have been impossible to accomplish everything I needed to get done without a little angst and a whole lot of swearing. But fortunately and thanks to Charlene, things were looking up. At least in the computer department. There was, after all, a spanking-new computer in Sarah's apartment, and when Eve cleaned out the place and donated Sarah's clothes and furniture to a women's shelter as Charlene had requested, she'd also remembered that Charlene had said we could keep anything we wanted.

"It's for a good cause," Eve had said, and as the Quick-Books program I'd installed the last time I'd been at the restaurant opened without a glitch and without the grinding of gears and whatsits I knew I would have heard from my old computer, I was grateful. With a cooperative machine, I'd have a big chunk of my work done before Renee finished eating. As long as I was paying for her meat, I wanted to be able to give her my full attention and find out all I could.

FORTUNATELY, I DIDN'T HAVE LONG TO WAIT. MAYBE Renee was a quick eater or maybe she was polite (or just easily pressured) and the fact that other folks were waiting for her table hurried her along. Within a half hour, she tapped at my door. I was in the middle of updating the Bellywasher's checking account, and I minimized the screen.

"It was so nice of you to ask me to stop by." Renee's comment was pleasant enough, but she was, after all, used to working in the halls of power. She glanced uncertainly around my teensy-weensy office. Eve stepped inside, too, and once the door was closed, there wasn't much room for any of us to move. I motioned Renee toward the chair next to my desk, and she sat down. Eve stood with her back to the door.

"We've been worried about you." I realized that my body language—sitting forward in my chair, bent toward Renee—was too patronizing. Slowly, I sat up and back. "Of all the people at the funeral luncheon, you were the most upset. Sarah was our friend, and we know she was your friend, too. We figured we should try to get through this together."

Renee opened her purse and plucked out a package of tissues. She pulled one out and dabbed at her eyes. "I know I should be over the crying part by now, but I just can't help it. Anytime anyone talks about Sarah, the waterworks start."

"That's understandable." Before I even realized I was doing it, I was leaning forward again. This time, I didn't make the correction. There was nothing condescending or insincere about the way I was treating Renee. I looked concerned because I was concerned. "She was your friend."

Renee sniffed and nodded.

"Which is why we wanted to talk to you." Even though

Renee's sudden appearance at Bellywasher's had caught me off guard, I knew what Eve had been thinking and why she'd invited her. It was a brilliant idea, really, just what we needed to help nudge our investigation along. At the same time I scolded myself for not thinking of the strategy myself like a real detective would have, I tried to ease quickly into the topic of Sarah and Dougy and the cruise. Eve was in the room—I knew if I waited too long, she'd say something she shouldn't.

"Because you were Sarah's friend . . ." I gulped down my mortification and reminded myself that if I was ever going to be a real detective, I had to get over my reluctance to poke my nose into people's private business. "We figured you'd know about her personal life. You know, about the man she was going on that cruise with."

Renee was a middle-aged woman with doughy features. Under the heavy coat of hide-the-wrinkles foundation she was wearing, her cheeks turned red. "Oh, I don't know." She scooted back in her chair. Just as I understood my own body language, hers was loud and clear.

"You're not dishonoring her memory," I said, jumping in before Renee could convince herself that there was no way she was going to talk about this. "In fact, you might be helping."

"That's right." For all her social skills, there was nothing subtle about Eve. She nodded enthusiastically. "You see, we don't think Sarah killed herself."

"You can't think Dougy—" Renee hadn't meant to let the cat out of the bag. Her eyes bulged. The color in her cheeks drained and left her chalky.

"It's OK," I said with an understanding smile. "We know about Sarah and Dougy. We know they were going on a cruise together."

Renee nodded. She still had a tissue in her hands and she shredded it in tiny pieces. A few bits of debris floated off her lap and to the floor. I controlled the urge to sweep them up and concentrated on Renee. "We don't think Dougy had anything to do with Sarah's death," I told Renee, not that I was certain of it, but because I knew it would make her feel better. "We just want to understand everything that happened. We figured Sarah's relationship with Dougy is a good place to start."

Renee's eyes glistened with unshed tears. "Nobody else knows this so please don't spread it around. I'm not supposed to know it, either, but Sarah, she was feeling a little guilty early on and one night when we went out for drinks, she told me. Sarah and Dougy had been seeing each other for a few months. Since you know about the cruise, you probably know that, too. From what Sarah told me, neither of them meant for it to be anything more than a fling. But then they got close. They loved each other. Truly."

"Even though Dougy had to keep cleaning up the mistakes Sarah made at the office?"

Renee, apparently, was an unrepentant romantic. "It didn't make any difference. Not in Sarah and Dougy's relationship."

"He told us he didn't know there were any problems with Sarah's work."

"He was being kind. Of course he knew." Renee rolled her eyes. "Jennifer had to clean up the messes, and Jennifer isn't quiet. About anything. No way Dougy didn't know. He just wanted to protect Sarah's memory. You understand."

I nodded. "So what was the problem with Sarah's work?" I asked.

Renee shrugged. "I never understood it. She had always been so thorough and so careful. Then, suddenly, everything just fell apart. Her information was scanty, her sources were unidentified. It was as if she couldn't hold it together any longer."

Affairs of the heart were, after all, Eve's bailiwick. She pushed away from the door. "We heard it was because she was upset about her breakup with Dylan Monroe."

"Then you heard wrong." Renee looked from Eve to me. "See, Dylan didn't break up with Sarah. She broke up with him."

"But he told us—"

Before she could say any more, I put up one hand to stop Eve. Once again, our investigation—and our suspicions—had come around to Dylan. We didn't need to broadcast them. Not in front of a woman who was practically a stranger.

"Sarah broke up with Dylan because of Dougy," Renee said.

"Was Dylan angry?" I countered.

"Not that Sarah ever said. She cared for Dylan, but she wasn't in love with him. Not like she was with Dougy. It was really hard for her to tell Dylan there was someone else in her life, but once she did, he understood. He knew they could never be happy together."

"Then Dougy was the one who made it possible for Sarah to live the way she did."

Renee looked away. "You mean the fancy apartment and the dog and the clothes. I don't think so. Dougy's wife, Lorraine, she keeps pretty tight control on him. At least when it comes to finances. No way he could have been spending that kind of money on another woman without her knowing about it and no way she knew about it. Lorraine's one tough lady. She'd never put up with a cheating husband."

"Then didn't you wonder where the money came from?"

Another shrug from Renee. "I thought maybe Sarah had sold some of her photographs. You saw them, didn't you? In her apartment? She loved to take her camera out on her lunch hour and roam around taking pictures. Some of them were pretty good, too, and I figured she'd found a gallery to sell them. Then there was that story about her aunt, too. You know, the one who she said left her all that money."

"But you didn't believe it?"

Renee gave another shrug. I wondered if her shoulders were getting tired. "It was none of my business," she said. "I figured if Sarah wanted to talk, she'd talk. If not . . . well, then I guess she had nothing to say. But now you're saying . . ."

She thought back over everything she'd learned since she walked into my office. Her dark brows dropped low over her eyes. "You think someone killed her? You think Dylan

Monroe . . ." Renee dismissed the idea with a little laugh. "Come on, you've seen the guy. No way could he ever murder anyone. He's too good-looking."

I wasn't sure what handsome had to do with hateful, but before I had the chance to argue, Renee checked her watch and popped out of her chair. "I've got to get moving. I hope you understand. I've got tickets for a concert at the National Gallery this afternoon." She sidestepped her way between my desk and Eve, who had automatically moved away from the door. Her hand already on the knob, she stopped and looked back at us.

"I think what you're doing is really something," she said with a sniff. "I mean, it says something about your friendship with Sarah, and I know how much she would have appreciated it. You're good friends. I don't know if you're right!" She gave a little laugh. "But you're good friends. And you know . . ." Renee hesitated, and I sensed that she was trying to decide if she should say anything further. I knew the instant she'd made up her mind. Her jaw tensed. Her eyes hardened.

"If you're looking for somebody who could hate Sarah enough to kill her, try Lorraine Mercy. If she ever found out about Dougy and Sarah's affair, that woman . . ." Renee shivered. "I wouldn't put anything past her. She's a regular piranha."

I STAYED IN MY OFFICE ALL AFTERNOON WITH THE door shut. The better not to have to risk another confrontation with Jim. I tried not to think about him or about the way that just thinking about thinking about him tied my stomach in knots and made my pulse race. It was hard, but I managed. Partly because I kept busy plowing through all the work on my desk, partly because I kept thinking about everything we'd heard from Renee, and mostly because halfway through the day, with my stomach rumbling and demanding lunch and my ego telling me that if I dared a trip to the kitchen I might have to face Jim, I put my head down and took a nap.

I dreamed about piranha. They were circling in a lake, and I was swimming in the middle of them. The one with the biggest teeth was wearing a navy suit, and her jacket and her skirt didn't match. While the others kept their distance, she got closer and closer, flashing her pearly whites.

As only dreams can do, this one terrified me beyond all reasoning. I tensed. I was breathing hard. As Lorraine the piranha closed in on me, I got set to scream.

I never had the chance.

Just as Lorraine's scissors-sharp teeth were about to take a chunk out of me, I was miraculously pulled up out of the water by none other than Dylan Monroe. The fact that he was walking on the water no doubt says something about my psyche that I do not want to examine further.

"I'll save you," Dylan said, in a Dudley Do-Right sort of way that made me laugh, even in my sleep.

The next thing I knew, we were on land, and there was no water in sight. Dylan winked at me, "Get the message?" he asked.

Did I?

I was still wondering about it when I sat up and shook away the cobwebs.

My shoulders ached and I stretched and rubbed my eyes. I'd fallen asleep on top of a pile of bills, and I straightened them, smoothing out the paper on top that I'd crumpled when I used it as a pillow. No doubt, my cheek had a crease in it to match.

"Get the message?" I repeated the words in the same superhero voice Dylan had used in my dream and chuckled. "I might," I told myself. "If I knew what the message was and how I was supposed to get it."

I checked the clock and decided that I'd slip out the back door as soon as I was done with the bills from the linen service. I pulled the bills closer and double-checked the company's numbers, punching the figures into my calculator with one hand while with the other, I drummed a pen against my desk.

"Message, message, message," I mumbled to myself. Maybe it took that long for my subconscious to finally get through to my brain.

"Messages!" I sat up straight, pushed the paperwork aside, and reached for the computer mouse. There might be e-mail messages on Sarah's computer and if there were . . .

A few minutes later, I jerked back, stunned.

There were e-mails left on Sarah's computer, all right.

I was looking at one of them right then and there.

It was from Dylan Monroe, and it began with the words, "You bitch, if I ever see you again, I'm going to kill you."

Fifteen

✖

MY HEAD SPUN WITH POSSIBILITIES.
   "I can't decide between the fig and rosemary pot roast and the pea soup with crème fraîche."

Not those possibilities. Those were the menu choices being considered by the man sitting at the table closest to the bar. It was three days after I found the message from Dylan. Heidi had called out with the flu, Eve was taking a week's vacation, and as unlikely as it would have seemed to me a few short months earlier, I was standing at attention, pen and paper in hand, waiting to take the man's order. While he shilly-shallied and I waited, I thought through all that I'd learned thanks to Sarah's computer and the e-mail saved on it.

Was Dylan our guy? Had he killed Sarah in a jealous rage? The message I'd found certainly seemed to point that way. So did the fact that Dylan had lied. Any number of times. He claimed that his work in Afghanistan had caused him and Sarah to drift apart. He said the decision to break off their relationship was his. He told us flat out—hadn't he?—that he blamed himself for Sarah's death because he knew she was heartbroken, and it was all his fault.

"Tell me again, hon. Is the crème fraîche made here? Fresh?"

My teeth clamped tight around a smile, and firmly ignoring the *hon*, I pulled myself away from my own possibilities to handle those of the man I was waiting on. Don't get me wrong, I didn't mind customers asking questions. Like everyone who worked at Bellywasher's, I was proud of our menu selections and like the cook I wasn't, I was amazed at the magic that went on in the kitchen. But the word *again* was as much a clue here as Dylan's e-mail was to my investigation of Sarah's murder. This customer had already asked about the crème fraîche—twice—and always in the same tone of voice. Like he thought I was lying and if he pinned me down, I'd crack.

I kept my smile in place and went through the song and dance.

Fresh. Absolutely. Made on the premises. Every day.

Of course, I said it a whole lot nicer than that.

"I don't know." As if it would provide the answer he was searching for, he squinted at the menu in his hands. "Tell me about the pot roast one more time. Those figs, are they dried?"

I could have been brutally honest and admitted that I didn't know. Instead, I did a quick eeny-meeny-miny-mo, decided on dried, and told him so.

While he thought about it, my mind wandered back to Dylan. His e-mail had provided me with proof that when it came to his relationship with Sarah, he wasn't just stretching the truth, he was pulling it apart and cobbling it together into a whole new shape.

Yeah, the big breakup had come while Dylan was in Afghanistan. A quick check of the date of the e-mail and a phone call to his producer at the TV network showed that much was true. The rest? Something told me the very fact that it was the only message Sarah saved said something about the situation. And it wasn't something pretty. I wondered if she felt as if she might need a little insurance once

Dylan returned from overseas. Thinking that Sarah had been afraid of Mr. Big Smile and Perfect Hair gave me the creeps.

"Pot roast."

I jumped at the sound of the customer's voice, and wrote down the order quickly with the hope that once it was on paper, he wouldn't change his mind. That taken care of, I turned to his companion.

The woman had passed on my earlier offer to take her order first, saying that she needed time to think. Now, faced with a decision of her own, she played with the string of pearls around her neck and pouted. "Well, I wanted a Pisco sour," she said. "But the man at the bar . . ." She looked over to where Jim was chatting with a customer. "He claims you've only got Chilean Pisco."

What's that saying about discretion being the better part of valor? I'd been around Bellywasher's enough to know that Pisco was a type of South American brandy. As to whether Chilean Pisco was a good thing or a bad one . . . well, I couldn't say, so I didn't respond.

It was apparently the wrong move.

Disgusted, the woman flicked her menu across the table in my direction. It slid and skittered and ended up on the floor. I bent to retrieve it and saw out of the corner of my eye that Jim had taken notice. He'd stopped talking and was watching what was going on.

All the more reason for me to behave like the employee of the month.

Struggling to get a smile in place and keep it there, I stood. I found the woman looking at me with her chin raised and her lips pressed into a thin line. I wondered if she realized how the expression accented the wrinkles at the corners of her mouth.

"Peruvian Pisco is far superior," the woman said. "If you have any aspirations toward ever being a decent restaurant, I'd think you'd know that."

Smile or no smile, boss watching or not, there was only so much I could take. "We aren't a decent restaurant," I said, and just as I expected, her eyes went wide. "We're better than a decent restaurant."

She didn't like being shown up. Her top lip curled. "Of course, it all depends on your definition of decent. In my mind, that means a restaurant where the staff is trained to treat customers with respect," she said. "Either that never happened here or you were absent that day. If your proprietor had any class at all, I think he'd pay attention and hire staff that minds its manners."

Criticizing me was one thing. I could live with that. And let's face it, I probably deserved it. But questioning Jim's reputation and his professionalism?

I knew better than to respond to the acid in her voice, just like I knew better than to care if Chile or Peru held bragging rights in the grape-growing contest. None of it mattered. I couldn't help it—I snapped.

"Oh, Jim knows all about manners and professionalism," I assured the customer, my voice as sweet as the smile I cast down on her. "He just isn't interested in catering to snooty people with no manners and bad attitudes and—"

Before I could get another word out, Jim's arm was around my shoulders. With a hurried, "Excuse us," to our customers, he spun me around, whisked me into my office, and closed the door behind us. It wasn't until I heard it snap shut that I realized what I'd just done.

The blood drained from my face. My legs turned to rubber. I guess Jim knew what was bound to happen next. He pulled my chair away from the desk and tucked it behind me. When I collapsed into it, he told me he'd be right back and went out into the restaurant.

For a couple minutes all I could do was sit in stunned silence, listening to the rough sounds of my own breathing. When I heard the door open again, I didn't bother to look. I knew it was Jim.

"I'm sorry," I said. "I lost my temper. I should go out

there and apologize." When I started to get up, he put a hand on my arm.

"No need," he said. "They're gone."

I was relieved that I didn't have to face the customers again but sorry that I wouldn't have the chance to set things right. I was appalled at my own bad behavior. I could imagine how Jim felt, and the least I could do was save him any further discomfort. I grabbed my purse.

"It's all right," I said. "I won't make you fire me. I'll quit first and save you the trouble."

"OK." He crouched down in front of me. "If that's what you want to do, I will'na stop you. But just for the record, I had no intention of firing you."

"You didn't?" I was pretty sure I'd heard wrong, and I stared at him, just to make sure. His expression was somber. Except for the glimmer in his eyes. "Why not?" I asked. "Why aren't you going to fire me? I deserve it. I'll prove it. I'll go after those people and tell them I'm quitting because of the way I treated them."

His hand was still on my arm, and he tightened his hold to keep me in place. "No need. I asked them to leave."

"You asked—" Of all the things he could have said in response to the situation, this was the most surprising. I thought it over for a few seconds, but no matter how I tried to make sense of the situation, I was more baffled than ever. "You asked? Them? To leave?"

Jim laughed. "They had a lot of nerve talking to you that way."

"But you asked? Them?"

"I knew she was trouble the moment I seated her, and when I saw her chuck that menu at you . . ." Jim's hazel eyes darkened with annoyance. "I told them if they couldn't treat my employees well, I did'na want them back."

"And they said?"

"Something about what a Philistine I was and how they'd take their trade elsewhere."

"And you said?"

"I'm fairly sure it was good riddance." He laughed and sat back on his heels. "Sorry to have to put you through that."

"You're sorry?" I scrubbed my hands over my face. "I'm the one who should be sorry. I never should have lost my temper."

"They never should have pushed you into losing it."

"And you're being very kind."

"No. Kind is not what I'm being." Jim got to his feet. He turned away from me, and I suspected that if my office was bigger, he would have taken a turn around the room. The way it was, with my chair pulled away from my desk, there was barely room to move. He drew in a breath. "What would you say," he asked, "if I told you I wanted to change a few things around here?"

"A few things, but one of them isn't that you want to fire me?"

"I don't want to fire you." He said it slowly, and maybe that's what finally got the message to penetrate. Feeling a little less mortified, I sank back in my chair.

"I'm tired of the likes of them," Jim said, glancing toward the door. I knew he was picturing the man and the woman who'd made me lose it. "I've always dreamed of a fine restaurant, but I never thought . . ." Again, he hunkered down in front of me. This time, he took my hand in both of his.

"Annie," he said. "I don't like these people. They're rude and demanding. They're ill-bred and ill-mannered. I've tried to make a go of it. I've tried to tell myself that I'm being too particular and that if I just give it another few weeks . . . none of it has made any difference."

"You're closing Bellywasher's?" I guess I'd never realized how much the restaurant had come to mean to me. The very idea made my stomach sour. Tears filled my eyes. "You can't," I said. "We're turning a profit. Not much of one, of course, but the bills are getting paid and the salaries are getting paid and—"

"Not closing it." Jim gave my hand a squeeze. "Changing it. I'd rather have the likes of Larry and Hank and Charlie in here any day than the variety of people we've been attracting. It looks like I'm meant to be an old-fashioned pub keeper. Not a newfangled fusion cooking restaurateur."

"That's why you've been hanging Angus's things back on the walls!" The revelation came to me in a flash. I knew I was right, because Jim smiled sheepishly. "You're more comfortable with homey than high style."

"Aye." Jim nodded. His expression was solemn. "And it's sorry I am to disappoint you."

It was my turn to laugh. With my free hand, I caressed Jim's cheek. "I'm not disappointed. If it will make you happy . . ." I thought of how strained our relationship had been of late. It had happened so gradually, I hadn't even re- alized how much I missed our easy friendship until it was gone completely. "No wonder you've been cranky."

Jim's spine stiffened, but he didn't look offended. At least not too much. "Cranky, is it? Well, if I've been cranky, you've been preoccupied."

I couldn't deny it. It was my turn to look sheepish. "You were right the night of the drive-by. I still don't know if the shooting had any connection to our investigation into Sarah's death, but you were right about us investigating. I took your comments too personally."

"And I didn't take your special talents personally enough. This investigation is important to you. I'm sorry, Annie. I shouldn't browbeat you because of it or try to stand in your way. You're good at this sort of thing. You proved that when you solved Drago's murder. It's just that I dunna want to see you get hurt."

"And I have no intention of getting hurt. That's the ab- solute truth!" To prove it, I crossed my heart with one finger. "But there's something that's not right about the way Sarah died. Eve and I are sure of it. You understand, don't you? You understand how I have to keep searching for the truth? To make things right for Sarah."

"I understand that if you have questions and you don't try to find the answers to them, you wouldn't be the special person you are." Jim leaned in and brushed my lips with a kiss. "I will back off, totally and completely, if that's what you want."

I could have taken the comment to mean back off from our relationship, but honestly, when Jim was looking at me that way—a tiny smile on his lips and a spark in his eyes—I knew that couldn't be true.

"You mean about the investigation." I nodded, sure that was what he'd meant. "I don't want you to back off; I just want you to stop worrying. We're being careful."

"We?" He looked at me with a gleam in his eyes that reminded me of the way he used to watch me back in cooking school. As I burned and scorched and seared my food to death and beyond, Jim didn't look disgusted or like he was going to throw in the towel. He simply looked fascinated and slightly amused.

"As far as I can tell," he said, "there isn't much *we* in your investigation. Not these days. Eve's abandoned you."

I knew he didn't mean it to sound harsh, but I have to admit, I was feeling a little sensitive. I tamped back my hurt feelings. "She's been spending an awful lot of time with Senator Mercy these last couple weeks."

"That's for certain."

As one, we glanced at my guest chair and the pile of newspapers that had been brought in by well-meaning customers. It seemed like every day, another one was added to the stack. The front page of that day's *Washington Post* featured a photo of the senator at a Kennedy Center concert with Eve on his arm. The Style section of the *Baltimore Sun* showed a picture of Eve and the senator at a ribbon-cutting ceremony for a children's health clinic. The local Alexandria paper had gotten caught up in the frenzy. Eve was front page news there, too.

As for the tabloids . . .

I looked over the array of yellow journalism rags that had

been dropped off by Monsieur Lavoie, who seemed to be getting a real kick out of Eve's newfound celebrity. I shook my head, honestly amazed that word could spread so far, so fast. "The Bureaucrat and the Beauty Queen" one headline screamed. "Could She Be Our First Lady Someday?" asked another.

"I'm glad Eve is having the time of her life," I said, and I meant it. "But I miss having her around. I miss having her with me when I investigate. It's always easier for me to think out loud, you know? Without her here to listen to me, I feel like I'm getting nowhere fast with this investigation."

"Then tell me."

I guess my expression must have said it all.

"No, I mean it," Jim said. "Come on."

Before I could protest, he had me by the hand and was leading me into the kitchen. He draped an apron over my head, tied it behind my back, and walked me to the stove.

"Oh, no!" I locked my knees. "Been here, done that. Remember?"

"I do." Jim's smile was bright. "That's why I'm going to do the cooking." He reached for one of the carrots sitting near the cutting board and pointed at me with it. "You," he said, "are going to do the talking. Go ahead, Annie." He turned and got to work, chopping carrots and quartering heads of cabbage. "Tell me what you've found out. Run your theories by me the way I run my menu ideas by you. Maybe if I understood more about what you're doing and how you're doing it, I'd worry less that it's going to get you in trouble."

"That's sweet." It was, and I didn't mean to downplay the offer. "But if I stand here and talk, I'm going to slow you down. There are plenty of people waiting for drinks and dinner."

"Aye, and one of them is none other than Jacques Lavoie himself. When I went to your office to talk to you, I asked him to take over for me behind the bar."

"Are you sure?"

"There are some things more important even than Bellywasher's." Jim finished with the carrots and whisked the chopped pieces into a pot. "You're one of them. And if you're hell-bent on being a detective, who am I to stop you? Tell me, Annie. Tell me everything."

I did, up to and including the e-mail message from Dylan threatening Sarah.

By the time I was done, Jim had already added chicken breasts and seasoning to the pot where he'd put the carrots. He carried it over to the stove and turned it on to simmer.

"That's serious, no doubt of that," he said when he turned back to me. "Do you think that message from Dylan means he might have killed her?"

I shook my head. "I honestly don't know. But it could mean he was jealous, and if he was, it could mean that he knew about Sarah's relationship with Dougy Mercy. And if Dylan knew about Sarah and Dougy, I bet that means other people did, too. Like maybe Lorraine Mercy."

"And there's another bit of jealousy we have on our hands."

I liked the way Jim said *we*. Just knowing he was on my side made me feel better about succeeding with my investigation. "That gives both Dylan and Lorraine motive," I said. "Of course, we don't know if either one of them had opportunity. And we don't know anything about the money, either."

Jim had been paying attention as I talked. He nodded. "You mean the money Sarah must have needed to live the lifestyle she did. And to buy that little yapper of hers a diamond collar."

I remembered the trip I'd taken to the groomer with Eve and Doc. "A diamond collar engraved with his initials. And—"

When I stopped talking in the middle of a sentence, Jim was immediately concerned. "Annie?" He reached for my hand. "Are you all right?"

"I'm fine. Really. I was just thinking. About the diamond collar. It had Doc's initials inside."

"And?"

"And I've been such an idiot! They're Doc's initials, all right, but they aren't only Doc's initials. DM. That could mean Doctor Masakazu. It could also mean Dylan Monroe. Or Dougy Mercy."

"Or Douglas Mercy."

"Do you think one of them gave her the money to buy that collar?"

Thinking, Jim pursed his lips. "It's most likely to be Dougy. They were having an affair, after all."

"But Renee doesn't seem to think he could slip the money past Lorraine."

"Which leaves us with the other two to consider."

"Or the fact that DM really does stand for Doctor Masakazu."

Jim tapped a finger against his chin. "This detective business, it's not as easy as it looks on TV. I'm impressed. I, for one, could never make sense of it all."

I wasn't sure I could, either, but I was too busy basking in the glow of that "I'm impressed" to point it out. "What we need is a break in our case," I said.

"Be careful. When the cops on TV say that, someone else dies."

I cringed. "Not what I meant at all. I mean another clue. Something to point us in the right direction. Either Dylan or Lorraine could be our killer. If this was TV, we'd find a letter written by one of them."

"Or blood on their clothing."

"Or we'd be invited to an island with all the suspects."

"Or a spooky old castle."

"Or a—"

"Fabulous, beautiful, glamorous ball!"

Do I need to point out that neither Jim nor I made that last comment? It came from Eve as she threw open the door and bounded into the kitchen. "I feel like Cinderella," she said, and she twirled around in the center of the room. No mean

feat, considering that we were surrounded by racks of pots
and pans, and that both the grill and the stove were in use.
She stopped when she realized she was going to do one of
us—or herself—some serious harm.

Her cheeks glowed. Her eyes gleamed. "I'm going to a
real, live, honest-to-goodness black-tie, formal ball," she
said. "It's a fund-raiser. Well, it's *the* fund-raiser of the year.
And you . . ." She reached into her Kate Spade bag, pro-
duced two tickets, and handed them to me with a flourish.
"You two are coming along."

IN A CITY LIKE WASHINGTON, FUND-RAISERS ARE
literally a dime a dozen. Pick a night—any night in
any week—and my guess is you can find at least three wor-
thy causes holding three different functions in three separate
places around town. More on weekends.

What made the one Eve invited us to different? Well, a
couple things.

Number one, Eve was right. This was the real deal. A
black-tie affair where the vice president was going to be the
guest of honor and the featured speaker.

The political connection, of course, explained how Eve
got invited and how she had snagged Jim and me a couple of
the coveted tickets, but it wasn't the only reason I was excited. As she did only once each year, Lorraine Mercy was
sponsoring the event, a black-and-white ball, as a way to
raise awareness and funds for a breast cancer survivors'
group. Any event Lorraine associated her name with was
bound to be not only successful but classy as well.

We might be from the almost-seedy side of Alexandria,
but suddenly we were A-list all the way.

I was jazzed, all right, because along with Eve and the
senator, Jim and I were to be seated at Lorraine's table.

I wondered how Lorraine would feel if she knew that
someone she was set to break bread with was planning to use
the opportunity to find out if she knew about Sarah's affair

with Dougy. And if she did, was she mad enough about it to kill?

As we got ready for the big event in my apartment, I mentioned that fact to Eve. She was just slipping into her gown, a white silk sheath that clung to every curve and in the front was cut down nearly to her navel. She poked her head out of what there was of a neckline and made a face at me.

"No way," Eve said. "You can't possibly suspect Lorraine."

In logic-be-damned mode, I had bought a gown for the occasion. I was just unzipping the garment bag from the tailor's where I'd taken it to be hemmed when Eve made her comment I glanced over my shoulder. "What do you mean, we can't suspect Lorraine? Lorraine and Dylan, I thought they were our two best suspects?"

"That was before." Eve fluffed her hair and skimmed a hand over her hips. She looked like a million bucks, and she knew it. "Before I got to know Lorraine so well. I told you, Annie, when we were at Doug's horse farm for Thanksgiving, I helped Lorraine with some of the grunt work for the fund-raiser. You know, special invitations and all. And I've been at the hotel a couple times this week with her, too, helping with the final stage setup and the flowers and the centerpieces. Oooo!" Eve's eyes glowed. "Wait until you see those centerpieces. Black-and-white, of course. Like the rest of the party. And these huge candelabra and twinkly stuff and flowers and . . ." The mere idea of it was enough to make her sigh. I reminded myself to tell her not to do that too often or too quickly at the ball. Her dress was not designed for it.

"Lorraine is a loving and caring person," Eve said. "She dedicates herself to all kinds of good causes. And she runs that sleep clinic, too. Really, she runs it, she's not just a figurehead. She's terrific. You'll see. You'll talk to her tonight. If you want, you can help us backstage, too. I promised her I'd do a final walk-through with her right before the festivities start. You'll see that there's no way she could have had anything to do with Sarah's death."

"I hope you're right." I took my gown out of the bag. I have to admit, when I did, my hands shook. Aside from my wedding gown, I'd never owned anything as beautiful. Or as expensive.

Because I knew Eve would be wearing white, I decided it didn't make any sense to try to compete. I'd only come out looking like an also-ran and besides, white was bound to make my complexion look pasty. I'd chosen floor-length black chiffon with a belted waist and a sprinkling of rhinestones on the skirt and across the bodice. Of course, when it came to necklines, mine wasn't anywhere near as daring as Eve's. The neckline was high enough to be modest and just low enough to show off a little décolletage. As Eve had told me when we shopped for the gown, "If you've got it, honey, you might as well flaunt it."

I wasn't used to flaunting. Anything. I slipped into the gown and scooped my hair off my shoulders so Eve could zip the dress for me.

I stared at the woman who looked back at me from my mirror. Except for the fact that I recognized my bedroom furniture behind her, I wasn't sure I knew her at all. Her cheeks were bright with excitement, her eyes glowed, and the gown . . .

"Well? What do you think?"

Behind me, I saw Eve smile. "He's gonna love it!"

I whirled around. "You know that's not what I meant."

She giggled. "Of course it is! Annie, you look amazing. And he's gonna notice, too. I guarantee it." Her cell phone rang. She answered, talked for a moment, and flipped it shut. "My driver is here," she said. "I'm meeting Doug at the dinner." She pulled me into a quick hug, then reached in her purse. "I got Doc's collar from the jeweler just like I said I would." She handed it to me and hurried out of the bedroom. "I'll see you there. Don't be nervous."

"Nervous?" I slipped the collar over my hand. It really did look like a bracelet. I reminded myself that walking around wearing a few thousand dollars' worth of diamonds on my wrist was the least of my worries. "What do I have to be nervous about?"

Just as Eve opened the door and stepped out into the hallway, my phone rang. She paused to listen to my conversation. Just as I suspected, it was Jim calling to be buzzed into the lobby.

"You ready?" he asked.

I gulped down a little spurt of nervousness the likes of which I hadn't felt since that long-ago day when I took hold of my dad's arm and waited to walk down the aisle of Saint Charles church to where Peter was waiting for me at the altar.

I banished the thought. "And the restaurant—"

"Oh no!" On the other end of the phone, Jim chuckled. "We made a pact, remember. Tonight, no talk of business."

"But you checked, right? Lavoie—"

"He's there. He's in charge. He knows exactly what he's to do and what he's not to do. Now, will you let me into the damned building?"

I buzzed Jim up, and with a wink, Eve closed the door behind her. A couple minutes later, Jim knocked.

I took a deep breath and smoothed a hand over the skirt of my gown. I wondered if my hair looked OK or if I should race into the bedroom and pin it up and—

I told myself to get a grip and opened the door.

Jim grinned at me from out in the hallway. I looked over his dapper tux and blindingly white shirt. The only detour he'd taken from tradition was his bow tie. It was black-and-white tartan plaid.

"You look fabulous."

"That's funny." I laughed. "That's what I was going to say to you. You look like Prince Charming."

"Then that's just perfect." He bowed. "Because, Annie, to be sure, you look like a fairy-tale princess. Madam." He offered me his arm. "Your carriage awaits."

Every cell in my body tingling with excitement, I stepped into the hallway and closed the door behind me. I didn't even double-check to see if it was locked.

But still, it seemed some old habits die hard. Halfway to the elevator, I stopped cold. "You didn't bring your motorcycle, did you?" I asked Jim.

I got the answer I deserved. Jim laughed.

Sixteen

✖

I PROMISED MYSELF I WOULDN'T GET CAUGHT UP IN the Lorraine Mercy mystique, and the whole idea that since she was in charge of the event, we were sure to find ourselves in rarefied territory, high-society speaking.

I was, after all, not attending the black-and-white ball to mingle with the cream of D.C.'s upper stratosphere but to investigate. This was the perfect opportunity for me to interview Senator Mercy again and see if I could find out more about what Eve was reluctant to bring up with him: why he'd noticed the decline in the quality of Sarah's work when his chief of staff had not. Best of all, since Eve had been Lorraine's right-hand man (so to speak) these last few weeks and had actually helped with the seating arrangements, she'd put me right next to Dougy for dinner. That meant it was also a chance for me to get up close and personal with him. Did he turn a blind eye to Sarah's shoddy work because they were sleeping together? Was he the one financing Sarah's lavish lifestyle? And if he wasn't, did he know who was?

I thought about my plan as I waited for the valet to open the door of the silver Jag Jim had borrowed for the night from none other than Monsieur Lavoie. When I stepped out of the car and looked over to the main entrance Ritz-Carlton in Pentagon City, another of Arlington's many neighborhoods, I fingered Doc's collar (it was still there, it was still safe) and thought more about my plan.

What would Dougy say when he saw the diamond collar? Or would Douglas Mercy himself be the one who would react? Would I catch that fleeting look of recognition, the one that betrayed the fact that one of them had seen the collar before?

Jim came around from the other side of the car, and I automatically took his arm. Yes, it was a formal and old-fashioned sort thing thing to do, but when two guys in tuxedos hopped to it and opened the hotel doors for us, I knew it was right. Need more proof of just how fancy-schmantzy the whole thing was? How about the fact that the first person I saw once we were inside the lobby was the White House correspondent from MSNBC. The second person was a senator from Arizona. He was chatting with the secretary of labor, who stood near the reception dcsk along with a woman in the most incredible full-length sable coat I'd ever seen (especially since I was pretty sure it was the only full-length sable coat I'd ever seen) and a man whose name I didn't know but who I recognized from the newspaper as the ambassador from Great Britain.

Did I lose my cool composure or the smooth smile that would have fooled anyone who happened to glance my way into thinking I actually belonged with these people?

Did I forget my resolve to keep my mind on my investigation and nothing else?

No, I did not.

At least not until I stepped inside the ballroom.

"Oh my gosh!" I sucked in a breath of pure wonder and clutched Jim's arm a little tighter. "Can you believe it? It's like something out of a fairy tale!"

When I'd first heard about the black-and-white theme, I'd thought the ballroom was sure to look dull. I was wrong. All around us, people in the requisite attire chatted and sipped champagne and nibbled on the exquisite appetizers being passed by waiters in tuxes. The colors (or lack of them) swirled and blended—contrasts, sure, but so perfect together. The whole scheme was reflected in the centerpieces on every table that were every bit as spectacular as Eve had promised, and even in the gigantic flower arrangements set up on the stage in front of the closed curtain. The flowers were something exotic I couldn't name, their color as pale as snow. They seemed to float magically in black metal bowls as big as Volkswagen Beetles.

Though he was the least likely person I knew to be impressed with pomp and circumstance, even Jim wasn't immune. Our arms still entwined, he leaned nearer and whispered out of the corner of his mouth, "Something tells me we're not in Kansas anymore."

I was still grinning about it when I saw Eve. She might be standing with Douglas Mercy and chatting with the anchor from the local six o'clock news, but Eve was Eve, through and through. As soon as she caught sight of us, she grabbed the senator's hand and headed over.

Did I mention that Eve looked fabulous? I wasn't the only one who noticed. When a photographer cruised by, she and the senator posed and smiled. I have to admit, when she first announced that they were dating, I'd been a little unsure about the Eve/Mercy combo. But Eve was as happy as I'd ever seen her. Things were apparently going well, and damn, but she and the senator looked good together! I was thrilled for her.

Finished with the photo op, Eve pulled me into a brief hug before she reintroduced us to the senator and said, "I wondered if you two got lost."

"Not lost. Just . . ." I couldn't help it. The atmosphere was so magical, I had to look around again. I breathed out the single word: "Overwhelmed!"

Senator Mercy was enough of a politician not to point out how plebeian I was. Or maybe, like Eve insisted, he was just a nice guy. A waiter came by with a silver tray filled with

champagne flutes, and he signaled to the man, took a glass
for each of us, and passed them around. I reached for mine
with my left hand and held it out so long, there was no way
the senator could miss the bracelet.

He didn't miss a beat. "If there's one thing my daughter-
in-law, Lorraine, knows how to do," the senator said, "it's im-
press a crowd. As always, she's thought of everything.
Enough variety in the appetizers to appeal to the carnivores
and the vegetarians, flowers that are beautiful but not heavily
scented so as not to offend those who are easily put off by
odors, even the color scheme." He laughed. "In spite of what
my colleagues on the other side of the aisle say, my head is
not so swollen that I think Lorraine did it just for me, but it
has worked out perfectly. For once, I don't have to worry
about complimenting a constituent on her aquamarine gown
only to find out later that I got the color all wrong." Still
smiling, he raised his glass, and we all did, too, in tribute to
Lorraine's party-planning genius.

"Of course, you both know that Lorraine has had a lot of
help these last weeks." Senator Mercy turned to Eve and
smiled. They were still holding hands, and he tugged her
closer. He raised his glass again. This time, to Eve. "She
couldn't have done it without you, honey."

Eve blushed. "Lorraine's a dream to work with. And we've
had such fun."

"Exactly what she's been saying about you! She said your
help today was invaluable."

Eve blushed. "It was nothing," she said. "We've just been
putting the finishing touches on the stage. You know, the
vice president will be here early to speak, before dinner. We
had to make sure everything was perfect before everyone
arrived."

"Perfect it is!" More gushing would have sounded insincere, so I didn't go on. "If you had anything to do with those
flowers . . ." I looked over at the huge arrangements again.
"They're spectacular."

"Not only did she have something to do with them, she

helped Lorraine decide where they should be placed and . . ." As if he were sharing a secret, the senator leaned nearer. "She's going to walk the speakers out onto the stage."

"Like the Academy Awards!" Eve sparkled like the bubbles in our champagne glasses. "Isn't it fabulous? Lorraine just asked a few minutes ago. Seems the model they'd hired to do it didn't show and—"

"And no model could be lovelier or more perfect for the job." The senator gave her a peck on the cheek, and Eve giggled like a teenager. "You're going to outshine the vice president, that's for sure, honey. But maybe . . ." The senator chuckled. "Maybe not the next vice president, huh?"

Fortunately, the discussion didn't have a chance to melt into politics. A youngish man with a mustache who I remembered seeing at Sarah's funeral luncheon came up and whispered in the senator's ear. "You'll have to excuse me." Douglas Mercy stepped back. "The Dalai Lama wants a word." He winked at me and hung on to Eve. "My money's on the fact that he doesn't want to talk to me as much as he wants to meet my dinner date."

They started to cross the room, but at the last second, Eve pulled away from the senator and hurried back over to where Jim and I stood.

With a tip of her head, she indicated the table nearest the stage. From the engraved seating card we'd been handed when we walked in, I knew that's where we'd be sitting. Eve bent her head closer. It should have been my first clue that something wasn't on the up-and-up. Second clue? She whispered. "Check on Doc for me, will you? He's—"

"Here?" The word exploded out of me. My heart sprang into my throat, and my blood ran cold. "Eve, you can't be serious. You didn't—"

"My dog walker is sick, and I couldn't leave him home alone all night. I wouldn't have had any fun thinking of him all by his lonesome. Plus, I wanted him to see how pretty everything was. I mean, I've been telling him about it for days, you know? The least I could do was show him." She pouted. "I tucked him right underneath your chair at your table. And don't worry, I got a new bag for him. It's big and roomy, and there's no way he's going to jump out. He loves snuggling in there—I bought him a new blanket and a chew toy to keep him busy, too. Besides, he'll only be here for a couple minutes. Micah, Doug's driver, he's going to take him. He had to pop into the kitchen first. Lorraine arranged for a dinner for him to take home. And, Annie, I remembered what you said. Both you and Jim." She looked back and forth between us, automatically making us part of the conspiracy.

"You two are the ones who told me that dogs don't belong in kitchens, aren't you?"

We were indeed.

Before either Jim or I could remind her dogs didn't belong in ballrooms, either, Eve turned away.

"Oh!" The senator was waiting twenty feet away, and she waved to him in a way that told him she'd be right there. She hurried back to my side. "There's another thing, Annie. About Lorraine." Eve looked all around to make sure no one was listening. "No way did she do it. You know. You-know-what to you-know-who." She mouthed the name, "Sarah."

I was relieved. If there was no real reason for me to investigate, I could relax and enjoy the party.

Except . . .

I gave Eve a probing look. "And you know this how?" I asked her.

She held up one finger to tell the senator she'd be right there. "She's too nice," she said and hurried away.

"The soul of logic, as always," Jim commented wryly. He glanced uncertainly toward our table. "Shall we—"

I had already made up my mind. I whirled toward the door. "I'm out of here."

"You are not." Jim held me firmly in place. "Just because she brought the dog—"

"Who even as we speak could be out of that bag and munching on someone's thousand-dollar wingtips."

"Then we really owe it to all these fine people to check on him, don't we?"

I surrendered with a sigh. "Now who's the soul of logic?"

He beamed a smile. "I'm learning from the best."

"Not Eve."

"Not Eve. You," he said, and before I had a chance to even realize he was schmoozing me to get his way and that I was letting myself get schmoozed because Jim's compliments always made me feel like I was on top of the world, he had me by the hand and was leading me toward our table.

Dougy was already there. So was the big new bag Eve had told me about. In keeping with the theme of the party, it was a black and white leather tote studded with rhinestones, plenty big enough for Doc, his blanket, and his new chew toy. As promised, the bag was on the floor beneath my chair. At the same time I shook the senator's son's hand, I nudged the bag with my foot. The tiny yap that came from inside soothed my worries.

"So . . ." With a look at Jim that told him to not let the bag out of his sight, I lowered myself onto the seat next to Dougy's and, manners be damned, I propped one elbow on the table to make sure that my wrist—and the diamond bracelet on it—was easy to see. "How are you enjoying the event, Mr. Mercy?"

As I've mentioned, our table was near the stage, and the flash of the spotlights that were trained on the closest humongous flower arrangement glittered off the diamonds like a million twinkling stars. It was a wonder Dougy wasn't blinded.

But just like with his father, if I expected some *aha* moment of recognition when he saw the bracelet, I didn't get it. Squinting a little, Dougy adjusted his position, the better to keep his corneas from being fried. "My wife is a whiz when it comes to things like this. Imagine spearheading all this and running a successful clinic, too. She's really something."

"She had help, of course."

Dougy thought I was somehow belittling Lorraine's accomplishments. His shoulders went rigid, and he cocked his head. "Of course she had help. No one can pull off something like this alone. That would be impossible."

"Not what I meant." It wasn't, and I figured I'd better get back on track before I offended Dougy and he clammed up. "I know she's the genius behind it all, and I'll tell you what, I'm blown away. Eve's been helping, you know. And every day, she's got another story about Lorraine and her incredible ideas, and how she knows exactly who to go to to get things done. I was just thinking that a thing like this takes a team of workers and months of planning."

Dougy softened a bit. He nodded. "Sometimes years."

"And I was just wondering, you know, if Sarah ever helped."

This time, when Dougy narrowed his eyes, it wasn't because of the glitter off the diamonds. I had the feeling he was trying to read my mind. "Why would you ask that?"

I shrugged. Maybe the atmosphere went to my head. Maybe it made me think I was better than I was. A better detective. Maybe that's what made me think I could lay my cards on the table. "No reason, really. But I know you and Sarah were going on a cruise together and—"

Dougy pushed his chair back from the table and got to his feet. "It was nice to see you again, Miss Capshaw," he said, and before I could scramble for the words to make him sit back down again, he was gone.

"So much for that plan," I told Jim.

"At least Doc's still here." He pulled the bag between us, peeked inside just to be sure, and gave the dog a quick pat on the head. "And once dinner is over . . ." He looked across the room to where an orchestra was setting up and tuning their instruments. "You'll dance with me?"

I felt heat color my cheeks. Gliding across the floor in Jim's arms sounded like heaven on earth. Just imagining it made me fizzy all over.

Until I reminded myself that I wasn't as much a glider as I was a stomper of feet.

"Oh, I don't know." I twisted Doc's collar on my wrist. "I'm not a very good dancer."

"But you'll dance with me anyway."

It was no longer a question. "It's so easy to do something wrong when you're dancing," I said, wondering why Jim didn't understand this. "I'll trip. I'll fall. I'll stomp. I'll look ridiculous."

"And you'll dance with me."

"I would, but—" My words washed back at me, and for the first time, I actually listened to what I was saying. They sounded a whole lot like every excuse Peter had ever used. Not for just not wanting to get out on the dance floor, but for not buying a house back when prices weren't sky high, and for not starting a family, and for never thinking that I had talents for being anything but a bank teller.

I reminded myself that I was a new woman. A woman who no longer lived with the flabby excuses of the past.

I pulled in a breath for courage. "I'd love to dance with you," I said. It was true. And terrifying. "Maybe in some dark corner where nobody can see us?"

"Aye, if that's what it takes." Jim laughed. He skimmed his hand up my arm. In the reflected light of the stage spots, his hazel eyes were flecked with green. His hair, a rich mahogany color, was touched with auburn. Even if I tried, I couldn't have resisted his invitation. And yes, I'll admit it: I didn't even try. Especially when he added, "And when we're done dancing—"

Well, I actually don't know what he was going to add. Because before he had a chance to finish, I heard Lorraine Mercy call to me from over near the stage.

It was the first time I'd seen her that evening, and I have to say, her outfit went right along with her image. She looked like a queen (and a little like a mermaid) in an off-the-shoulder black gown that hugged her hips and thighs and flared at the ankles. Ever practical, I wondered how she could move so quickly in a dress that tight.

"Oh, Annie!" In a half waddle, half spring, Lorraine hurried over to where we sat. "I'm so glad I found you. Eve needs your help. Come on."

She tugged me out of my chair. Before I could ask what had happened and where we were headed, she hurried over to the exit doors on the far side of the ballroom. If I had any hope of catching up, I couldn't afford to dawdle. I left Jim with a quick, "I'll be right back" and a reminder to keep an eye on Doc. Then I went after Lorraine.

Apparently, a lifetime of privilege and a trust fund big enough to fill the Capitol Rotunda had a way of instilling talents common mortals never even dream of. Even in stilettoes, Lorraine moved like the wind. I scampered to keep up, and big points for me, I only tripped a time or two.

"What happened?" I asked as I closed in on her. I was breathless from the effort. "Where's Eve and—"

Lorraine didn't take the time to answer. She punched through the doors and sped down a long hallway on the other side. This was the utilitarian part of the hotel. No fancy carpeting here, no paneled walls or oil paintings. The heels of my shoes slid against the linoleum. When Lorraine got to another set of doors, she waited for me to catch up.

"Where is Eve?" I asked again. The sling back on my left shoe cut into my heel, and I was limping. I hoped my panty hose hadn't run. "And why—"

"Here." Lorraine pushed open the door, and we stepped inside. It only took a moment for me to realize that we were backstage. "I tried to help her out, but she insists you're the only one who can do it. We don't have much time. The vice president is scheduled to arrive any minute. You're going to have to take care of this, Annie."

"OK. I will. I just need to know—"

There was a maze of pulleys and curtains and backdrops ahead of us. Lorraine maneuvered through it all while I brought up the rear. By now, I pictured every calamity imaginable, and as each presented itself inside my mind, my panic climbed and my heartbeat increased.

Eve had fallen and broken a leg. Eve and the senator had quarreled, and she was inconsolable. Eve had an uncharacteristic case of stage fright. She'd gotten kidnapped. She was—

"Stuck." The moment I laid eyes on her, Eve shrugged and explained. She was standing just behind the curtain in the shadow of a huge flower arrangement that looked just like the ones in front of the curtain. From the other side of the curtain, I heard the hum of the party.

Eve's cheeks flamed with embarrassment. She put one hand on the skirt of her gown and gave it a delicate tug. "There must be a nail or something sticking out of the stage. I can't move."

"And I'm relieved! Thank goodness that's all it is. You scared me to death." I turned toward Lorraine just so she'd know, but she was already gone.

Eve shifted from foot to foot. "The Dalai Lama really did want to talk to Doug," she explained. When she made a move to give the gown another tug, I waved her off and took over. I knelt at her side and peered down at the place where a hem stitch had caught against an exposed nail, wondering how I could unstick it without tearing the gossamer fabric.

"So I figured I'd see if Lorraine needed any help, and she did. But honestly, Annie . . ." Eve squirmed to see me better. "I've been over this stage a dozen times this evening. Why did this have to happen now? It's almost time for the vice president to get here. It's nearly time for the curtain to go up. I hate to be responsible for delaying everything. You know how people are, they'll find out, and they'll know it was me, and somehow, Doug will get blamed. Politicians have to be so careful. About everything." She wrung her hands. "What if I'm responsible for him not getting the vice presidential nomination?"

"That's not going to happen," I told her. I made sure to keep my voice level and my hands where she couldn't see that they were shaking. "I'll have you unstuck in a second. I've got my little traveling sewing kit in my purse, so if you need any fixing—"

"I don't have time for fixing!" Eve's eyes filled with tears. "I don't want to be responsible for Lorraine's fund-raiser being a flop."

"You're not. You won't be. Don't worry." Like a burglar preparing to crack a safe, I scraped my thumbs over the tips of my fingers and got down, stomach to stage, for a closer look at the tangle of thread. "Just hold still," I warned Eve. "You don't want to make it any worse. And don't worry about time. Nobody's going to try to rush us. Nothing can get started while we're still here."

It came down to that whole soul of logic thing again. All that sounded perfectly logical, didn't it?

That doesn't explain why at that very moment, the curtain started to rise.

Or that as it did, we heard a desperate yapping coming from one of the tables very close by.

"Oh no!" Though I tried to stop her, I couldn't move fast enough. Eve spun around to see what Doc was up to. Her dress ripped up the side.

I chanced a look out at the ballroom and saw about a thousand people who couldn't decide which was the biggest show: the two women looking like fools up on the stage, or the little dog that bounded out of Eve's purse, yapping its head off.

They didn't have long to consider it.

Before I even had the time to be mortified, I heard a bang that reverberated through the room like thunder and a thousand collective gasps.

Right before one of those giant flower arrangements toppled off its perch. The last thing I saw was the big-as-a-Volkswagen metal bowl and a tumble of white flowers. Just as it all came right down on us.

Seventeen

⊠

THERE WERE TWO JIMS STARING DOWN AT ME.

OK, I'll go out on a limb here and say this should have struck me as odd. Or at least it should have been my first clue that something was very, very wrong. But honest, at the time, it never occurred to me to question it.

I liked Jim. Twice as much as I liked any other guy. Blame it on a head filled with what felt like old and sticky cotton candy and a noise in my ears as loud as the roar of a jet engine. To my way of thinking, it made perfect sense that there would be two of them.

Two Jims equals twice as nice. And Jim—both of them— looked delectable, in spite of the fact that one sleeve of his (their?) tux jacket was ripped, and there were white sprinkles in his hair and a streak of dirt across his cheek that made it look as if he'd forgotten to shave one side of his face.

This was all very un-Jim, but I didn't wonder about any of it. Maybe I would have tried if my head wasn't pounding, and my stomach wasn't flipping and flopping, and my left arm didn't hurt like hell. When I tried to move, the room spun and tipped like one of those masochistic Tilt-A-Whirl rides at the amusement parks. The kind that always make me sick.

Better to concentrate on Jim and on the fact that he was there with me—wherever *there* was. Just seeing him made me smile.

Neither one of the Jims smiled back. They glanced up and over to my right. Anxious to see where I was and what was going on, I turned my head that way. The room spun a little more.

There was a handsome African American man with salt-and-pepper hair and a natty goatee standing at my shoulder. In fact, there were two of them. They were twins.

"Good to see you awake," they said. They spoke with one voice. OK, it took a while, but I was beginning to get the picture. Or should I say, both the pictures? Once I realized I was seeing double and accepted the fact as an aberration of my eyes, not my mind, it was a little easier to concentrate. My stomach settled a bit, too.

"I'm Dr. Lawrence Anderson," the man said at the same time I noticed that he was wearing a white lab coat. He had a stethoscope around his neck. "You're in the ER at Virginia Hospital Center. Can you tell me your name?"

No-brainer. At least it should have been. But when I tried to nod, a shower of stars burst behind my eyes. "Annie," I said. My voice was as dry as dust. "Annie Capshaw."

I scraped my tongue over my lips. Dr. Anderson must have known how parched they were. He had a little sponge on a stick and he dipped it in water and brushed it against my lips.

"Can you tell me what day it is, Annie?" he asked.

"The day of the party." Carefully, I turned my head to look at Jim for confirmation. "Isn't it?"

He checked his watch. "Aye, but just barely. It's nearly midnight."

"No." This wasn't possible, and I thought it only right to point out Jim's error. "That would mean I've been knocked

out for—" Though numbers were my forte, the mental calculations didn't compute.

"It's been a couple hours. We were worried." Dr. Anderson supplied the information. "Some of us more than others." He did not make this sound like a bad thing. When a
smile tickled the corners of his mouth, I knew who he was
talking about.

I couldn't move my left arm. Lifting my head enough to
peer down at it, I saw the fuzzy outline of a cast. So much for
escaping unscathed. Jim put his hand over my good one.
"Sorry we didn't get to dance," I said. "Or maybe we did? I
didn't trip on the dance floor and end up flat on my face, did
I? Is that how I ended up here?"

"You don't remember?" The question came from the
doctor.

"I remember the party, but I'm in the hospital, and my
arm is broken because a dog was barking."

"Yeah, that's pretty much how it happened." Jim chuckled and smoothed a hand over my forehead. "Is that all you
remember?"

"No, I remember . . ." I squeezed my eyes shut. No easy
thing, since the left side of my face was swollen. "Eve!" I
would have bolted upright and jumped out of bed, but with
Jim on one side and Dr. Anderson on the other, I didn't have
a chance. In desperation, I looked at Jim. "Where is she? Is
she OK? What happened?"

"Exactly what we were hoping you could tell us."

It was the first time I realized there was someone else in
the cubicle with us. I looked toward the foot of my bed. It's
a good thing I'd already figured out the double-vision part of
the equation. I would not have liked to think that there were
two Tyler Coopers in this world.

When he saw me looking his way, Tyler pushed off from
the wall and stepped closer to the bed. "Do you remember
anything about what happened onstage?" he asked. "Anything at all?"

"I'm not even going to try." Because I knew Tyler wouldn't understand, I said this to Jim. "Not until you tell me about Eve. Is she—"

"She's fine." Jim smile was soft. "Better than you, as a matter of fact. Seems when you saw that flower arrangement headed at you, you had the presence of mind to push her out of the way. Unfortunately, you weren't so fast on your feet yourself. Your high heels tripped you up, and the flower container toppled right over and caught you on the left side of your body. A couple more inches . . ." Jim looked away and cleared his throat. "A couple more inches in the other direction, and you would have been crushed."

"Now that you've contaminated her memories . . ." Tyler sighed with exasperation. "How about you go check on Miss DeCateur." He made it sound like a suggestion, but I knew Tyler well enough to know he wouldn't take no for an answer. He looked from Jim to the doorway, his message anything but subtle. Typical Tyler. But maybe my nearly mushed brain was playing tricks on me, because the next second, I swore that what was almost a smile crossed his face.

"You can have Annie all to yourself," he told Jim. "In just a couple minutes. I'd like to get a few words in with her before the Secret Service shows up."

Another piece of my memory clunked into place. I looked toward Tyler. "The vice president. He's—"

"He was just getting out of his limo in front of the hotel when the flower arrangement came tumbling down, so yeah, he's fine, too. Everybody's fine. And as strange as it seems, it's all because of that damned dog some moron brought to the party."

Tyler didn't have a warm and fuzzy bone in his body. No way could he understand Eve's affection for Doc, so no way was I even going to try to explain.

"It was the dog's yapping," Tyler said. "That's what made you and Eve look to see what was going on. I guess that means that dog saved your lives."

"And Doc—"

Jim kissed me on the forehead. At this close range, I saw that what I'd mistaken for snow in his hair were bits and pieces of blasted flower petals. "Doc is back in his tote bag where he belongs. He's gone home with the senator's driver. This time, for certain."

"And nobody else—"

Another quick kiss, and Jim backed away. "Nobody else was hurt. Just you. And Eve, but just a bit. It seems a bit suspicious, don't you think?"

"I'll be the one to decide that." As soon as Jim was gone, Tyler took his place. The look he aimed at Dr. Anderson told him it was time for him to head out, too.

"A minute," the doctor told Tyler. "I just want this young lady to know . . ." He glanced toward the doorway where Jim had just disappeared. "You're bound to hear it from somebody else, but I thought you should know. The story I got from everybody who was there is that your young fellow was the one who rescued you from under that flower arrangement. Worked like the dickens to make sure you were OK. It wasn't easy. Or without danger. See, when that arrangement came down, the curtain did, too. And all the heavy pulleys and weights that make it work. Risked his own neck to save yours." He gave me a wink. "Thought you might rest better knowing that."

I thanked him with a smile and watched him leave. I would have liked to have some time to think about what Dr. Anderson had told me, but of course, Tyler was still there. And like I said, Tyler didn't have a warm and fuzzy bone in his body.

He flipped open his notebook and took out a pen.

"What happened?" he asked.

When I shrugged, every muscle in my body screamed in protest. "The flowers fell."

"We know that. The question is why."

"Gravity?"

Tyler didn't get the joke. Or maybe he did, and he just

wasn't in the mood to laugh. Then again, he hadn't nearly been killed by a bouquet of flowers as big as the Jefferson Memorial. Maybe he didn't understand how living through something like that made a person feel grateful and just a little slaphappy.

I apologized with a quick smile that I swear Tyler didn't even notice. "Eve was stuck," I said. "Her gown got caught on a nail, and I went onstage to help her. The next thing I knew, the curtain went up, and the flowers came down."

"Just like that?"

"Just like that."

"You didn't see anyone near the flowers when you got to the stage?"

I knew better than to shake my head. It hurt too much. "Lorraine Mercy was with me. She's the one who told me Eve needed my help. But then . . . then she was gone. I'm sure she had other things to do. You know, before the vice president arrived. But I never saw her anywhere near the flowers."

"And you have no idea why anyone would want to hurt either you or Miss DeCateur?"

I was starting to see where Tyler was headed with his questioning, and I didn't like it one bit. "You don't think it was an accident."

"I know it wasn't an accident. You want to tell me what you're up to?"

"You want to tell me how you know it wasn't an accident?"

He gave in with a brittle smile. "The flower arrangement was rigged. As soon as the curtain went up . . ." Tyler demonstrated, lifting one hand into the air. "The flowers came down." He brought his other hand down against the bedside table with a slap. "Of course, the curtain wasn't supposed to go up until the vice president walked out. That's what's got everyone feeling a little antsy about this whole thing. Fortunately, it was just you and Eve . . ." He twitched his shoulders. Enough said.

"Some Secret Service agents are going to come and talk

to you," Tyler told me. "They think the sabotage was aimed at the vice president, and for all I know, they're right. But just so you know, I did a little digging. I'd heard about the drive-by in Alexandria, of course, but being the reasonable person I am, I never thought you or Eve were involved. But after what happened tonight, I called a buddy of mine over on the Alexandria force and found out you two just happened to be standing outside the restaurant when the shooter did his thing. I'm putting two and two together here, Annie. I know you understand, because I know that's how your brain works, too. If there's anything you want to share with me . . ."

His brows raised, Tyler waited

"The drive-by, it was random. It had to be." Was I trying to convince Tyler or myself? "And the flowers . . ." My mind flashed back to the moment when I saw the huge black bowl headed straight for me. "Eve doesn't think Lorraine Mercy can be involved, because she's too nice. Lorraine, not Eve."

"No kidding."

"Eve's nice, too." I felt duty-bound to remind Tyler of this. "But that's not what I'm talking about. The only other person with something to hide is Dylan Monroe . . . but well, he wasn't even at the party, was he?"

Of course, none of this made sense to Tyler. Not much of it made sense to me, either, but I blamed it on the thwack on the head.

"Dylan Monroe, the news anchor?" he asked. "What does he have to do with Lorraine Mercy?"

"Nothing."

"And so . . ." Impatient, Tyler paced back to his place near the wall. I knew what the motion meant. He would have been happy if I could have explained more.

Hey, so would I.

Before I could work through it, though, there was a commotion outside the cubicle. A second later, a cotton hospital blanket around her shoulders, Eve rushed in.

"You're OK!" Tears slipped down her cheeks. Her hair

was a mess, and she'd bitten off all her lipstick. "Oh, Annie!" She threw herself at me.

Which wasn't the wisest thing to do, considering that every little movement of my hospital bed made my stomach lurch.

"I was so worried. I thought you were—" Eve hugged me harder. "You saved my life, you know. If you hadn't pushed me out of the way—"

"The way I heard it, Doc saved both our lives." I knew that mentioning the dog would take her mind off what had happened and, hopefully, keep her from doing any more damage to my already sore muscles. "He's OK, isn't he?"

Eve sniffled. "He's fine. He's home. Doug's driver took him." Smiling, she looked over her shoulder, and I saw that the senator was here, too. She held out her hand to him, and when he stepped into the cubicle and took it, she turned back to me. "The media is already calling Doc a hero. Imagine that! His picture is going to be on the front page of tomorrow's *Washington Post*. They're calling him the dog that saved the vice president."

"I should have known you had something to do with the dog being there."

Needless to point out, this comment came from Tyler. Eve had been so worried about me, she hadn't even noticed he was there. Now she turned to him, and her cheeks, already chalky, got a little paler.

"Why, if it isn't Lieutenant Cooper." Eve raised her chin. "Fancy finding you here. Like a vulture circling the scene of an accident."

Tyler tipped his head. "Just doing my job, ma'm."

Eve's smile was sleek. "I don't believe you've met Senator Douglas Mercy."

"I don't believe I have." Tyler didn't offer his hand. Which was just as well, since Eve was hanging on to the senator's so tight, there was no way he could have shaken it. Tyler looked my way. "I may have more questions. Later?"

And before I could tell him I had a feeling I wasn't going anywhere anytime soon, Tyler walked out.

"Well!" Eve rolled her eyes. I knew that in front of the senator, it was the only comment she was going to make. "It's so good to see you, Annie. We were so worried. Weren't we, Doug?"

"So are the fellows from the Secret Service." The senator looked toward the doorway of the cubicle, and I saw that there were two men in dark suits waiting out there to talk to me. A senator apparently trumped a civil servant, but I knew they weren't going to wait long. "Eve and I are going to get some coffee," he said. "We'll be back."

Eve bent to kiss my cheek. "And then we'll talk," she whispered.

I didn't know what about. Which was pretty much what I told Mike and Alex, the two Secret Service agents who questioned me about the accident. Were the tumbling flowers aimed at the vice president, and had Eve and I just gotten in the way?

Honestly, I couldn't say, and I told them so.

"But if the flowers were meant for him . . ." Thinking out loud, I turned the thought over in my head. "Well, you must have realized it, too. That's an awful lot of trouble to go through. I mean, rigging the flower arrangement and such. But then the flowers came down before the vice president was even in the hotel. That seems like really bad timing to me."

It also seemed to indicate that maybe the vice president wasn't the intended target.

This, I did not mention to Mike and Alex. It wasn't their job to worry about Eve and me, and I needed to think about this a whole lot more before I pointed fingers. Besides, I still didn't know who I was pointing fingers at.

I was still mulling it all over when the agents left, and a nurse came in to check my vital signs and tell me that there was a room ready for me. I was going to be transferred upstairs for an overnight stay and observation. By then, Eve was back. This time, without the senator.

"I gave Doug the slip." She winked like it was some big accomplishment. For all I knew, it was. "Told him we had girlie things to talk about. We do, don't we? I mean, about our investigation, right?"

I yawned. "We still don't know squat. Except that we were in the wrong place at the wrong time."

"But Dylan—"

"Wasn't even there."

"But he could have been. Earlier. He could have—"

"So could a thousand other people. No." Fatigue washed over me like a wave, and I yawned. "It's no use, Eve. You say Lorraine didn't have anything to do with Sarah's murder."

"No way." She nodded. "I tried to bring it up in conversation, you know, about how some men cheat on their wives and how it ruins relationships. Lorraine never batted an eyelash. I don't think she knows. And besides, I told you, she's too nice."

"And we didn't get any reaction to the bracelet—"

In horror, I looked at my wrist. It was bare.

Eve patted my arm. "Not to worry. I've got the collar. I sent it home with Doc."

I breathed a sigh of relief. "Nobody reacted to the bracelet," I said. "Not Dougy and not—"

"Of course Doug didn't." Eve was indignant. "I told you, he didn't have anything to do with Sarah other than being her boss. No way did he buy her that collar."

I was too tired to argue. "So we know it wasn't Dougy. We know it wasn't Lorraine. We know it wasn't the senator."

"That leaves Dylan Monroe." Eve was insistent.

"Maybe."

"Maybe?" She made a face. "He's the only suspect we have left."

"Or not."

At the sound of Jim's voice, we both looked toward the doorway. "I've just been in the waiting area," he said, walking into the cubicle. "And the TV was on. The reports are all over the news. I don't think you'll be proving anything about Dylan Monroe. He was found earlier tonight, you see. Shot dead and dumped in the Potomac. And that's not all."

As if that wasn't enough?

I braced myself for the rest of Jim's news.

"According to the report I just saw, there were notes and things found in his apartment. And more on his computer at work. It seems that Dylan was conducting an investigation of his own into Sarah's death. I don't know about you two . . ." Jim looked from Eve to me. "But my guess is that he found something. Something somebody doesn't want anyone else to know."

As hard as I tried, I couldn't reason my way through any of this. Facts swam through my head. Dylan was looking into Sarah's murder? It didn't explain why he'd threatened her, but it sure went a long way toward helping me figure out why he'd been so uncooperative. Dylan had his own agenda and his own investigation to conduct. No wonder he was less than helpful.

And now he was dead.

My head pounded like a high school marching band drum line.

"It doesn't make sense," I groaned. "None of it makes sense."

"And none of it has to. At least not tonight." Jim stepped between Eve and the bed. "You're staying here. You'll rest, and in the morning, your head will be clearer. Until then, don't worry about it. Nobody else is going to bother you."

As if.

No sooner were the words out of Jim's mouth than I saw Tyler and the senator jockeying for position outside the cubicle. The senator got through the doorway first, and Tyler didn't look happy about it.

The senator took Eve's hand. "Did you tell her?"

Eve's cheeks turned a pretty shade of pink. "I was going to wait until morning. You know, when Annie's feeling better."

"Great. Wait until Annie's feeling better." Tyler moved forward. "Until then, if you'd all just excuse yourselves, I've got a couple more questions to ask her."

I sighed. "And I'm so tired, I can't keep my eyes open."

"And we really should tell her now," the senator said. "If the news gets out . . ."

Tyler snorted. "If this guy's bothering you . . ." he told Eve.

"This guy . . ." Douglas Mercy's eyes snapped. "Is a United States senator, detective, and I think the least you can do is control your jealousy."

"Jealousy? You think that's what it is?" Tyler snickered. "I'm here to tell you, Senator, I was just trying to do you a favor. This woman is—"

"What?" The senator stepped up, toe-to-toe with Tyler. He raised his chin, and his hands curled into fists.

Even muzzy-headed, I knew trouble was a-comin'. Fortunately, so did Jim, and he hadn't been bonked on the bean. He stepped between Tyler and the senator.

"It's been a long night," Jim said. "I think you'll both agree."

"Which is why Eve needs to get out of here." Tyler never took his eyes off the senator. "My car is right outside the door," he said, and we all knew he wasn't talking to Douglas Mercy. "You go on ahead; I'll get you home."

"You'll do no such thing." The senator's eyes flashed lightning. He leaned around Jim, the better to aim a laser look at Tyler. "A woman returns home with the man who was her escort for the evening. I don't know about where you come from, but in the more refined segments of society, that's how it's done."

"Refined, huh?" Tyler put a hand on Jim's arm to push him out of the way. "Well, if that's what you call it—"

"Boys! Boys!" Eve stepped forward. "I think we need to settle this once and for all. Tyler . . ." She looked his way. "You're just gonna have to face facts, sugar. You don't have any claim on me. Not anymore."

Tyler's mouth thinned. "And this guy—"

"This guy is who I'm going home with tonight." Eve wound her arm through the senator's. "And not only that, but we have an announcement. Tyler, Jim, Annie . . ." She looked at all of us and grinned. "Doug and I are engaged!"

Eighteen

✖

NEAR-DEATH EXPERIENCES, ENGAGEMENTS, AN ALMOST-fistfight between Senator Mercy and Tyler . . . It was too much excitement for one night, and I was really feeling it. By the time I was taken up to a private room on another floor, it was past two, and I was completely wiped out. I knew Jim must have been tired, too, so after the nurses had me settled, I fully expected him to say good night.

Which is why I was surprised when he plunked down in the chair next to my bed.

"Staying for the night," he said.

I attempted one shake of my head, then decided it wasn't the best idea. "Don't have to," I said on the end of a yawn. "Go home. Sleep. I'll be fine."

"Yes, you will be." He sounded more certain of it than I felt. "And I'm going to make sure of it." He snapped off the light. "I'll be as quiet as a mouse, so I won't be any bother, and if you need anything, I'll be right here beside you."

"Won't need . . . anything." My words wandered along with my thoughts, and sleep wrapped me like a wooly blanket. "Won't . . . bother you. Just . . . sleep."

I couldn't see much in the dark, but I heard him slide forward in his chair. He kissed my cheek. "Good night, Annie," he said. "I'll see you in the morning."

When I drifted off, I was smiling, but not for long. A weird dream engulfed me.

In it, I was walking down a long church aisle in a pink matron-of-honor gown that was too tight and cut way too low for my curvy figure. Doc was barking louder than the organ music playing in the background. People in the pews were throwing flowers at me, and one of them clunked me on the head.

It made a sound loud enough to jerk me awake.

I stared into the dark. Had I been asleep for minutes? Or hours? I knew I wasn't in my own bed, and for a few scary seconds, I wasn't sure where I was or what I was doing there.

Until I heard Jim's gentle, even breaths from the chair in the corner.

Glancing that way, I breathed a sigh of relief, and automatically, I found myself smiling again. In the dim square of light that seeped into the room from the window, I saw that Jim's tartan bow tie was loose and hanging around his neck. His tuxedo shirt was unbuttoned at the throat. His head was thrown back against the high back of the chair, and there was a lock of hair hanging over his forehead. A wave of peace washed over me. I closed my eyes again.

Until I heard a sound.

The same sound that the dream flower made when it bonked me on the head.

Since I wasn't asleep and no longer dreaming—at least, I didn't think I was—this didn't track quite right. Even in my mixed-up brain. Carefully, I lifted my head off the pillow so I could look around. I was just in time to see a woman step into the room and close the door behind her.

"I'm awake," I whispered. "You don't have to worry about disturbing me if you need to take my blood pressure or something."

Except for the dim glow of her white lab coat and a thatch

of dark hair, I couldn't see much of the nurse. She didn't speak a word.

She didn't check my blood pressure, either.

Or my temperature.

Or feel for my pulse.

Instead, I saw a glint of light against the syringe she held in one hand. She moved toward the IV line attached to a bag of fluids that hung above my bed.

"This will teach you to mind your own business," the nurse growled. While I was still wondering what was going on, she plucked up the IV line with one hand and put the needle of the syringe against it.

I still wasn't sure if I was dreaming or not, but I wasn't going to take any chances.

My head might be busted, but my lungs were working fine, and just to prove it, I let out a scream loud enough to wake the dead.

Fortunately, it also woke Jim. More fortunately, he's one of those morning types who wakes bright-eyed, bushy-tailed, and ready to take on the world.

Or in this case, the mystery nurse.

The second Jim's eyes flew open; he knew something was wrong, and he wasn't about to take any chances as to what it was. He leapt out of his chair and tackled the nurse.

We weren't exactly subtle, what with me screaming and the commotion Jim and the nurse made as they wrestled around the room knocking into the bed and the dresser across from it. A second later I heard footsteps racing down the hallway. The door flew open; the overhead lights went on. When they did, I saw that Jim had control of the situation.

And of none other than Lorraine Mercy.

"Dr. Mercy!" The floor nurse who'd turned on the lights looked from Dougy's wife to the syringe she still had in her hand. "What on earth are you doing here at this time of night? And what . . . ?" Don't ask me how the woman had the presence of mind, but before Lorraine could move, she snatched the syringe out of her hand and held it up for a better look. "Air?" The nurse looked past the syringe to me. "You weren't—"

"She sure was." Jim was standing behind Lorraine with his arms wrapped good and tight around her. I was glad. When she looked my way, her eyes flashed with hatred. I gulped down a wave of nausea. "I saw her. She was going to—"

"You little bitch!" Lorraine squirmed and kicked. She elbowed Jim in the ribs. His cheeks darkened, and he puffed out an *oof* of surprise, but no way was he going to let her get anywhere near me. His determination only made her more angry. "You were going to ruin everything," she spat. "You were going to tell everyone about Dougy and Sarah. Once word got out and the media got wind of it . . ." She screeched her frustration. "You were going to ruin my chance of ever being First Lady!"

I sucked in a breath of complete surprise. "Then you were the one? The drive-by shooting? And the flowers coming down on us? You were the one who tried to kill us!"

"Damned straight." Lorraine's eyes flashed. "I had to keep your mouths shut. And now . . ." She shot a nasty look over her shoulder at Jim. "You weren't supposed to be here. You weren't supposed to stop me. Nobody is supposed to stop me. And now you—all of you—you're going to ruin everything."

It was Jim who had the presence of mind to set her straight. When she banged her heel into his shin, he never even flinched. "Ruin everything, eh? Sorry to tell you, Mrs. Mercy, but you just did that all by yourself."

The truth slammed into Lorraine. Eyes burning, mouth thinned with fury, she went rigid. Then like a balloon pricked by a pin, she collapsed.

"You were going to tell," she screamed, tears sliding down her cheeks. "You were going to ruin everything."

She was still crying and screaming when hospital security showed up and hauled her away.

* * *

MONSIEUR LAVOIE WAS IN ON THE CONSPIRACY WITH me. So were Larry, Hank, and Charlie. And Heidi, Marc, and Damien, of course. Damien was the one who'd lured Jim to Bellywasher's with an early morning phone call about an emergency—the only thing, we'd figured, that would get him out of my apartment, where he'd been playing mother hen since my return from the hospital. (Just for the record, I was loving every minute of it.)

As soon as he was gone, I slipped out with Marc. While Damien and Heidi kept Jim busy in the kitchen, we got to work. When we were done, I signaled from the restaurant, and they led Jim out, blindfolded, to the sounds of Larry, Hank, and Charlie thrumming their hands against the bar like a drum roll.

"This is making me very nervous!" Jim laughed like it was no big deal, but I could tell he wasn't kidding. Not completely. I couldn't blame him. And I couldn't stand the thought of keeping the surprise a moment longer.

"OK," I said. "It's time," and when I did, Monsieur Lavoie stepped forward and pulled the blindfold off Jim's eyes.

"So, what do you think?"

I would have liked to twirl around like a model at a car show, but even though it was two days after the incident at the fund-raiser and Lorraine's middle-of-the-night attack, I wasn't taking any chances. Not with my head, or with my broken arm. Instead of twirling, I made a Vanna-like gesture (with my good arm, of course) toward the walls of Bellywasher's.

Jim's mouth fell open. He looked over the pictures that jammed the walls, and at the kilts and the old broadswords, the Scottish flag that had been hung above the door, and the thistle border that had been stenciled on every single wall just that morning. "It looks just like it did when Uncle Angus owned the place. Only there's even more junk!"

We all applauded.

"It's your junk," I said, stepping back (but not too

quickly) to admire it all. "I couldn't have done it without everyone's help." I smiled at Monsieur and the rest of them. "It's gorgeous."

"Nah. You're gorgeous. Even with that cast on your arm." Hank gave me a gap-toothed grin. "This place . . ." He sighed with contentment. "Thank goodness, this place finally looks like home again."

"You did this? All of you?" Jim's astonishment might be complete, but I could tell he wasn't totally convinced. He turned a skeptical eye on me. "Do you need to go back to the hospital to have your head looked at again, woman? What were you thinking? This isn't the place we envisioned."

"No. It isn't. But the place we envisioned wasn't a place that made you happy. You told me so yourself. Besides, it was the least I could do."

"All this, just for saving her life!" Charlie slapped a hand against the bar and laughed.

"Not just for saving my life." I smiled up at Jim. The old Annie would have been embarrassed to lay her emotions out on the table, especially in front of Charlie, Hank, and Larry and the rest of them. Not to mention Jim. But I was a new Annie. Or at least I was trying to be. Just so he'd know it, I gave Jim a hug. "For being there for me. For being there with me."

His grin never faded. "Then you'll be happy to know that I've made some decisions about Bellywasher's, too." Like he was making a speech, Jim cleared his throat. He wrapped an arm around my shoulders and we faced our friends. "We're closed on Mondays, you all know that. So after Christmas, we'll be starting something new. Every Monday night." He reached in his pocket for a piece of paper, unfolded it, and handed it to me.

I looked at the crest like a coat of arms at the top of the page. Instead of the usual charging lions and crowns, this crest had a chef's hat, a spatula, and some vegetables on it.

"Bellywasher's Academy." I read the words under the crest. "A cooking school?"

Jim's eyes glinted. "What do you think?"

"I think . . ." Quickly, I read over the information on the flyer. It was all about providing hands-on opportunities to create delicious meals using the freshest ingredients, and about sitting down after every class and enjoying the food and friendship with fellow classmates. "I think it's brilliant!"

"Will it fit into your business plan, do you think?"

"Will it make you happy?"

His smile inched up a notch.

It was the only answer I needed. "Then we'll make it fit with our business plan," I told him.

Jim's smile softened. "I miss teaching," he said, and he looked at Monsieur. "This will give me the chance to keep my fingers in it, so to speak, and still keep the restaurant going. It will give Marc and Damien experience at being instructors, too."

"And we'll get to sample." Charlie applauded.

"It's perfect." Jim pulled me closer and kissed me. Through the ringing that started up all over again inside my head, I heard more applause. "All because of you."

"Not perfect. Not yet." I'd saved the biggest surprise for last. Taking it slow and easy, I untangled myself from Jim and went around the bar to the new menu board we'd installed that morning. There was a tablecloth covering it, and I whisked it off and watched Jim's eyes light up.

"Today's hot dog special!" He punched a fist into the air. "Yes! Bellywasher's is back."

We were all still hooting and laughing and applauding when the front door opened. Eve and Tyler were standing outside. One look, and I knew this was a chance meeting.

As if he'd just bitten into a sour apple, Tyler's mouth was puckered. And Eve? She had the same little grin on her face that had taken up permanent residence ever since Doug proposed. Only it was brighter than ever. I had not one scrap of doubt that this was for Tyler's benefit. I also didn't doubt that he knew it. Of course, he would sooner have been boiled in oil than admit that it was driving him crazy.

His shoulders rigid, Tyler stepped back to let Eve walk into the restaurant first. She knew what I'd been planning to do that morning, of course, and she breezed inside, glanced around, and nodded her approval. Tyler stepped inside after her, closed the door, and stopped right there.

"Looks like I'm interrupting a party," he said.

"There's so much to celebrate these days," Eve cooed.

"And it's just the first of many celebrations around here." Jim smiled in my direction. "What can we do for you, Lieutenant?"

"You could get me a cup of coffee." Nobody had chutzpah like Tyler had chutzpah. He looked right at Eve when he said it. She ignored him, but Heidi didn't. While she went into the kitchen, Tyler chafed his hands together. "Just thought I'd stop in," he said, "to wrap things up."

After the disaster at the fund-raiser, Eve was convinced she needed a deep pore cleansing and her hair an intense oil treatment. Her skin glowed, and her hair was sleeker and glossier than ever. She tossed her head. "Or maybe, Tyler honey, you were just hoping for the chance to see me again. You know, before I'm officially Mrs. Senator Douglas Mercy."

Tyler did not grace this comment with a reply. He pulled out his notebook, and when Heidi arrived with the coffee and set it on the table nearest to where Tyler stood, he sat down and got to work.

"Dr. Mercy has been hospitalized and is being kept under close observation," he said.

"And isn't that a shame." Eve slipped out of her coat. She was wearing her brown suede skirt along with an ivory silk blouse and the diamond ring—it was as big as my apartment, I swear—that she and Doug had purchased only the day before. She stepped far enough away from the table so Tyler couldn't fail to get a good look at her. "The good news, of course, is that the whole crazy daughter-in-law thing doesn't seem to be hurting Doug's political standing. He's always had a concern for the mentally ill."

"Except that this mentally ill person tried to kill Annie."

Tyler didn't need to point this out to Eve, who already felt bad enough that her future daughter-in-law had nearly murdered her best friend. Of course, that's exactly why he'd mentioned it. "We found the gun," he added, looking past Eve to where I stood. "The ballistics match. Lorraine Mercy is definitely the one who took the potshots at you outside the restaurant. Lucky for you she was in a moving vehicle. I've talked to the folks over at her country club. She's a champion skeet shooter. They say she has a dead-eye aim."

"And all this because she didn't want anyone to know about her husband's affair with Sarah." I shook my head—carefully. "It's really sad, isn't it? She's a brilliant woman. She had an impressive career and a successful business."

"And, Dougy Mercy? We've learned that he's had a string of these affairs." Tyler supplied the information. "As long as he was discreet, Lorraine never cared. But this time, you two . . ." He barely spared Eve a look before he turned back to me. "You two might have ruined all that. You found out about Sarah and Dougy, and she was convinced that was going to hurt Dougy's image and his chance to follow in his father's footsteps." The smile Tyler aimed at Eve was as sleek as a sharpened knife. "In the senate, Eve, honey, not with you."

I sidestepped the sarcasm. Eve could give as good as she got, and I didn't have the energy to get tangled in the Eve versus Tyler mess. "And do you think she killed Dylan, too?" I'd been trying to think my way through this part of the mystery ever since I heard about Dylan's death.

This time, Tyler didn't even bother to glance at Eve. He kept his eyes right on me. "He was investigating Sarah's death, too, and Lorraine must have known that meant the truth was going to come out. A news reporter was even more of a threat than you. She had to kill him."

"But she couldn't have, could she?" I tipped my head, thinking this through. "Killed him, I mean. Lorraine was at the fund-raiser."

"Coroner's not exactly sure about time of death," Tyler

said. "Monroe could have been dead long before the fund-raiser ever started. And we already know Lorraine was a crack shot, so there's no problem there." Tyler narrowed his eyes and studied me. "You don't look convinced."

Didn't I? I chewed over the thought and realized that for once in his life, Tyler was right. I dropped into the chair across from his. "You think she killed Sarah?"

"Do you?"

I knew better than to be fooled into thinking Tyler might actually be asking my opinion, detective to detective.

"Why didn't she admit it?" I asked Tyler.

He, of course, didn't have an answer to this, but fortunately, Tyler didn't have to worry that anyone would think less of him because of it. Before he could say a word, Eve's cell phone rang. She answered it, listened, and smiled.

"Uh-huh. Yes. I understand." I knew something important was up because Eve was using her best beauty pageant voice and her thickest Southern accent. "Of course. We'd be honored. We'll be there."

Before she'd ever hung up the phone, she was across the room and pulling me into a hug. "That was the producer from Oprah," Eve said, laughing. "They've invited me and Doug and Doc to Chicago. They're calling Doc a national hero. And doing the show live in his honor. We're all going to be on TV tomorrow!"

Nineteen

✖

"I'M SO NERVOUS, I CAN'T SEE STRAIGHT!"

This was news to me, because Eve didn't look nervous. In fact, in a pink suit and a choker that matched Doc's collar (I hoped hers was rhinestones), she looked like a million bucks. She set Doc's carrier down on the floor outside my Bellywasher's office. "I had to stop and see you before I left for the airport, Annie. Doug is used to this kind of publicity, but me . . ." She squealed and jumped up and down. "I feel like I'm gonna burst!"

"You'll do fine. Really." It was early, and Bellywasher's wasn't open yet. I'd stopped in early on my way to the bank to catch up on some of the work I'd left undone, thanks to my hospital stay and recuperation. As it happened, it worked out perfectly, because Eve and I just had to see each other before she left for Chicago, and it was more convenient for Doug to pick her up in Alexandria. Perfect, all the way around.

"I'll be watching," I told Eve. "Pioneer Savings and Loan or no Pioneer Savings and Loan. I already called my supervisor and told her I'd be taking my lunch break late today. Just in time for Oprah."

"I wish you could come, too." Eve sighed. "It would be so much fun."

"But more romantic if it's just you and the senator."

She blushed. "I'm nuts about him, Annie," she said. She dug around in her Kate Spade bag and made a face. "He may not be so nuts about me if he realizes I left my driver's license at home."

"Here." Eve had her raincoat over her arm, and I took it from her so that she could look through her purse more easily. She unloaded her wallet, a comb, a compact, and three tubes of lipstick, then came up smiling.

"Got it!" She held up her driver's license. "And I've got what I need for Doc, too. I think. I hope." She had a small package of dog treats in her purse, a new chew toy, and a tin of doggy breath mints. She bobbled them in one hand.

"You know, there's plenty of room in Doc's carrier for all this stuff." I took it all from her, and while she worked on getting her things back into her purse, I stepped into the restaurant. There was a snap-to-close compartment on the top of the carrier, and I opened it. "Right in here," I said.

Except that there was already something in there.

I peered at the eight-by-ten black-and-white photograph.

It showed two men on a park bench, their heads bent toward each other, deep in conversation. The man on the left was handing a thick manila envelope to the man on the right.

The man on the right was Douglas Mercy.

The man handing the senator the envelope looked vaguely familiar. He was a hefty guy with heavy jowls, a wide nose, and eyes that were too small for his face. The hand in which he held the envelope was as big as a ham. His fingers looked like fat pork sausages.

Ivan Gystanovich. I recognized the man who owned our linen service company—who was also reportedly the head of the Russian mob in the area—from the picture Eve had once pointed out in the newspaper.

And the pieces of the puzzle clicked into place, along with the truth that had been staring me in the face since the night we found Sarah's body in the bathtub. My heartbeat sped to an improbable rate. My head spun, worse than it had when I had the concussion.

I stared at the photo, wondering how to break the news to Eve, and oblivious to where I was and what was going on around me.

Too bad.

It meant that when the front door opened and Senator Douglas Mercy walked in, I wasn't ready for him.

"Good morning!"

At the sound of the senator's voice, I jumped. I hid the photograph I was still holding behind my back.

"Is Eve here? Is she ready?"

My mouth opened and closed in response to the senator's questions, but I couldn't get any sound out.

"She is going to Chicago with me, isn't she?"

I managed an anaemic laugh and closed in on the senator. "She changed her mind. She's too nervous. She says she just couldn't do it. She—"

"Annie, what in the world are you talking about?"

Eve came up behind me. "You're talking crazy, girl! Of course I'm going to Chicago. And what is that you're holding behind your back?"

Before I could react, Eve snatched the photo out of my hands.

My formerly racing heartbeat stopped cold; I swear it did. The blood drained from my face. By the time I spun to warn Eve to keep quiet, it was already too late.

"It's you," she said, turning the photo so the senator could see it. "And some other man. Look, Annie." Eve pointed. "He looks just like Ivan Gystanovich, the guy who owns the linen service. You remember him. Well, that doesn't make any sense at all." In an attempt to order her thoughts, Eve shook her head. "Why would you and Ivan Gystanovich be sitting on a park bench in the middle of nowhere? And why would somebody take your picture?"

"Not just somebody; it was Sarah." It was too late to bluff, so I didn't even try. I turned to the senator. "That explains the money, and once the money is explained . . ." I would have slapped my forehead if not for my recent head injury. "It all falls into place. Sarah loved to spend her lunch hour roaming around town taking pictures. And one day, she just happened to come upon you and Gystanovich. She was a smart woman. She knew exactly what was going on. She also knew this picture was going to mean a lot of money to her."

Eve still wasn't getting it. "A picture of Doug and this Ivan guy? But that doesn't make any sense, Annie. Why would Sarah care? And how could it get her any money? I mean, yeah, maybe it would if she was blackmailing Doug or something. Like if Doug was meeting with Gystanovich secretly and taking payoffs or . . ." Eve blanched. Her voice faltered. When she looked at her fiancé, there were tears in her eyes. "Doug? Tell me we're wrong, will you?"

I knew we weren't. And I couldn't bear the thought of Eve hearing it from the senator, so I spoke before he could. "In case you're wondering," I said to him, "the photograph was in the dog's carrier all along. That's probably the one place you never thought to look."

"Thanks for saving me the trouble." His smile was sleek. "Now, honey . . ." His words were sweet, but the look he aimed at Eve was anything but. "If you'll just hand over that picture . . ."

"Don't." I stopped Eve before she even had a chance to think about it. "It's proof that the senator is taking bribes from the mob. No wonder you didn't recognize Doc's collar when I wore it to the fund-raiser. You didn't give it to her. Sarah took the money you were giving her and bought it herself. That's why your initials were inside it. It was Sarah's way of sticking it to you, a little reminder that you were under her thumb."

"She always was smart." The senator snapped his fingers, motioning for the picture, but Eve was still too stunned and too confused to move. All she could do was twist her brand-spanking-new engagement ring around her finger.

"Tell me we're wrong here, Doug," Eve pleaded. "Please! Tell me we're making some kind of mistake."

"The only mistake you two made was not keeping your mouths shut." The senator moved quickly. He yanked the photograph out of Eve's hands so violently she gasped. "This would have been a whole lot easier—for all of us—if you never found out what Sarah was up to."

I suppose I should have been surprised when the senator pulled a gun.

Not too surprised to stop talking, though. "You gave Sarah plenty of money, and my guess is you finally got tired of it. That's why you killed her, isn't it?" I asked the senator.

"Shut up!" He aimed the gun at me, then slid it in Eve's direction.

Staring down the barrel, she finally came to her senses. She sniffled. "But, Doug, you said you loved me!"

"I loved the idea of a wife not being compelled to testify against her husband in a murder trial even more. Now, if you ladies will get moving . . ." With the gun, he directed us back to the kitchen, far away from the front windows and anything a passerby might see.

I stood my ground. "It's why you killed Dylan, too. It wasn't Lorraine. Oh, she might have tried eventually, when she realized Dylan's information would expose Dougy's affair. But you realized first that Dylan was looking into Sarah's death. He found out, didn't he? About the payoffs from the mob."

"He did." The senator's smile was sleek. "And I couldn't let word get out. Now, if you two will get moving . . ."

Again, he tried to point the way with the gun.

Again, I wasn't about to budge. I wasn't about to give up without a fight, either. The trick was figuring out how. Until I did, I had some major stalling to do.

"There was nothing wrong with Sarah's work, was there? You put the word out that her work was suffering. So people would start talking. So when you killed her, they'd think it was because she was depressed because she might get fired.

And Dylan? Did you put the word out about their breakup, too?"

"Didn't need to." The senator's smile was as sleek as a knife. "She broke up with him, you know. Hurt his ego. That's why he lied to everyone and told them the breakup was his idea. And it was all because of that harebrained son of mine. If Sarah hadn't started an affair with Dougy and then made Dylan angry, he never would have started looking into her death."

"A death you engineered." Just thinking about what must have happened at Sarah's that night made me shiver. I wrapped my arms around myself. "You gave her extra Valium, right? In the wine. Then you dragged her into the bathroom and—"

"No." Eve sobbed. "It isn't possible. Doug, there's no way you—"

"Shut up! And get moving. Get into the kitchen."

"Sure. But you're sadly mistaken if you think that's the only copy of that photograph there is."

The senator called my bluff with a smile. "It's the only copy of the photograph there is. I know; I took apart Sarah's apartment. If there was another picture, I would have found it."

"Just because there's not another picture doesn't mean nobody's going to know what happened," I told him. I hoped the edge of defiance I added to my voice was enough to fool him. "After the drive-by," I said, "we had security cameras installed."

Just as I was counting on, this was something he hadn't thought of. The senator looked in the corners near the ceiling and over near the bar. "You're lying."

"You willing to take that chance? They're hidden." I backed up a step. We were standing near where a green plaid kilt was draped over one of the sandalwood screens.

"Over there," I said, and I played my trump card. If I was right, Eve and I would live. If I wasn't . . . I gulped in a breath for courage. "Right by that red kilt."

Just as I'd hoped, the senator looked at the green kilt. His head wasn't turned long, but it was long enough. The instant he looked away, I darted to my right. I grabbed Grandpa's walking stick from its place of honor on the wall and whacked the senator over the head with it. Too bad I didn't remember my broken arm first. A pain like a thousand bolts of electricity shot up my arm, but hey, the strategy worked. The senator staggered and went down in a heap.

"Annie! Annie!" Eve crumpled to the floor, but I didn't run to her. Carefully—just in case he wasn't as knocked out as I thought he was—I looked at the senator. When I was sure he was out cold, I kicked the gun across the room. Then I called the cops.

"EXPLAIN AGAIN."
I groaned and dropped my head into my hands. Or more specifically, into one hand. My other hand—and the arm it was attached to—hurt like hell. It was being looked at by a paramedic, who was making tsk-tsk noises that did not sound promising. "I've already explained," I told Eve. "A thousand times. I told the uniformed cops who came when we called. I told the detectives who interviewed us. I told—"

"Annie!" Jim burst through the kitchen doors, got past the cops there with a quick, "I own this place," and raced across the room. He looked at the paramedic, who was kneeling on the floor next to where I sat.

"Are you all right? Tell me you're all right!"

I wasn't, not exactly, anyway, but I popped out of my chair, and when Jim pulled me into a hug, I didn't object. And I only winced a little.

"They told me there had been an incident. That's all they said. They mentioned two women and—"

"We're fine." I wasn't sure how long I'd remain fine, since I couldn't breathe with my nose pressed against Jim's chest. I backed out of his arms. Since there were cops and paramedics milling around inside and lots of people out on the sidewalk ogling the scene and I wasn't sure who knew what, I kept my voice down.

"They came and took the senator away," I said.

"Mercy?" Jim looked as surprised as I must have when I first found the picture of the senator with Ivan Gystanovich.

"He killed Sarah. Because she knew he was taking bribes. She was blackmailing him."

"And Annie hurt her arm again," Eve explained, even though Jim surely had that figured out. There was an ambulance waiting outside, and the paramedic said I had to have more X-rays taken of my arm.

"But before she goes to the hospital . . ." With one look from Eve, the paramedics backed off. "Explain it again, Annie. How did you know Doug would look the wrong way?"

"Don't you remember? At the black-and-white ball. The senator said he was grateful to Lorraine for coming up with idea. He said he was always afraid he'd tell some constituent her gown was aquamarine when it was really some other color. At the time, I thought he meant shade. He'd tell her it was aquamarine when it was really some other shade of blue. But he didn't mean shade, he really did mean color. He's color-blind."

Eve sniffed. "Huh?"

"He was the one who messed up the clothes in Sarah's closet," I explained. "He put a green jacket in with the red ones. Only a color-blind person would have done that."

"So you told him red because you knew he'd look at the green kilt and when he did . . ."

"Exactly." The paramedic would no longer take no for an answer. He took me by my good arm to lead me out to the waiting ambulance. Jim walked at my side.

"And if you weren't right?" he asked.

I didn't want to think about what might have happened, so I didn't answer him. At least not directly. I got into the ambulance, and Jim climbed in next to me. I rested my head on his shoulder.

"I'm glad everything at Bellywasher's is back to the way it used to be," I told him. He knew I wasn't talking about the food. Or the decor.

"Aye." Jim wrapped an arm around my shoulders. "So am I, Annie. So am I."

RECIPES

✖

**Sarah's Goat Cheese
and Artichoke Bruscetta**

**Jim's Split Pea Soup
with Bacon and Rosemary**

Annie's Easy Fennel Salad

**Damien's Roasted Asparagus
with Crisp Prosciutto**

Doctor Masakazu's Delights

**Marc's Chicken
with Black Pepper Maple Sauce**

**Mercy's Maryland-Style
Crab Cakes**

Eve's Flourless Chocolate Torte

Eve's Lavender Pound Cake

**Larry, Hank, and Charlie's
Blue Plate Special**

Sarah's Goat Cheese and Artichoke Bruscetta

18 baguette slices, cut on the diagonal about ¼-inch thick
extra virgin olive oil
1 clove garlic
2 jars (6 to 6 ½ ounces each) marinated artichoke hearts
½ cup plus 2 tablespoons chopped parsley
½ cup grated Parmesan cheese
freshly ground black pepper
6 ounces creamy goat cheese, crumbled

Preheat oven to 375 degrees. Brush baguette slices on both sides with olive oil and place on a baking sheet. Bake slices until just crisp, about 3 minutes a side. Remove from oven and rub one side of each piece with the garlic and set aside.

Drain artichokes and place them in a food processor fitted with a metal blade. Add 2 tablespoons of the olive oil, ½ cup of the parsley, Parmesan, and several grindings of black pepper. Process, pulsing machine, until mixture is a coarse puree.

Spread each bread slice with artichoke puree and top with goat cheese. Return to the oven and bake 5 to 6 minutes or until the cheese is melted and bruschetta is warmed through. Sprinkle with additional black pepper and the remaining parsley and serve.

Makes 18 bruschettas.

Jim's Split Pea Soup with Bacon and Rosemary

Serves 4 to 6

4 bacon slices
1 large onion, finely chopped
1 large carrot, peeled, chopped
2 garlic cloves, minced
4 14½-ounce cans low-sodium chicken broth

1¼ cups green split peas, rinsed
2 bay leaves
½ teaspoon chopped fresh rosemary or 1 teaspoon dried, crumbled

crusty bread, warmed

Cook the bacon in a large pot over medium-high heat until crisp. Transfer to a paper towel–lined plate and reserve. Spoon off and discard all but 1½ tablespoons of the bacon drippings. Return the pan to medium heat, add the onion and cook until slightly tender, 4 to 5 minutes. Add the carrot and garlic and continue cooking for 4 minutes. Add broth, peas, bay leaves, and rosemary and bring soup to boil. Reduce heat to medium-low, and simmer covered, stirring occasionally until peas are tender, 40 to 45 minutes. Season soup with salt and pepper and serve with crusty bread.

Annie's Easy Fennel Salad

Serves 4 to 6

2 medium fennel bulbs, sliced paper thin
1 small granny smith apple, cored and sliced paper thin
juice of one lemon (2½ to 3 tablespoons)
3 tablespoons extra virgin olive oil

⅛ teaspoon kosher salt
¼ teaspoon black pepper
2 tablespoons fresh parsley leaves, torn
⅓ cup thinly shaved Pecorino Romano cheese

In a large bowl combine the fennel, apple, lemon juice, and olive oil. Season with the salt and pepper and toss to combine. Gently fold in the parsley and cheese and serve.

Damien's Roasted Asparagus with Crisp Prosciutto

Serves 4

1 pound pencil thin asparagus, ends trimmed ½-inch
1 tablespoon olive oil
¼ teaspoon kosher salt
¼ teaspoon black pepper
⅛ pound thinly sliced prosciutto

Heat oven to 400 degrees. Place the asparagus in a single layer on a rimmed baking sheet. Drizzle with the oil and sprinkle with salt and pepper. Cook until tender, 12 to 15 minutes depending on thickness. Meanwhile, in a skillet over medium heat, heat the prosciutto until crisp, 1 to 2 minutes per side, then transfer to a plate and let cool. Transfer the cooked asparagus to a serving dish. Break the prosciutto into pieces and sprinkle over the top of the asparagus.

Doctor Masakazu's Delights

2 cups whole-wheat flour
1 tablespoon baking powder
1 cup milk
1 cup peanut butter (chunky or smooth)

Heat the oven to 375 degrees. Combine flour and baking powder in a bowl. In another bowl, mix milk and peanut butter. Add to dry ingredients and mix well. Place dough on a lightly floured surface and knead until totally combined. Roll dough to ¼ inch thickness and use a cookie cutter to cut out shapes. Bake for 20 minutes on a greased baking sheet until lightly brown. Cool, then store in an airtight container.

Good enough for people—and dogs!

Marc's Chicken with Black Pepper Maple Sauce

Serves 4 to 6

1 3½ to 4-pound chicken, cut into 8 pieces
1 medium yellow onion, cut into wedges
2 small sweet potatoes, peeled and cut lengthwise into wedges
1 tablespoon fresh rosemary needles
3 tablespoons olive oil

2 teaspoons cider vinegar
1 teaspoon salt
¼ teaspoon black pepper
¼ cup maple syrup
8 sprigs fresh thyme

Heat the oven to 400 degrees. Rinse the chicken and pat it dry. Place the chicken, onion, sweet potatoes, and rosemary in a roasting pan or baking dish. Drizzle the oil and vinegar over the chicken and vegetables, season with the salt and pepper and toss to coat. Drizzle with the maple syrup and sprinkle with sprigs of thyme. Roast, occasionally stirring the vegetables, 60 to 70 minutes or until the chicken is cooked through. Let rest for at least 5 minutes before serving.

Mercy's Maryland–Style Crab Cakes

Serves 4 to 6

¼ cup olive oil
1 medium onion, finely chopped
1 small bell pepper (any color), finely chopped
½ teaspoon kosher salt
¼ teaspoon black pepper

5 scallions, (white and light green parts only), thinly sliced
1 clove garlic, finely chopped
2 teaspoons Cajun seasoning
2 large eggs
1 tablespoon Dijon mustard

⅓ cup breadcrumbs
¾ cup grated Parmesan cheese
1 pound lump crabmeat
coleslaw

Heat oven to 400 degrees. Heat 2 tablespoons of oil in a pan over medium heat. Add the onions and cook until slightly soft, 4 minutes. Add the bell pepper, season with the salt and pepper, and continue cooking for 2 minutes. Add the scallion, garlic, and Cajun spice and cook 1 minute. Remove from heat, transfer to a large mixing bowl and let cool. Stir in the eggs, mustard, bread crumbs, and Parmesan cheese. Add the crabmeat and mix to combine. Form the crab mixture into patties. Heat the remaining olive oil in a large skillet over medium-high heat. When the oil is hot, add the crab cakes and cook until golden brown, 2 to 3 minutes per side. Transfer to a parchment lined baking sheet and cook in the oven until heated through, 4 minutes. Transfer to a serving platter and serve with coleslaw.

Eve's Flourless Chocolate Torte

Serves 8

unsweetened cocoa

2 (8-ounce) packages semisweet chocolate
  squares, coarsely chopped

½ cup butter

5 large eggs, separated

1 tablespoon vanilla extract

¼ cup sugar

Grease a 9-inch spring form pan, and dust with unsweetened cocoa. Set aside.

Melt chopped chocolate and butter in a heavy saucepan over low heat, stirring until smooth. Whisk together egg yolks and vanilla in a large bowl. Gradually stir in chocolate mixture and mix until well blended.

Beat egg whites at high speed in an electric mixer until soft peaks form. Gradually add sugar to the whites, beating until sugar dissolves and stiff peaks form. Fold one-third of the beaten egg white mixture into the chocolate mixture. Gently fold in remaining egg white mixture until just blended. Spoon batter into prepared pan, spreading evenly.

Bake at 375 degrees for 25 minutes. Cool on a rack for 10 minutes before removing sides of pan.

Eve's Lavender Pound Cake

Serves 8

2½ cups unbleached all purpose flour
1 teaspoon baking powder
½ teaspoon baking soda
¼ teaspoon salt
1 cup sugar
1½ tablespoons dried lavender
   blossoms

1 cup (2 sticks) unsalted butter plus
   one tablespoon for melting
1 tablespoon vanilla
4 eggs
¾ cup sour cream
1 teaspoon finely shredded
   lemon peel

1 cup sifted confectioner's sugar
3–4 tablespoons freshly squeezed
   lemon juice
eggs, butter, and sour cream should
   be at room temperature

Heat oven to 325 degrees. Grease and flour two loaf pans (8×4×2 inch size) and set aside.
   In large bowl, mix flour, baking powder, baking soda, and salt. Set the mixture aside. Blend ½ cup of the sugar and dried lavender in a food processor. When fully combined, transfer to an electric mixer. Beat the lavender-sugar, the rest of the granulated sugar, butter, and vanilla on high speed until light and fluffy (about 3–4 minutes). Slow the mixing speed to medium; add the eggs, one at a time. Slow the mixing speed to low; add flour mixture and sour cream, and mix until just combined. Stir in lemon peel. Divide mixture between the two loaf pans.
   Bake for about 45 minutes. Remove and cool on a rack for 10 minutes, then remove from the pans.

Glaze: Melt one tablespoon of butter. Mix in confectioner's sugar and lemon juice. Spoon over the cakes and serve.

Larry, Hank, and Charlie's Blue Plate Special

Serves 4

4 hot dogs

1 small jalapeno, seeded and sliced into strips

4 slices bacon

1 medium tomato, finely chopped

½ small red onion, finely chopped

¼ teaspoon salt

¼ teaspoon black pepper

juice of one lime

1 tablespoon olive oil

4 hotdog buns, warmed

½ cup shredded cheddar or Monterey jack cheese

salsa

Using the tip of a paring knife, carefully make a slice into each hot dog, about ¼-inch deep. Place the jalapeno strips into the slices in each hot dog. Wrap entire hot dog with bacon. In a pan over medium heat, cook the hot dogs, turning occasionally, until the bacon is crisp, 5 to 7 minutes. Meanwhile, in a small bowl, combine the tomatoes, onion, salt, pepper, lime juice, and olive oil. Arrange the hot dogs in buns on a platter. Top with the shredded cheese and fresh tomato salsa and serve.